Pride Publishing books by Jackson C. Garton

Single Books
Avalon's Last Knight

I0681204

AVALON'S
LAST KNIGHT

JACKSON C. GARTON

Avalon's Last Knight
ISBN # 978-1-83943-890-5
©Copyright Jackson C. Garton 2020
Cover Art by Louisa Maggio ©Copyright April 2020
Interior text design by Claire Siemaszkiewicz
Pride Publishing

Published in 2020 by Pride Publishing, United Kingdom.

AVALON'S LAST KNIGHT

Dedication

This book is dedicated to my editor, Ann Leveille,
for helping me turn a pumpkin into a carriage,
to Liam Mayhugh, who is the first person I turn to
when I need a solid opinion, and to anyone who
still believes that the Appalachian Mountains are
made of magick.

Chapter One

The Beginning of the End

Avalon, KY

No one expected me to come home this summer.

Hell, *I* didn't expect to come home this summer.

Until a week ago, I had been apartment hunting in Lexington, looking for a one-room studio with a balcony and fire escape — maybe next to a park, certainly something close to campus. But rent is so outrageous in this college town that it just wouldn't be worth it. So when Gwen asked me to come home, to spend my summer vacation in Avalon, it didn't take much convincing. I was on a bus within hours of our phone call.

On the second day after my arrival, I decided to look for a job. Luckily, my old boss from a summer job I'd had in high school offered me a new position at Camelot Crafts, a little hole-in-the-wall store that sells scrapbooking materials to Sunday school teachers and bored housewives. I accepted the position immediately... but now that I've completed an entire shift, I'm not sure it was the right decision.

The boredom might literally kill me.

Gwen isn't being helpful, either. She was supposed to text me around three to let me know when she would be here to pick me up, but she hasn't responded to any of my texts.

Because she is a flaky asshole. *This is just like her. Classic Gwen.*

When it comes time for me to leave, I look down at my phone once more to see if Gwen has texted me. She hasn't. So I make the decision to walk home instead. I throw on my hoodie, grab my black side bag and make my way to the front door.

I look down at my feet. *Wearing Converse to work was a bad idea.*

Standing outside next to an old, rusted pickup that's more rust than actual metal is my best friend from high school, Arthur. Our eyes meet and he dashes over to the door to greet me. I wave once behind the tempered glass. *Sometimes my sister can be such an asshole, I swear.*

After I lock the door from the outside and turn around, Arthur scoops me into his arms with lightning speed. He's enormous now, muscles everywhere, a mountain of a man, the boy I once knew wholly lost to long days of manual labor.

"Lance!"

"I see that Gwen texted you instead of me," I say, gently untangling myself from his bear hug. "How very responsible of her. Is this your noble steed?"

Arthur grins and pats the side of the truck. "He is. I call him Percy. Do you wanna lift?"

Of course I have to say yes, because I live like seven miles from the shop, and because Arthur is looking at me with the most beautiful, dreamy brown eyes I have ever seen, knowing full well just how bewitching they are. I shrug.

"Yeah, I guess," I say. "What's her excuse this time?"

"No excuse," Arthur admits. "I just wanted to see you, is all. You look good, by the way. I feel like I haven't seen you in like a year."

That's because it has been a year, but I don't tell him that. "Yeah," I reply. "It's been a while since I came home." Arthur helps me into the truck, then rushes to his side and opens the door in a frenzy.

"You gonna be all right there?" I ask, pushing a safety helmet onto the floorboard.

Arthur removes his orange protective vest and runs a hand through the top of his blond, sun-bleached hair before starting the truck. "I'm better than all right. I'm great. Goddamn, I can't believe you're actually here," he says. "Queenie told me you were thinking of moving to Lexington."

"I do live there," I say, trying to pull the seat belt across my lap, but it snags, and I have trouble getting the strap to release. Arthur slides over real close and takes the belt into his hands.

"You know what I mean," he says. "Here, let me get that for you. It's not the best truck in the world, but it gets me from point a to point b. There ya go."

A whiff of sweat and dirt from a hard day's work fills my nostrils when he brushes against my stomach, and I have to talk myself out of closing my eyes and savoring the intoxicating scent. Arthur smells so good, so familiar. He hugs me again and tells me how glad he is that I'm here, with him, in his truck. That he hopes we can spend all summer together. I doubt it, because my body dysphoria is a roadblock on a route riddled with endless repairs, and I'm not sure Arthur would understand how to navigate all the signs and detours, but I keep that part to myself and nod instead. I sigh.

On the drive to my house, Arthur and I discuss school—his graduating, my upcoming junior year. He graduated two weeks ago. I know this because I follow him on Instagram, and every single picture he posted that day had a different girl in it. I suddenly feel guilty and think about how he attended my high school graduation with a smile. But I've always been kind of petty, I guess, and I just couldn't bring myself to see him, not when I'm a mess, a crippling mass of confusion and heat.

"Well," he says, reeling me back into the conversation. "At least that's over. I'm just glad that I don't have to take any more stupid tests for a while. You know what I mean?"

I nod, and watch him drive up the hill that I've called home for nearly twelve years now. "Yeah, I feel that," I say. "College is nothing but tests and papers. It can be really shitty sometimes. But hey," I reply, suddenly remembering, "Gwen tells me that you have your own place now. Look at you being an adult and everything, mister construction worker."

Arthur laughs and places an arm across my chest while the truck takes a sharp left turn. I briefly consider leaning into his arm, but think better of it. *I don't want him to think I'm a weirdo.*

"Okay," he says, both hands now on the steering wheel. "It's a goddamn trailer. We ain't talkin' about no palace here. Sturgill's Mobile Homes, you know, by that used tire store? And construction sure beats the hell out of unpaid volunteer work. At least I'm getting good money outta this."

While Arthur talks about his new job, I watch his lips move, how he bites on the inside of his cheek, how he licks his lips twice, how his bottom lip trembles every time he says my name. Watching him speak never gets old.

"Oh, yeah," I say, finally. "Gwen mentioned a bonfire tonight, and something about a seance, maybe? I'm not sure I'm really ready for that. You know how people get at these things, especially when they're drinking. They take Ouija boards way too fuckin' seriously, and fights always break out because someone gets freaked out."

Arthur slumps slightly and makes a noise. "Pretty please," he says. "With sugar on top? I haven't seen you in forever. Don't you want to hang out with me? Didn't you miss me at all?"

Other than Gwen, Arthur is the only person in Avalon I care about, and it's been that way for the past five years, but any time he gets brought up, or the status of our friendship gets brought up, I choke and have a difficult time verbalizing a response.

"I did miss you," I say, my mouth suddenly dry. "But you know how I feel about her bonfires. The music is always terrible and loud, and you can't hear anyone talk. Everyone's drunk and being obnoxious, touching you and stuff."

"I'll stand real close to you so that you can hear me, and we can hang out on the porch if it gets to be too much. I won't let anyone lay a finger on you. Or we can check it out and leave if things get dumb. Please, Lance."

I love this man, and I have been in love with him since my junior year of high school. The perpetual sincerity in his voice shakes my steel core every time.

"All right," I say, caving in without putting up much of a fight. "But I swear, if someone calls me Linda, I'm out of there immediately. Do you hear me?"

"We don't have to stay the entire time if you don't want. I just want to hang out with you."

Against my better judgment, I agree to let him shower and change clothes before heading to the bonfire, but now that we're here in the trailer park, I'm not so sure it was a good idea.

Arthur pulls into the gravel driveway of a small mobile home, then hops out of his truck and hastily opens my door. His excitement is a little jarring, honestly, because I am not used to bright, bubbly personalities, not after having been away at college for the past year. I'm used to keeping my eyes glued to the sidewalk and walking with my earbuds in, to avoid any unnecessary — or necessary — conversations.

Arthur helps me down from the truck and hugs me again, this time pressing his chest against mine.

"I've missed you so much," he says. His voice cracks a little, like he's about to cry. "You have no idea."

Arthur's trailer is small, but clean and tidy, with lingering scents of bleach and Pine-Sol in the air, and I'm surprised to see a bag of cat food sitting on his kitchen table.

"Do you have a cat?" I ask, half-shouting so that he can hear me in the backroom. "I thought you were allergic!"

"Two," he says, the sound of his voice mixing with other noises. "Yin and Yang."

Arthur returns from his bedroom, walking down the narrow hallway, two kittens — one black, one white — in his arms. I notice he's not wearing a shirt and that his ponytail has come undone. My pulse speeds up.

Coming here was a terrible idea. I've made a huge mistake.

I try not to look at Arthur's large forearms, or the blue veins coming to the surface of his heavily tan skin, or the surprisingly large tattoo of a claymore on his biceps that he must have gotten sometime this past year. But there's just so much of him now that averting my gaze would be too obvious.

"I'm going to take a shower," he says. The kittens jump from his arms onto the table and chase after each other. "Feel free help yourself to anything in the fridge. I've got some filtered water, and some chocolate soy milk, I think. There might be a beer in there, but I'm not sure. It's been a few days since I've actually had the time to sit down and eat a home-cooked meal."

I pour myself a glass of water and look at a wall calendar next to the refrigerator. Today's date is circled in bright red ink, and below is written the word LANCE accompanied by two underlines. Arthur must have asked Gwen in advance if he could pick me up from the store. Those two are always up to something.

When Arthur emerges from the bathroom, I smell him instantly—a familiar mixture of patchouli and cedar announcing his existence. I would know that scent anywhere, because it's one that I've associated with him since the eleventh grade. *It never gets old.*

Walking into the kitchen now, wearing a tight black T-shirt that fits snugly around his biceps and a pair of black skinny jeans that hug his lean frame, Arthur could easily be mistaken for the witch responsible for tonight's séance and bonfire.

When he calls my name, I blanch, because I have no idea how long I've been staring at him.

"Oh, huh?" I ask, placing my glass in the sink, my back now turned toward him. "What was that? I'm sorry, I spaced out. I didn't get enough sleep last night."

Arthur laces up his other boot and says, "I asked if you were seeing anyone at the moment."

The question slithers its way up my neck and squeezes at my throat, cutting off my oxygen. Arthur has a way of doing this to me, and I know by the way he asked the question that it's been on his mind for some time now.

"I don't really have time to do much other than study, you know?" I say, taking a seat on the black futon in the living room. "I'm kind of boring."

Arthur straightens his back and unbuttons his pants, then tucks in his shirt. "Well," he replies, "I don't plan on doing anything this summer other than working, and trying to spend as much time with you as I can. How does that sound?"

My phone buzzes and I pull it out of my pocket. Gwen has finally responded, but instead of an apology, she's texted a picture of two men dressed in black leather, kissing. I roll my eyes and shove the phone back into my pocket. *Ass.* When I raise my head, I see Arthur staring at me.

"What?" I ask, hoping that he didn't see Gwen's text. "What is it?"

He sits down beside me on the futon and fixes my shirt collar.

"I'm just waitin' for you to ask me if I'm seeing anyone," he says, not meeting my eyes.

Arthur hasn't always been so forward, but in the year that I've been away, he's become a proper man. Working a full-time job, living by himself, driving his own car and paying all of his bills — a truly admirable thing for a man who's not quite nineteen years old. I don't know how he does it.

I swallow and look down at the relatively fresh tattoos on my knuckles. They're not peeling anymore, but they have started itching, and I silently chide myself for not keeping lotion in my bag. The moon on my thumb is the worst offender.

"Are you seeing anyone?" My question is barely audible.

"Nope," he says, buttoning and unbuttoning my collar. "I'm as single as it gets."

"That's not what your Instagram suggests," I say, catching his hands mid-buttoning. Our eyes finally meet. "Looks like you have a different girl every week."

Arthur bites his bottom lip and wags his head. "You know everythin' posted on the Internet ain't real life. And besides, I wouldn't lie to ya."

Arthur has asked me out twice now, and both times I have turned him down because I'm not ready for a relationship. Or rather, I'm not ready to have my heart broken by this man. It's one of the reasons why I didn't come home this past year. Actually, he's the main reason, if I'm being completely honest with myself.

The moment I first laid eyes on Arthur, I knew he would be my undoing. I can't resist a man with blond hair and brown eyes—they make for a deadly concoction when combined.

At first I told myself to resist his charms because of our age difference—he was in the ninth grade when we met—but then last year he texted me on his birthday at midnight, an image of a pack of cigarettes and two porno mags. An announcement to me—and the world, I guess, as the image later popped up on Instagram—

that he was of consenting age. I never saw so many people like an image of a Playgirl in all my life.

"I didn't call you a liar," I reply. "But you ain't exactly some sweet, innocent boy no more."

Arthur exhales loudly and sinks into the futon cushion. "Lance," he says. "I don't want to be turned down a third time."

"So then don't ask me if you think you already know the answer."

We sit in silence until Arthur reaches into his pocket and pulls out a lighter. The sound of the spark catching fills the small room. I turn around and see a joint in his hand.

"God, see how far you've fallen? When did you start smoking weed?" I ask.

Arthur answers, but hesitates at first. "September, I guess. Do you want some?"

I know my body—smoking weed will only act as an aphrodisiac, and I'm already at my limit.

"No," I say. "But it doesn't bother me. What time does the party start?"

"Are you that eager to get away from me?" Arthur asks, then starts coughing.

"No," I lie. "I was just wondering."

Arthur leans forward, puts the joint into an ashtray on the coffee table and slides his arms around my waist.

"Arthur," I protest. "What are you doing?"

"Can I hold you?"

Being in love with your best friend is literal torture, and I wouldn't wish it on my worst enemy. It doesn't hurt that Arthur is the world's biggest flirt, and that he doesn't always understand the necessity of boundaries.

"Yes," I say, cautiously. He wraps his arms around me, and I can feel his heart thumping through his shirt.

The last time I let him hold me like this, we fell asleep on his bed and awoke to his father bursting into his room like the mattress was on fire. We hadn't even been doing anything other than sleeping—we've only ever slept together on a bed. Hell, the door hadn't even been locked.

When his father had put his hand on my arm, I'd thought the night was going to end with Arthur going to jail. Arthur's parents' constant invasion of his privacy has been a sore spot for the past five years, and has further solidified my fears that no one will ever accept us as a couple. No one wants their son dating a trans man, at least not in this part of Kentucky.

Arthur is a fiercely loyal friend, but I hadn't expected him to respond to the incident by moving out of his parents' house the day after his eighteenth birthday and cutting all ties with his family, except for his mamaw. I never asked him to do that, and I refuse to believe that I'm the sole reason for his moving out of that hellhole.

"Is this okay?" he asks, sliding his hands under my shirt, keeping them carefully planted on my waist. He hasn't seen me since I had top surgery, and should know from past conversations with Gwen just how uncomfortable I am talking about it. Gwen can be an absolute dipshit at times, but she's my confidant and closest ally. A lovable dipshit, if you will.

"Yes," I whisper, and allow myself to lean into his warm body. He pulls me closer and rests his chin on top of my head, making me thankful that I washed my hair this morning before work.

"You smell good. Real good," Arthur says. "If you don't want to go to the party, we don't have to. There's this new Netflix documentary about the Salem Witch

Trials if you wanna watch that instead. I could order us a pizza."

Just knowing that Arthur might be into me at this point in time is enough to keep me sane — to keep me going. For the past year he's texted me regularly, despite my inability to respond at times, and interacted with me on Facebook and Instagram, sometimes even sending me stupid messages on Snapchat. We still haven't discussed the text he sent me, the one where he said he loved me, and I'm not brave enough to bring it up while I'm in his arms.

"I don't think that's such a good idea," I reply. "I mean, I'm sure Gwen wants us there for moral support. Besides, you know she can't start a fire to save her life."

"I didn't think you were into that kind of magick anymore," he says, running a finger over my fresh undercut. "Your hair is cute." He pauses, letting his hand rest on the back of my head. "Wait," he says. "I thought you were exploring your roots anyway, Mexican witchcraft or whatever."

"It's called *brujería*, and when you call it Mexican witchcraft like that, you sound ignorant as hell. Very white and very country."

"I've never been very good at hiding my flaws, you know that. Why don't you come home with me after the party then?" he asks. "I can drive you to work in the morning if you need me to."

Arthur isn't trying to be pushy — I know. Gwen is staying with her girlfriend while she's in town for the summer, and I hate going home because everyone still calls me Linda. But there's no way that I can spend the night here, because having sex with Arthur is always at the back of my mind when we're alone together, an ever-present reminder of the one and only time someone's tried making love to me.

The details are still fresh in my mind. I hadn't started medically transitioning yet, and despite his reassurance that he didn't mind my binder, we didn't go through with it. We couldn't. I couldn't.

Because I'm mental, and incapable of sharing any part of myself with anyone.

It had started out innocently enough, a simple game of tickling on his bed during some TV commercial, then before I'd had time to react he'd had me pinned to the bed, his mouth on mine in a matter of seconds, and I'd unleashed four years' worth of bottled-up, neatly packed desire. I'd torn at his clothes like they were made of paper, and he'd done the same. The botched attempt had ended with me bawling myself to sleep in his arms. Waking up to his father shouting about diablo and the eternal pits of hell had been an added bonus — the sour cherry on top of an already melted sundae.

"Arthur, I'm only going to say this once, so please listen to me." I pull away from him and slightly twist my torso so that we're facing each other. "I have missed you — a lot. You mean the world to me, and I want to spend as much time with you as I can." He nods and reaches out to touch my face, but I catch his hand before it lands on my cheek. "But you're super busy at the moment with work and everything, and I do not want to be in anyone's way. I want this to be a chill summer."

"You won't be in the way," Arthur protests. "Goddamn, I haven't seen you since August. You've been gone for almost ten months. Almost a whole fuckin' year. I followed you online like some creepy stalker guy because you weren't returning my texts, and I didn't know what else to do."

"I know," I say. "I'm sorry. I was in a pretty dark place for a while there."

"You could have texted me. You could have called me. I know you hate talkin' on the phone, but fuck, I missed your voice. Your laugh. I wasn't even allowed to be there for your surgery. Do you know how much that hurt?" he asks, his voice cracking. "Gwen had to tell me everything, every minute detail, every update. Then I nearly had a breakdown when I saw your post-op pictures on Instagram because I was so relieved—you have no fuckin' idea."

I want to touch him, to tell him everything is going to be all right, but everything I touch turns to ash, so I can't. I won't. I have wanted to be with Arthur ever since I could remember, but our story, the legend of King Arthur and Lancelot, has prevented me from telling him how I really feel.

Everyone knows Lancelot betrays Arthur in the end. It doesn't matter that Gwen is my sister—something bad will come from our relationship. I can feel the wrongness of it all deep inside, lurking in my bone marrow. No one is fast enough to outrun fate.

"I love you," he says. "And I have been in love with you since God knows when." The ice inside has started to thaw, and I can feel water pooling at the corners of my eyes. "But you keep me at a safe distance, and I don't know why. I won't hurt you, I promise."

His confession, the words I have waited so long to hear, confound and thrill me, and remind me that no matter what happens, Arthur is a dependable friend, someone I will have by my side regardless of how we define our relationship in five years, in ten years, or even in fifty years.

Looking thoroughly agitated, and seemingly not wanting to explore or discuss these feelings any further, Arthur leaves my side and saunters off to the back of the trailer. We don't normally fight, so I'm not sure how to handle the situation. I've never had a serious boyfriend, for obvious reasons—I believe that my best friend is a reincarnation of a legendary British monarch, I have horrible body dysphoria and I'm an amateur *brujo*, a half-white, half-Mexican witch.

I get up from the futon and walk to the bathroom. It still smells like pot everywhere, but I remain surprised by how spruce Arthur keeps his house. *The man can clean.* I fish around in my side bag until I snag a container of liquid eyeliner, hoping that I remembered to switch it out, since the last container was almost empty.

When I'm finished applying eye makeup and fashioning my freshly dyed black hair into a bun, I pull the necklace I've been wearing out of my shirt and let it dangle from my neck. A black Magic 8-Ball charm attached to a simple steel chain—an old Christmas gift from Arthur—my most prized possession. After I've fastened a black choker around my neck and slid several black jelly bracelets down my arm, I emerge from the bathroom, only to find Arthur leaning up against the cabinet, drinking a glass of water.

"I'm sorry," he says. "I shouldn't have unloaded all of my shit on you. You didn't deserve it. It's not your fault I'm clingy and insane."

Then my phone buzzes as if in response, and I pull it out of my back pocket.

"Gwen says she wants us to pick up some orange soda on our way to the fire," I say, thankful for the change of subject. "Do you mind? She says you owe her any way."

"Ah," Arthur replies. "She must have scored some vodka. Ask her what kind she wants. Caffeine-free or…?"

I walk over and join him, forgetting about the stupid gay-biker-leather image that Gwen sent earlier.

"If that's supposed to be us," Arthur says, peering over my shoulder, "you can tell her that it's inaccurate, because I prefer latex."

I tear my face away from the text messages and look up at his big, toothy grin.

It's going to be a long summer, and I'm not sure I came fully prepared.

Chapter Two

The Invite

"You absolute slut!" Gwen sails across the dirt road to meet Arthur's truck as we pull up to the house, her long white skirt billowing in the wind. "Did you bring me anything to smoke, Art?" she asks in a high-pitched, childlike voice. "Did ya?"

Arthur pops his head out the window sideways. "Dammit, Queenie, I brought you soda. Now you want my smoke? I thought you got a job last month."

I ignore their playful back-and-forth and survey the scene.

There are people everywhere. People I've never seen, and people I've known since I was first adopted by the Lotte family. Most are recent high school graduates, and a few are my age or older. I spot a small group of people I graduated with and sink into my seat. *Shit.*

"Hey," Arthur says, shifting the manual transmission into first gear. It makes a short, faint grinding sound and he laughs, then turns his eyes on me. "I'm still getting the hang of driving this thing. Sorry."

I instinctively pull my black hoodie over my head and groan. *Coming to this party was an outright mistake. Fuck.*

"Um, are you okay?" he asks.

No, I am not okay. There are several people here that know me as Linda, or rather, knew me as Linda, and it doesn't matter that I legally changed my name to Lance as soon as I graduated from high school. I don't want to put up with the stares, or the questions. I just want to eat some Doritos and maybe drink a Pepsi. And I certainly do not want to be dead-named by people who are otherwise nice, thoughtful folks, because honestly, that's the worst part — their ignorance of just how much it hurts.

When I don't answer right away, Arthur unbuckles his seat belt and slides across the torn leather seats. He puts his arm around my neck and whispers, "If you wanna leave, I'll take you anywhere you wanna go. We don't have to stay. We don't even have to get out of this truck if you don't want to."

I pull on my hoodie strings, and tighten them to the point where only my nose is exposed. *Something in the air tells me that I'm going to regret coming back to Avalon.* Then Arthur kisses the tip of my nose, thoroughly unraveling any defenses I've knitted for protection, and I let him pry open my hood.

"But don't let a few dumbasses spoil your night. You have a right to be here. We all do."

"That's easy enough for you to say," I reply. "You never went by another name. You've always been Arthur."

"And you've always been Lance. Look, you're like a superhero, only you got rid of your alter ego, and we all know who you are now."

Arthur's support is like an ever-flowing fountain — crystal clear, everlasting, and always there — a tall glass of water whenever I'm feeling parched.

"How many tranny superheroes are there in the Marvel Universe?" I grumble. "Right."

"Hey," he says. "Don't call yourself that."

His tone is serious, and the frown on his face tells me that he's not joking.

"I'm kidding." I nudge him with my shoulder. "You know I'm allowed to call myself that if I want," I say. "It's you who isn't allowed to use that word."

"But I read this thing on HuffPo, and they were like, don't use it, like ever. How the fuck am I supposed to know what to say, or what to do when there's so much conflicting info out there?"

Arthur is so close to me now that I'm practically sitting on his lap. I reach up and run my index finger along his prominent jawline. He is perfect in nearly every way — even his naïvety is endearing and charming, a flower to water and watch grow.

"I'm right here," I say. "Your very own trans man. You can ask me anything."

"Anything?" he replies. I move my finger and he catches it, then turns it over. I feel like we've been sitting in the truck forever. "Do your finger tattoos still hurt?"

I shake my head, my attention too focused on his gentle touch. When he kisses each individual finger, I'm certain that I'm going to dissolve into the shitty leather interior.

"Arthur," I say, "we'd better head inside."

"You said I could ask you anything," he says, his lips lightly brushing my cheek. "What will happen if I ask you out again? Are you gonna break my heart?"

The insides of my thighs suddenly burn, and I can barely breathe. But I'm trapped in between the car door and his massive chest, so I lay a hand on his stomach and reply, "Do we really have to rush into this? I've been here for less than a week. We have the entire summer." I'll need the entire summer to prepare for this, for Arthur's body—for any consequences we may face.

"Yes," he pleads. "We've already wasted a year. I haven't slept in six days because I can't stop thinking about you. I freaked out when Gwen called me. I must have cleaned my house from top to bottom at least twenty times, I was so fuckin' nervous."

"Um, why were you nervous?" I ask.

"Because," he says, "I haven't seen you since last summer. You never respond to any of my texts, or messages on Snapchat. I feel like an asshole. What...what if you found a sexy, super-smart college boyfriend? What...what if you didn't want anything to do with me anymore because I'm trailer trash?"

The ridiculousness of his thinking forces me into a fit of hellish laughter.

"Hey, it's not funny." I've never seen Arthur like this, so vulnerable and timid. "I'm being serious here," he says.

"What do you want me to say?" I reply, wondering how I can stop the torrid sensation now roaring in between my legs. "Do you want me to give you an answer right now? Like right this second?"

Arthur slides a hand slowly across my chest and tilts my chin up to meet his.

It's the first time I've allowed anyone this close to my scars. His mouth finds mine and wages war against the space separating our bodies. I'm the first to seek relief.

"Do I want you to be my boyfriend, as corny as it sounds?" he asks. "Hell yes. A fucking-thousand-times yes. Am I capable of waiting until you're ready for me to call you that? Yes." He pauses and sighs. "I can wait a little longer, I suppose."

Before I'm able to respond to Arthur's admission, two fists rain down on the hood of the truck, and a slightly-but-not-quite-intoxicated Gwen dances her way around the front of the vehicle, doing her best Stevie Nicks impression. Or at least that's what I call it.

"Are you planning on staying in there for the whole party?" she wails, and I can feel her eyes seeking answers to unasked questions as they wander across Arthur's hands, which are now hugging my chest. "Because we're getting ready to burn a whole bunch of shit and release some negative energy. If not," she says, scrunching her nose, "well, then there's a big bag of condoms sitting on the kitchen counter, and you can help yourself to them. But be advised, the strawberry ones straight-up taste like chalk."

"You are a huge asshole," I say, while lights in the old farmhouse behind Gwen flicker on and off like someone is tinkering with the breaker. She must see my mouth twitch, because within seconds she yanks on the door handle of Arthur's truck, and I fall forward into her hands after it opens.

"What are you doing?" I ask, catching myself on the side door. "Gwen!"

"Why, stealing my precious Lancelot from his King Arthur." She locks our arms together and takes two steps forward without waiting for me to catch up.

"Come with me, little knight. We have much to discuss."

"You are three sheets to the wind, girl." I hear Arthur say as we hobble around a couple making out on the paved part of the driveway. "I hope you ain't drivin' tonight."

Gwen dismisses his comment with a languid wave of her hand.

"Are you two fucking? Because you sure took a long time getting here, and then he was practically in your cervix when I saved you from his clutches."

"What are you talking about?" I ask, pulling my arm from her now-loose grip. "We were just talking about stuff."

"Not even a hand job? He looks like he could use one. I bet he's ready to burst."

"Stop it," I say, clenching my side bag and doing my best not to step on fingers splayed out in the grass. "That's Arthur you're talking about."

"Young, dumb and full of cum!" Gwen laughs, and stumbles up a set of stairs that are in desperate need of repair. Her sandal catches the splintered wood and she stumbles forward. The wrap-around porch is crowded, and we have to push our way through a sea of red Solo cups and plumes of clove smoke.

"You are drunk," I say. It sounds like an accusation, even though I don't mean it that way. "It's only nine o'clock. How are you going to make it until midnight? Who is going to lead the séance?"

Hip-hop music, which grows louder each time we walk through a room, is making it difficult to hear Gwen's drunken ramblings. When she ducks her head and disappears into a herd of intoxicated teenagers, my pulse quickens and I hopelessly search for a way out of the room. The lights flicker on and off again, and girls start grinding on one another like they're at a rave. *I have to get the fuck outta here.* The stale scent of gas station incense and cheap weed is giving me a headache.

I turn around to head back out the way we came in, and my eyes accidentally land on two guys who are leaning up against a couch. Both men have a joint in one hand and a beer in the other. We lock eyes, and one of the men recognizes me and straightens up immediately. *Todd. Todd Butcher.* I avert my gaze and try to push my way through two girls who are standing in the doorway. I'm sure I've just wandered into another part of the house, but I don't care.

"Linda!" Todd's deep baritone voice booms over the music. "Linda, wait!"

His voice triggers several unpleasant memories. Todd was my boyfriend during ninth and tenth grades. He and I broke up the summer before I started eleventh grade, after I told him I was transgender. Of all the people I expected to run into at this stupid séance, he was the last. Hell, he hadn't even been on the list, because I had purposely forgotten about him.

A firm grip finds my wrist and I turn around. Todd is drunk and smells like bourbon. I wriggle my hand, trying to break free from his hold. We haven't spoken in over a year and a half. I don't know what he could possibly want.

"I thought that was you. How the hell are ya?" His words are slurred, and spit flies from his mouth onto my cheek. A girl pushes us together, trying to make her way to the kitchen, and our faces are now an inch or so apart. "Gwen told me you'd be here, but I told her I'd believe it when I saw it. I thought you hated parties," he says, and plants his hand on the wall just above my head. "So you're a man now, huh? No more Linda? You weren't kidding." I can feel his eyes raking across my chest.

Every time someone says the name Linda, indentations form on the hard-earned armor that I've worn with pride for the past two years. Talking to Todd about my gender is the last thing I want to do at this party.

"Do you remember that time I fingered you on Jackie Thompson's porch swing? Her parents were gone for the weekend, and she had the whole house to herself, just like this." He bends forward and brushes his lip against my ear. "We had just smoked a blunt and were sitting on the porch. You gave me head afterward. Do you want to go outside for a little bit?"

"Fuck off, asshole," I say. "And move your hand." I shove his chest as hard as I can. Things like this always happen at these parties. I always run into assholes from my past.

"Your pussy was wet then and I bet it's wet now." Todd slides his hand down the wall and rests it on my shoulder, then places his other hand on my hip. "Come on, just the tip."

Before I can respond to Todd's crude suggestion, two arms slide around his torso and he is lifted up like a toy in a claw machine.

"That's about enough of that!" Arthur tosses him aside without much effort and rushes over to me. "Dick! Are you okay?" he asks. Worry paints his forehead, and I all but fall into his chest. "What did he say to you? Did he follow you over here? Did he do anything?"

"I'm all right," I reply. "You know how he gets when he's drunk. Bastard."

"Oh, you mean how he turns into a rapist? Yes, I do know that," he says. "And I'm sure he's looking for his next victim right now. I have been waiting for an opportunity to kick his bony ass."

I turn my head from side to side. "Arthur, no. Let's not get into any fights while we're here."

"If he touches you again, I'm going to break his fucking arm. I mean it."

"Just help Gwen light that goddamn fire, and then we can get out of here."

Arthur's jaw muscles relax and the light returns to his eyes. "Okay," he says.

Gwen is in the kitchen when we find her, yelling at some kid who has made balloons out of condoms left on the counter. He can't be any older than fourteen, fifteen at the very oldest.

"Do you know the statistics for teen pregnancy in this state?" she shouts at him. "Do you? Well, I can't think of them off the top of my head, but they're pretty fucking high. Get out of here, and take this, because I sure as hell don't want *you* getting someone pregnant. Goddess help me!"

After she's popped each individual condom balloon, she stands up, her hands spangled in lube and latex. She mutters to herself and throws two handfuls of rubber into the garbage.

"Little prick. Oh hey," she says, finally realizing that we're standing there. "Where have you been?" She eyes Arthur for a second, and slowly focuses on our hands. Her eyes narrow and I break free from his grasp, then shove my hand into my pocket, because I'm not ready for this—I'm not ready to be seen, I'm not ready to answer more questions.

I'm not ready to live this dream that's slowly coming true.

"Bonnie said there's pizza in here," Arthur says. "Is there any cheese left? Jesus, what the hell was that?"

Gwen and I exchange heated glances. I don't know what she's thinking, nor do I truly care, but I'm sure it has to do with me and Arthur, or how I'm hiding something from her, when I'm not.

The overhead lights blink twice before going completely out, and vibrations caused from the loud music in the next room over viciously rattle the bones inside my chest like a human maraca. The only rational explanation for this power surge that I can think of is magickal in nature—a convergence of too many energies in one place, perhaps.

"Shit," Gwen says. "Help me light these candles. And be quick about it."

Arthur removes two pizza boxes and several empty soda bottles from the kitchen counter, and Gwen drops six glass candles onto the clean surface. The candles make loud thunks on the granite countertop, and one nearly rolls off the counter before I catch it.

"You sure you wanna clean up broken glass in a poorly lit room, Queenie?" I ask, now shouting over the loud hip-hop music blaring from the other room. "Did it just get louder in here, or is that just me?"

"No!" Gwen says. "There's some heavy energy here tonight. Some powerful witches, I guess. I have no idea who half these fucking people are, though. Olivia is going to be so pissed when she comes home and sees everyone here. I said plus one—plus one—not plus ten."

"Yeah," I say. "I ran into Todd Butcher out there." Arthur grunts and folds his arms. If I hadn't stopped him, Arthur would have started a brawl right there in the middle of the house. I love him, but he does let his emotions get the best of him at times, and I have to remind him to keep them in check.

"What?" Gwen asks, straining her neck to look through the doorway. "Is he still here? Lance, I swear I didn't invite him. I wouldn't. What did he say to you?"

"It's not a big deal. That incident was a little over three years ago. I'm okay. I just didn't expect to run into him here." I put up my hand, a physical dismissal of her concerns. "And who the hell is Olivia?" I ask. "I thought your girlfriend's name was Lena."

Gwen lights the individual candles, and stops to say a prayer into each flame. The music in the next room returns to a decent volume, and the kitchen suddenly fills with light as if the power surge never occurred. My sister is finally becoming a witch—her powers must have awakened sometime this year when I was away. I smile at her.

"Olivia," she says, "is my boss. She owns Baubles."

I sneer at her. "Your boss? There's an orgy about to happen out there on the lawn, and this house belongs to your boss. Are you out of your damned mind? What are you thinking?"

"Relax, grandma. Olivia is super chill. She asked me to house-sit for her this weekend, and told me that if I wanted to have a get-together, it was okay. Power surges aren't that big of a deal."

Arthur joins my side, a piece of cheese pizza in each hand. "It's not the electricity I'm worried about, dude." I point to the people standing in the doorway. "It's the massive swelling of energy in this house. Did you intend on calling a coven tonight?"

Gwen's smirk vanishes from her face, only to be replaced by a scowl. She's going to lose her temper — it's easy to spot when she's been drinking.

"All we're going to do is eat some acid, maybe do some shrooms, and dance outside under the beautiful moonlight. No one is going to get hurt. Jesus, you worry too much."

My phone buzzes in my side bag and I check to see who's calling. I don't want to bicker with Gwen, and I'm thankful for the distraction. I didn't come to the party to argue with anyone, especially not my little sister and best friend.

A Facebook notification alerts me that someone has just sent Camelot Crafts a message.

Shit. I guess I didn't log out of the store account before I left the store.

Emmett, my boss, has asked me to manage the page while I'm at work, because he's too stubborn to actually learn how to maneuver the damn site for himself. I open the link and a message from someone called Mordy Lafayette pops up. They want to know if Camelot sells candles, stones and-or rubbing oils. I send a reply, stating that we sell wax to make candles, and glass stones for aquariums, that kind of stuff — adding that if they're looking for something else, to check out Baubles & Books, the store next door to ours.

As soon as I send the message, I hear the faint sound of a Facebook notification. I look up from my phone and scour the scene. Other than Gwen and Arthur, there are only two other people in the kitchen.

My phone buzzes again. I look down at the message. Mordy thanks me for the advice and wishes me a good night. The message intrigues me for some reason, so I send another text expressing that they're welcome, and as before I hear a notification. While Gwen and Arthur busy themselves with collecting pizza boxes to burn in the fire — something I do not approve of doing — I meander from room to room, looking for anyone who might be on their phone. It takes all of five seconds to discover that most everyone is on their phone, and there's no way of telling if this Mordy person is at the party.

The rooms are as tightly packed as a box of crayons, and being confined in such a small space with so many people is freaking me out, so I decide to get a breath of fresh air. City life, even in a smaller city like Lexington, is different from life in the mountains. The air is cleaner here, or at least smells better, and you can actually see the stars at night.

After a quick glance up at the twinkling sky lights that have held my admiration for these past twenty-some years, I take a seat on the soft grass. I pull out my phone and scroll through pictures on Instagram, cute pics of cats and dogs, pictures of girls in bathing suits and pictures of people at this party. I stop on Gwen's account and watch a video of her licking white powder off some girl's nipples. I roll my eyes and keep scrolling.

Gwen was not like this before I left to go to college. While not exactly prim and proper, she had been sweet and shy, especially around girls she liked. Then something had happened to her, and she'd gone off the deep end, I guess. When I'd come home for Christmas during my freshman year of college, she'd been several inches taller, had gotten her braces removed, and had

had pastel pink streaks in her near-white hair. She had become a woman in the six months I had been gone.

"Excuse me," someone says, stealing my attention away from the illuminated screen in my lap. "But do you have any idea where the bathrooms are?"

Two people, dressed completely in white, stare down at me from the porch. I crane my neck back to get a better look at them. They don't sound like they're from around here, and I'm certain I've never seen them in school or in town.

"Oh," I say. "I think there's one downstairs, right beside the kitchen, and maybe one upstairs? I'm not sure. You should ask my sister. She's the one in charge, I guess."

One of the two guests takes a step forward. "Gwen is your sister?" they ask.

I put my phone away and squint into the dark, letting my pupils readjust to the darkness. "Yeah, she is. I'm her brother, Lance." I get up from the ground and wipe off my palms, then extend my hand. "Nice to meet ya," I say.

"Lance and Gwen Lotte." The other person finally speaks. They exchange glances with each other. "You live here, in town?"

"Yep, sure do." I gesture to my left, using my chin. "About four miles that way. Where are y'all from? I've never seen you around here before."

People of color are few and far between in Avalon. There are black families that I know of in town, but I don't recall any of them having kids my age, or anyone remotely close to my age.

"California," they both say at the same time.

When one of them tries to take my hand, the other slaps their hand out of the way. "No. We are not even supposed to be outside, and you want to touch *his* hand? Have you lost your mind?"

"Who will know, Morgan?" The question is like a hiss, aggressive and serpentine, and not meant for my ears, I think. "Tell me."

"Our ancestors, the spirits. They will know."

"You're taking this Iyawo shit too seriously, you know that? That old man has filled your head with fairy tales."

"No," Morgan erupts and jams her finger into the other person's chest. "You are the one who is not taking it seriously enough."

"Lance," the unnamed one says. "It was my pleasure to meet you. Hopefully this will not be the last time our paths cross. Be safe tonight." The one who appears to be male—maybe?—pulls his hand out of Morgan's grasp. "I'll meet *you* back at the car."

Morgan calls out, "Mordy!" and chases after him as he swerves in and out of people on the porch.

Mordy. That was Mordy? I hastily pull my phone out of my bag and sign in to the Camelot Crafts account again. Most of his profile is set to private, but I can still see a set of dazzling white teeth smiling back at me. I click on tagged photos and scroll through the public ones. Mordy wears glasses and has perfect teeth, including the silver one in the front. He's tall and slender, not muscular like Arthur at all. I like the way his bottom lip juts out slightly, plump and ripe for the picking.

Handsome. Absurdly attractive.

In several pictures standing beside him is a girl, whom I assume to be Morgan. They must be twins, because she is absurdly attractive too, with long, well-maintained dreads that match his, and silver beads scattered throughout her hair. They're dressed in slim-fitting black clothes in all of the pictures — a stark contrast to the matching white outfits they now wear.

I return to the first image and for a second, an overwhelming feeling of déjà vu consumes me, followed by a strong desire to weep — to grieve — to mourn something that I've lost, or that I'm about to lose.

I drop the phone and cup my mouth. The sensation lasts only a few seconds, but it's powerful enough to knock me back into the railing. I have met those two before, but where? I cannot say.

"There you are," Gwen practically sings when she finds me. "Where's Arthur?"

"I have no idea. I thought he was with you." I drop to the ground and scramble on all fours, searching for my phone. *No. No. Please don't be broken.*

"No," she replies, firmly grasping one of the eight pillars on the porch with her hands. "I did see him come out here, though. I thought he was following you."

I shake my head. "Nope. Are you okay?"

Gwen swings her body around the pillar to stand in front of me. "I was just thinking the same thing, Lance."

"What are you talking about?" I ask. If I take one wrong step, I'll smash the phone screen. I've done it twice now, and I've run out of my student loans. A hundred-dollar screen repair is out of the question. I move my hands in a circular motion, praying that someone's foot doesn't find the phone before I do.

"He came here to be with you."

I don't like her tone. "Arthur is a free man. He can do what he wants. We're not joined at the hip."

"You know damn well freedom is the last thing on Arthur's mind."

"I don't care to talk about sex with you again, and I'm looking for my phone right now. So can we please not?"

Gwen pulls out her phone and uses it as a flashlight, holding it above me while I frenziedly look for mine. "I am not talking about sex. That man is desperately in love with you. Doesn't that bother you at all?"

"Ah ha!" I find my phone and kiss it, not at all caring that I just inhaled a lump of dirt. "He told me he loved me this evening."

"What?" Gwen asks. She swings her legs over the railing and balances herself on the metal pole. "And what did you say?"

"Nothing. I told him that I wasn't ready."

"When will you be ready? You'll be twenty-one in three months. Are you going to watch him from the bleachers for the rest of your life?"

"We both know I can't," I say. "You and Arthur both know."

Gwen clicks her tongue. "So...is this a trans thing? Or like a knight-of-the-round-table thing?"

Darkness has fallen so Gwen can't see me roll my eyes, but that doesn't stop me from doing it. We haven't discussed either matter in months, because I can't bring myself to admit these certain truths that I hold about myself and my friends may or may not be true. She knows I don't believe in coincidences, or the possibility that some things just aren't connected, so talking to her about predestination is out of the question.

When I came to Avalon, I was Linda Gonzales. A social worker placed me with six foster families before I was finally adopted by the Lotte family, my forever foster family. Gwen doesn't believe in legends, and certainly does not believe that the name 'Gwen Lotte' has any connection to Gwenhyvfar, the famed woman who notoriously betrayed King Arthur by falling in love with his best friend and confidant, Sir Lancelot, a love that led to widespread destruction and Arthur's ultimate demise.

"I do love you," she says, her voice soft and understanding. "But not that like. You're my brother, and I'm a dyke."

That didn't stop King Arthur from falling in love with his twin sister, Morgana.

Morgan. I dismiss the notion immediately that Arthur and the mysterious girl from earlier share a blood connection, but mentally set the thought aside for further investigation, because that's just how my brain operates.

"Arthur is dying for you to make a move," she says. "What is the hang-up?"

"I can't. We already know what happened the last time. It was a sign."

Gwen flips over the railing and lands beside me, her feet planting firmly on the ground like a gymnast. She places her hand on my shoulder and squeezes.

"Homophobia is not a sign," she says. "It's a mental disorder, and you're going to die a virgin if you continue to live like this."

"Virginity is a social construct, Gwen. It has meaning because we give it meaning. It doesn't actually exist."

Gwen sticks out her tongue at me. "You do realize that's precisely what a virgin would say."

I shake off her hand and pull out my phone. "It's nearly midnight. Aren't you supposed to be burning off negative energy or some shit?"

"Text Arthur, tell him you want to suck his big dick."

"What?" I ask. "I thought you were drunk, but now I think you're experiencing severe psychosis. Because you are absolutely bonkers."

"Why not?" she asks. "Do you want me to text him? I'll do it for you."

A screen door slams and someone calls out, "Gwen!" My sister bumps my head with hers and points at my phone.

"He would probably bust a nut just reading that text."

"Why are you like this?" I reply.

"Just sayin', is all. Bring that negative energy out back and prepare to get naked."

Gwen is always naked, or talking about getting or being naked. She jumps at any and all reasons to undress in front of others. I love her, but she's mental.

After she leaves, I walk around the house and find a spot to lean against. My head is swimming and my stomach burns. I haven't eaten anything since lunch, but I'm not really into the idea of possibly running into Todd again just for a slice of cheese pizza, so I'll wait to eat something when I get back to Arthur's.

I should probably text him to see where he is, so I send him a message, and decide to scroll through Instagram while I wait for a response. The third picture I see makes my gut sting even more — Arthur has two girls on his lap and they're both kissing. I can't really see his face, but he's smiling, so that means he's having a good time, enjoying himself and the view. The girls are closer to his age, and look like models. A splendid time being had by all, I'm sure.

I'm self-aware enough to know that everyone, not just me, finds the light in Arthur's eyes warm and alluring, that the things I admire the most in him are admired by many. But I am not in a good mental space, haven't been since my arrival, and I know now with utmost certainty that I should have gone home after work.

"Fuck this," I say to myself, and push off the side of the house.

I shove my phone into my bag and make the decision to walk home alone.

Chapter Three

The Dioscuri

A few days after the party, I find myself sitting in Baubles & Books, having coffee and eggs with Gwen. She hasn't shut up about the party since we got here, though, because apparently after I left, several people got really high, stripped naked and jumped into a creek that runs alongside the old farmhouse. The night ended in someone getting their ass bitten by a baby water moccasin. Must've been city folk, because everyone around here knows better than to do such a dumb thing. You never get into a creek at night, especially when you've been drinking.

"Have you heard from Arthur since Friday night?" Gwen opens two plastic containers of creamer and pours each one into her coffee. "Did you go home with him?" she asks. "I don't really remember much from that night, honestly."

I reach for the ketchup and squirt a dollop of dark red brilliance beside my eggs. Gwen makes a retching sound and points at it. I reply, "They're my eggs. And no, I haven't. I left before he did."

"What pissed you off this time?" she asks, never missing a beat. "You're ridiculous, you know that, don't ya?"

I survey the small, mostly empty store before answering, doing my best to contain the frustration I feel bubbling up from the pit of my empty stomach.

The store has been here since we were in middle school, but I have trouble remembering specific details about it opening, my memories hazier than usual for some reason. A colorful assortment of resplendent stained glass in all of the windows and wind chimes hanging from every open screen make it difficult to maintain a sour mood in here.

At the front of the store are two displays, one full of packaged, vacuum-sealed herbs for medicinal purposes, and the other full of calendars, journals and small charms meant for novice witches and those interested in casting spells. A purple calendar attractively adorned in stars and moons immediately catches my eye. Not because I'm a novice witch, but because I'm a sucker for Celtic-inspired art. The plastic-wrapped paper chart reminds me of a journal I have packed away in a box from my dorm room.

The rest of the store is pretty much just stocked with cheaply made wooden bookshelves and used books on various types of witchcraft. No real organizational skills or thoughts have been applied to the actual setup of the store. How Baubles & Books has managed to stay afloat this deep in the Bible Belt is beyond me. As unintuitive as it might sound, I suspect it has something to do with magick.

Gwen and I are seated by a large bay window that looks overlooks an empty parking lot, and wafts from the burning incense snake their way toward us. I love the pure, clean scent of sandalwood, so that smoke doesn't bother me at all.

"How can I put this, without sounding like a huge ass," I finally say. "I'm a very selfish person, I know this about myself, and I don't particularly like the idea of sharing Arthur with everyone, which is why I won't commit to the idea of being with him exclusively."

Gwen replies, her mouth full of hash browns, "Exclusively? I don't know what that means. Are you saying that you would be into an open relationship? Because that's very 'millennial queer' of you, if so."

I shake my head. "No," I say. "I don't want him to settle for me."

We have had this conversation more than once, and every time, it ends with us arguing about whether I have the right to make that decision for Arthur. I wait for Gwen's impassioned response, and take a sip of the Earl Grey tea that was just brought to me.

"I don't see how you can sit here and say these things about yourself."

Ever since I came out as Lance, I've struggled with these types of thoughts about myself and others. Gay relationships often seem off limits to trans people, especially among gay men. I'm not white, I'm a trans man, and I'm gay—the array of conflicting identities can be too much for me at times. I can't share that burden with Arthur, not here in Avalon, and I would never dream of asking him to move to Lexington just for me. I'm not worth the hassle.

"But I won't argue with you anymore," Gwen says. "It's your journey, and if you're dead-set on traveling it alone, I won't force you into doing somethin' you don't want. I just wish you'd let him love you once and for all. Oh, I meant to ask you—aren't Arthur's kittens cute?"

I scoff. "You mean Yin and Yang?" Just saying those words makes me feel uneasy.

"Yes! I helped him name them!" Gwen beams with pride. "Because they're black and white!"

I stare at her in disbelief. "You suggested those names? I can't believe it. Are you that dense?"

"Dense? I don't get it. What's wrong with it? They *are* black and white."

I pinch the bridge of my nose. "You've taken sacred Chinese philosophy and— You know what, just— never mind. I don't feel like getting into it with you right now."

Gwen pouts her bottom lip. "This is a 'I'm white and have done something horribly offensive again' thing, isn't it? I'm sorry."

"I don't live here anymore," I say. "I am not going to dictate how you or Arthur live your lives, but try to be mindful of this shit, won't you? You're like this close to being that dumbass who wears a headdress to the bar on Halloween night."

"God, Lance, give me some credit. I would never do that, I'm not that stupid."

"Just how stupid are we talking?" a voice from behind our table asks. "Mornin', Gwen, Lance."

Arthur and a girl wearing a plain, low-cut yellow sundress walk over to our table. She has blonde dreadlocks and a tattoo of a Japanese symbol just below her clavicle. I know the girl, or at least have seen her at the library a few times. The last time we actually spoke to each other was in passing, at the polling station, where she was helping folks vote. That time she had been wearing a shirt that said 'A Woman's Place Is In The White House', and kept fucking up my pronouns because I was still registered to vote as Linda. I think she was confused about the whole process. Hell, I was confused, and it made voting for the first time suck.

"Hey," Gwen says, and kicks me under the table. "Speak of the devil. How are you, Arthur? Tammy?"

I don't acknowledge either of them, keeping my eyes on my cup of tea, because I'm a huge baby and haven't been able to climb out of my dark feelings since Friday night. Besides, I am not particularly fond of Tammy, and just the sight of her irritates me.

Arthur does his best to ignore my low mood, though, and takes the chair next to mine, turns it around then sits on it, folding his forearms on the back. His leg brushes against mine and he keeps it there, making me acutely aware of his close presence. Normally I would say something and move it abruptly, but that would force me to acknowledge him, so I don't.

"Lance, do you know Tammy Dixon?" Gwen asks. "Tammy, this is my brother, Lance."

Tammy must not recognize me, because she is all smiles and giggles when she introduces herself, but that doesn't stop me from ignoring her greeting. Arthur rubs his leg against mine and I shoot a look at him.

"I'm glad to see you made it home okay on Friday night," he says, leaning over. "I would have given you a ride if you had said something. You didn't have to walk all that way. I spent the rest of the night thinking that Todd had done something awful again. Do you even know how to respond to text messages?"

Arthur isn't usually this disgruntled, or at least, frames his questions differently when it's just the two of us. The irritation saturating his voice is almost palpable. I'm not sure if it's vexation or disdain, but I'm not used to such a black, accusatory tone.

"Lance, I feel like I know you." Tammy must sense the beginnings of an argument, because she interjects before I have time to respond to Arthur. "Have we met before?"

"I'm not sure, maybe," I reply, my eyes still locked with Arthur's. "White people all look the same to me."

Arthur stifles a laugh and Gwen huffs.

"I'm sorry," Gwen says. "My brother is being very rude at the moment. Maybe he's about to be on his period?"

"Fuck off," I say to Gwen. "You expect me to be nice to some white chick with shitty dreads and a fucking Asian tattoo on her left boob that probably means 'barbecue'?"

Tammy shuffles uncomfortably in her seat, and when I think she's about to apologize for existing, she says something even dumber, sending me into a fit of rage. To make sure I heard her correctly, I ask her to repeat herself.

"Don't you think it's misogynistic to imply that your brother is about to be on his period just because he's mad?" Tammy asks Gwen again, in all seriousness.

The table falls silent, and Arthur, Gwen and I exchange looks. I scoot my chair back and stand up.

"Are you serious right now?" I ask. "Don't you think it's transphobic to suggest that men don't get periods? You know what? I actually don't give a damn about what you think because I'm leaving." I reach into my pants pocket and pull out two five-dollar bills, then toss them on the table. "That should cover my breakfast, tip and all. I'm out of here."

"Lance!" Arthur stands up. "Hey, wait!"

I can hear Gwen telling him to let me go, that I'm on one at the moment, that it's not worth it. *She's probably right.*

"Lance!" Arthur calls out once more, ignoring Gwen's sound advice. "Where are you going?"

I make my way to the front of the store, and throw up a hand, before opening the screen door. "Later," I say.

I don't know why I'm so mad, maybe Gwen's right.

The overhead sun is in full force this morning, so I reach for the sunglasses in my shirt pocket and take a few deep breaths before finding a shaded seat on the ground.

Outside, the streets are much busier than inside the shop, and while this would normally exacerbate my anxiety, there's something unusually calming about watching joggers and random folks with dogs share a sidewalk with one other. Sometimes life is so simple in this little Podunk town.

Across from Baubles & Books is a tiny vintage boutique that sells hats and scarves, called Hatsapalooza, and beside that is a candy store that specializes in making old-fashioned rock candy and homemade ice cream floats. I have no idea how some of these shops are still around. Who even buys hard candy in bulk anymore? Camelot Crafts is Baubles & Books' next-door neighbor, and the only store on the block that I know of with a steady stream of customers on the reg. *Thank God for church ladies and preschool teachers.*

Gwen has worked at Baubles & Books for the past two months, I think. It's her third job in the past four years. She's a hard worker, always on time, never calls in, that type of person, but doesn't take shit from customers who pinch her ass or call her sweetie. I wonder how long she'll last at this job. She has a cool boss and seems happy, but she's been at it for only a couple of months, so only time will tell.

I should probably text her, apologize for acting like a huge dick all the time. No one deserves that. She doesn't deserve it.

Because Gwen is my ride or die. My rock.

Gwen is my soulmate—and I don't mean that in a romantic sense of the word. She's just the type of person who will get in the face of a homophobe at a right-wing rally, someone who would drive three hours in a raging snowstorm just to have a cup of coffee with you, someone who would legit stare death in the face, on your deathbed, and say *fucking try me*.

I turn around and glance over my shoulder. Arthur and Gwen are discussing something, and Tammy is staring at the phone in her hand. I bet Tammy is the same type of person. They both share a similar kind of energy. I should probably apologize to her as well. God knows I need all the allies I can get at the moment. Maybe I'll ask Arthur if she has a Facebook, send her a message. Not right now, but maybe later.

I don't know why I'm such an asshole all the time. I hate feeling like this.

I find a spot on the warm sidewalk and take a seat, but it's so hot outside that I find it difficult to get comfortable. *Maybe leaving the store was a mistake, maybe I should just go back inside.*

"Hey!" a voice calls out from across the street, and I whip my head around, only to see Morgan and Mordy standing on the other side of the road, bags of candy in each hand.

"I'll be damned," I say to myself and get up from the concrete ground. "Hey, y'all! What's up?"

The two clad-in-white siblings cross the street and greet me with smiles and waves. I envy the way they look cool without even trying—Mordy's dreads are pulled into a single knot, and his sister's are fashioned into buns, one on each side of her head. It's not even so much the way they dress or how they look, but rather how they carry themselves. Tall and proud, completely oblivious to the outside world. A string of baby's breath in a bouquet full of black hydrangeas.

"Mordy, right?" I ask, extending my hand cautiously, hoping that a handshake is not a personal affront to Morgan. "And Morgan, was it?"

Morgan laughs and takes my hand with vigor. "Yeah, Morgan Lafayette. We're siblings. And I'd like to apologize for the other night!" she says. "I wasn't really feeling being around so many white witches, if you get my drift." Her eyebrow rises when she says the word 'white'. "This place is wild, though." Morgan gestures to the block with her hand. "I don't see how you remain sane. Everyone just—"

"Stares at you," all three of us say, simultaneously. Boisterous laughter follows, and I immediately feel completely at ease with these outsiders. Maybe it's because I've always felt like an outsider myself, or maybe it's something else, I can't tell.

"So what do you do around here other than hang out at loud parties with terrible music and shitty weed?" Mordy asks. He holds out his bag of candy and I stick my hand inside, grabbing a few pieces. "Are you a witch?" He gestures to the black jewel and Magic 8-Ball charm hanging from my neck.

The way he's looking at me with enormous green eyes full of curiosity reminds me of Arthur, and it doesn't make me uncomfortable necessarily, but it does make me self-aware of how I'm put together this morning. I didn't expect to run into anyone other than Gwen. I bet I look like a walking pile of wrinkled denim and black leather.

"Yeah," I reply. "I've been practicing witchcraft since I was a small child. How about you two?"

Mordy puts his arm around his sister and says, "Santería, which is why we're dressed like ghosts."

"Santería?" Last year I took an anthropology class on world religions, and while most of it had been whitewashed, ethnocentric bullshit, some of it had been interesting, like brujería. I recall liking aspects of Santería, too. "Like Cuban witchcraft, or whatever?" I say.

"Afro-Cuban witchcraft," Morgan corrects me politely. "Spiritual aspects from both of our peoples, you feel me?"

"Does that freak you out?" Mordy asks, his tone playful and airy.

I look up at him. His silver tooth glitters in the sunlight, adding to his unyielding composure, and I shift my sunglasses down ever so slightly, revealing my golden irises.

"Are you cool with curses and evil eyes, that kinda shit?" I ask.

Mordy and Morgan exchange looks. "We are totally cool with that kinda shit," Morgan replies. "And then some." She winks at me.

Black magick. Dark magick. Forbidden magick.

I look down at my phone and see that I have four missed texts from Arthur. One text apologizing for Tammy's behavior, another regarding hanging out tonight. I don't read the other two because I need to sort through my feelings and put a cap on them before I end up doing something really stupid, or saying something I regret.

"Why don't you text me your number?" Mordy asks. Morgan is already halfway across the road when I realize that it's just the two of us.

"Really?" I say, surprised that he would want anything to do with me.

"Yeah, really." Mordy pulls out his phone and taps mine with it. "Unless you're scared, that is."

"Scared of what?"

"Practicin' magick with a couple of weirdos from out west."

Much like Arthur, Mordy commands your attention when he's speaking, so much that you don't want him to stop, and I like his accent, his manner of speaking. He's a really cool dude.

A dimple forms in each cheek and he beams at me. I think he's flirting with me, but I don't know why, not when my hair is sticking to my face and I'm covered in sweat from the heat.

"I ain't scared of nothin'," I say. "You're the one who's messin' with Brown holler magick."

Mordy grins and replies, "Brown holler magick. Now that's the kinda shit I'm looking for."

Chapter Four

Le Morte D'Arthur

When I got called into work this morning, I didn't expect to be working by myself or pulling a double. Emmett has got the most incompetent fucking people working here. I actually don't know how he manages to keep any staff, or how Emmett gets anything done.

Who counts the inventory? Who unloads the inventory? Who stocks the inventory?

Unless he knows how to make a broom sprout arms, I don't see how things get done behind the scenes. Emmett can't upload a picture to Facebook — how could he possibly juggle scheduling people who simply don't show up for work when it's their turn? I honestly don't think he's ever fired anyone, either. Everyone just gets fed up and leaves on their own, except for maybe Caspian, but that's because Caspian thinks he's a wizard or something.

Truly mind-boggling.

Next to Saturday afternoon, Tuesday is our busiest day of the week. From sunup to sundown we have grannies coming through that door with clipped coupons from the newspaper, and Boy Scouts buying up all the construction paper to make things like paper cranes for patients in the hospital. It's nearly seven o'clock now, and I don't think I've sat down since I took a five-minute break right before it got busy again, around noon or so.

I'm exhausted and hungry because I forgot to eat this morning, and ended up eating the peanut butter sandwich from my packed lunch for breakfast. The bag of potato chips got me through the afternoon rush, but now I'm ravenous, ready to eat anything.

After I've finished counting the money in the register, the bell above the door rings, signaling the last customers of the evening—hopefully, anyway. I'm not exactly sure how to close the store, because Emmett is usually the one who handles that type of stuff—this is only my second time doing it—but I figure it couldn't hurt to keep track of how much money I made today. Besides, I like math, and I'm good at it.

"Good evening," I say, still on my knees, trying to remember the goddamn safe combination. "I'll be with you in a second!" I would normally just text Emmett, but I have no idea where he is, or what he's doing, or if he even knows how to use a smartphone.

"Take your time," a familiar voice says. "We're in no rush."

I pop my head over the counter, only to see Mordy and Morgan perusing the small selection of clay bowls we have stacked at the front of the store. Mordy picks up a red bowl and turns it over. Morgan shakes her head at him, and he puts it back where he found it.

"Anything I can help you with?" I ask. "Are you looking for a specific type of bowl?"

"84183," Morgan says, taking a small break from the milkshake in her hand.

"Huh?" I ask, stupidly. "84183?"

"The safe," she replies. "Try it."

I do as she says, and the safe clicks, then opens. She walks over to where I am and peers over the counter. "Was I right?"

"How did you do that?"

"Nothin' special. We're all witches here," she says. "Some of us are just more attuned to our environments, that's all."

Morgan and Mordy are dressed in white again, but this time Morgan is wearing a sleeveless crop top and a pair of skinny jeans. Like Mordy, her hair is pulled into a knot today, and sitting atop the mound of dreads is a pair of large white-framed sunglasses. Her fashion sense is on point.

I'm not into women like that — never have been — but I am certain that every time she walks past a hot-blooded hetero male, her soft curves turn heads. Gwen would stop dead in her tracks, I know that much. Mordy's wearing a tight T-shirt that hugs every part of his arms and upper torso, and a pair of off-white chinos.

His butt looks really good in the pants. *Really good.*

"Lance," Mordy says, breaking the spell I've found myself under. I blush and quickly meet his eyes, acutely aware that I've just been staring at his ass for God knows how long. The smile on his face indicates that either he doesn't care or didn't see me staring at him. I hope it's the latter, rather than the former. "Morgan said you might be hungry." He reaches into his shoulder bag and withdraws a damaged box of oatmeal cream pies — my favorite snack food — and I'm certain that if the box were given to me, I would eat every cake. "So we stopped at a gas station on the way here," he says. "This was the only box they had."

When he pulls out three bottles of Yoo-hoo, I gape at the both of them. Yoo-hoos are what I drink when I'm feeling stressed out or depressed. Something about the watery chocolate goodness just gets to me.

"Thank you," I say, accepting the gifts with caution. "But how? Why? Are you a psychic?"

Morgan laughs. "I prefer soothsayer, but yes, I am blessed with the gift of sight."

I gawk at the food in my arms. My stomach growls loudly in response to the cream-filled cookies I'm carrying, and I find the two of them staring down at me.

"Look, I know we don't know each other," Morgan says. "And I was a huge bitch when we first met. I'm sorry for that, it was entirely my bad. But the three of us share the same vibe. Our energy is the same. I know you feel it." Her eyes search mine, anxiously awaiting my response.

What she says is true. I do feel it, like some intangible magnetic force is constantly drawing me toward these two — but part of me is afraid to embrace it. Just looking at them pulls at something inside of me, some latent darkness that I've always known was there, but tried to hide. Sleeping nephilim just waiting to be summoned.

"Why don't we get together tomorrow?" Mordy asks. "We can get coffee. Or lunch. Whatever's good for you, Lance."

Morgan nods, then slowly shakes her head a moment later. "Wait. You know what, scratch that — I can't. I have to witness a *santiguó* with *Tío* Myrddin, and I have no idea how long that'll take. Mordred," she says, turning to her brother, "why don't you two get together instead?"

"Your name is Mordred," I interrupt, looking at Mordy, both of my hands now suspended in the air. "And your uncle's name is Myrddin?"

Morgana. Myrddin. Mordred. Lancelot. Arthur. Gwenhyvfar. Avalon.

For better or for worse, we are all connected.

There's no way this is purely coincidental. If I tell Gwen—and that's a big *if*—she won't be able to rationalize her way out of this. Legends that once were are no more, because they're being retold right before our eyes.

"Okay," I say, finally. "I can do coffee tomorrow before my shift starts, if that's all right. Does nine work for you?"

Morgan smiles at me and takes my hand. "We are going to learn so much from one another. You just wait and see. I thought this summer was going to be so fucking boring."

Her touch makes my skin prickle, but it isn't an unpleasant feeling necessarily, more like the feeling you get right before you sneeze.

Morgan and I exchange phone numbers and say goodbye.

As the twins exit the store, Emmett passes them, walking through the doorway. Morgan suddenly hisses at my boss, and Mordy rubs his hands back and forth vigorously. I'm not entirely sure what's happening, but the room suddenly grows dark and it feels like I just walked into a meat freezer.

"Get out of my store!" Emmett says, crossing his forehead, mouth and chest with his thumb, his gray breath detectable in the darkness. "This is no place for your kind."

"*Vete a la mierda.*" *Fuck off.*

Mordred takes a step in front of his sister as if to protect her, and pushes her behind his back so that he's completely blocking her way. "I will snap your goddamn neck like a twig, old man," Mordred says. "You'd better watch yourself, *juramentos.*" *Oathbreaker.*

"Lance." Emmett calls out my name, now pulling me into the situation. "You are not to let these two back into my store. Do you understand me?"

Morgan spits at Emmett. "Don't worry, you geriatric piece of shit. We won't be back." She then looks my way, fashioning a phone out of her thumb and pinky. "Lance, a pleasure always. Give me a ring whenever."

Mordred is visibly too angry to speak, and Morgan has to drag him by the arm out of the store. I still have no idea what just happened. When Morgan and her brother pass the large window up front, she makes a gesture with her hand, and the overhead lights blink once, then every bulb in the store bursts in the air like glass confetti. I cower beneath the counter, next to the safe, my hands gripping the sides of my head.

"Lance, you may go home." Emmett's voice is off. "There's no need for you to stay."

"But, Mr. Crabtree," I say. "The glass."

Emmett puts up one hand. "No worries. I can clean it myself. Just be careful when you leave."

"Are you sure?" I ask, surveying the floor that is now covered in glass shards. "I don't mind."

Emmett waves and locks the door behind me. Arthur had offered to give Gwen and me a ride home tonight after work, but her shift doesn't end until the store closes at eight o'clock, so that means I still have a little over a half an hour to fart around and do nothing.

I find a seat on the still-warm sidewalk and pull out my phone. For the last hour or so, Arthur has been texting me, sending memes and silly animal gifs. I guess I was so caught up in the madness that I didn't register the buzzing in my back pocket. The last text asks if I have any plans this evening, followed by a picture of him holding up a video game controller and a slice of veggie pizza.

Before I can respond to the multitude of texts, Arthur's truck pulls up out front.

"Hey," he yells out the passenger window. I get up from my spot and walk over to meet him. He turns off the truck. "What are you doing?" he asks. "I thought you had to close the craft store tonight."

The passenger window is already rolled down, so I lean my elbows on the metal frame and shake my head. "Not tonight," I say. "Some folks came in the store, caused a bit of a scene with the owner, and he sent me home early."

"What kind of scene? Are you okay?" Arthur is always worried that something bad has happened to me, or is going to happen to me. He slides across the bench seat and scans my bare arms, clearly amazed by the lack of injuries I should have suffered, but didn't.

It was almost as if I had been protected somehow from the violent display of power, but suggesting these two strangers might have created a magickal barrier could add some unnecessary speculation that I just don't want to deal with at the moment.

"Did you know the customers?" he asks.

"No, I'm fine, and kinda? Two kids I met at Gwen's party."

Talking about Mordy and Morgan with Arthur feels almost like a betrayal, and I'm not quite sure why, because I haven't done anything wrong. I'm not the one responsible for upsetting Emmett, or the layer of broken glass now lining the countertops and floor, and I'm not sure he'd fully understand the importance of their names—Mordred and Morgan Lafayette.

"What happened, exactly?" Arthur asks.

Emmett had said *'Your kind'*. But I'm not sure if he was being a huge racist, or if he was talking about witchcraft. Or both. Emmett Crabtree has been my boss off and on for the past five years, and if he's racist or prejudiced toward people of color, it's news to me. He's spacey and doesn't know how to delegate tasks, but he's never treated me differently, so I choose my words carefully.

"They were leaving the store, and Emmett was walking into the store. After they passed one another he told them to get out, then told me they weren't allowed in the store ever again, and they left."

"Did he send you home early because you knew them?"

"No, I don't think so," I say. "Once they were outside, the lights flickered immediately and then every bulb in the store shattered."

"Holy shit," Arthur replies. "That's super intense. Are they witches?"

"Yes? But it's more complicated than that. Morgan and Mordy are Santería initiates, I think."

"What's Santería?"

I don't feel like giving Arthur a lecture on world religions at the moment, and instead offer him a bottle of Yoo-hoo. "A form of witchcraft. Just Google it," I say. He takes the bottle, puts it in the cup holder and returns to the window, pulling me close. I barely have time to close my side bag, his actions are so fast.

It's been nearly a week since Arthur told me how he feels. In fact, he hasn't mentioned our conversation at all, but given how many times a day he texts me—a good morning text right after I wake up, a good night text right before I go to sleep and a bajillion texts in between—it has to have crossed his mind at least once or twice. I'm not complaining, though.

The streets are already deserted because all but one shop is closed, and this town doesn't know how to operate outside of the hours of eight a.m. and eight p.m. I allow Arthur to slowly run his hands up and down my arms. His touch sends waves of pleasure from one limb to the other. He looks me in the eye and says the same thing he's been saying since the night of the party. "Come over tonight. I can always drive you home if want me to."

But I never go home. We've ended up on his futon instead, watching reruns of *American Horror Story—Coven*, a personal favorite—and we sort of fool around until I kick him out of the living room and send him to bed.

"I've stayed on your futon for the past three nights," I say. *I'm not sure when things changed between us, but I have been trying to just go with the flow.* "If this keeps up, you might as well just buy me a toothbrush and keep it in your bathroom."

"Okay," Arthur blurts out, his answer instantaneous. I'd meant it as a joke, a jab at his insistence that we spend every waking hour together. "Done," he says. "I've got a six-pack under the sink. You can have the green one."

"Arthur."

"What? I'm just sayin'. It's yours if you want it."

Arthur traces my chin with his thumb and eventually finds his way to my mouth. He spreads my lips apart and slides the tip of his finger inside, gently caressing my tongue. The sensation is strong enough to bring me to my knees, so I plant my palms firmly on the side of the door and deliberately push away from him. He watches me do this, then reaches out, taking my wrists into his hands. I know by the way he's breathing that he feels the same.

Relief washes over me when Gwen pops her head out of the door, reducing a small fraction of our tension, and says, "Hey, guys! I'll be another twenty minutes or so. We've still got to do the floors and take out the trash. I hope you don't mind waiting."

Neither of us breaks eye contact, but I reply, "Yeah, that's not a problem."

After a loud clank on some metal patio furniture behind me, Gwen says, "My new pack of tarot just arrived. You should give Arthur a reading. I bet he'll be into this deck."

The door slams and it's just the two of us again.

"Do you like me, Lance?" Arthur asks. "Because I like you. A lot."

I don't think 'like' is a strong enough word for how Arthur makes me feel. Not even the word 'love' seems adequate. When I don't respond immediately, he lets go of my hands.

"Yes," I whisper. "I do. Very much."

Arthur opens the passenger side door and hops out of his truck. "Sometimes I want you so much I can't stand it." I'm not sure if he's talking about love or sex, or both, and I'm too afraid to ask. "You've been doing this to me since the fucking ninth grade, man."

I don't know where this sudden confession is coming from, or where he expects it to go.

I think back to when I was a student helper, one of the first memories that I have of Arthur. He had already been tall—over six feet—when he was fourteen, and gangly, not like he is now. I don't know where Arthur traded in his old model for this new one. Back then he had been all legs and arms—scrawny, not muscly.

When Arthur had come into the room the first day, with chin-length flaxen hair and sporting an old pair of busted-out Vans, it had been hard to miss him. He had just moved from Indiana, right across the bridge from Louisville, to be closer to his mamaw, who hadn't been doing so hot.

I still remember the first interaction we had.

We had been well into the school year, halfway through the first nine weeks, and I had been tasked with handing out papers. The last paper in my hand had been his, but I had never heard or seen his last name.

When I'd read the paper, I'd nearly dropped it. Pendragon.

'Your parents must really hate you,' I'd said, handing the exam to him. 'Are they really into King Arthur or something?'

'No,' he'd replied with a smile, his brown eyes twinkling under the florescent light. 'Monty Python.'

'Ah yes,' I'd said, my British accent cringeworthy. 'King of the Britons.'

'Well, that, and my great-grandfather's name was Arthur, I guess. I'm not sure if my family has a weird sense of humor or what, but...'

All it had taken was Arthur laughing at my stupid reference to seal the deal, because he wasn't just nice to look at, but he was nice, too.

'You know my name,' he'd said. 'I think it's only fair that you tell me yours.'

At that point, I had only recently come out as Lance, and had struggled with telling people my new name. Being put on the spot like that had felt awkward and scary.

'Linda Lotte,' the person sitting beside Arthur had said.

'I don't recall asking you for his name,' Arthur had replied, his tone as sharp as a blade.

'Lance,' I'd said, intervening, not wanting to cause a scene. 'Lance Lotte.'

'Ah, so you're Lance,' Arthur had said. 'You're a math tutor as well, right?'

After that, Arthur and I had hung out nearly every day before and after school. I'd snuck glances at him while he was correcting his homework during tutoring, and thought about how soft his hair must be, slowly but surely falling in love with every feature, every word spoken, every laugh laughed.

The memory of our first encounter never changes for me, but often leads to other memories that I'd rather forget.

"Do you know," Arthur says, "I failed all five of those quizzes at the beginning of the year so that Mrs. Ramsey would send me to tutoring."

"What?" I ask, sitting down on a rusted patio chair. "Why?"

"I even did the math, down to the very percent, of how poorly I would have to do in order to go to tutoring without Ramsey notifying my parents of my grades. I think the average was a seventy-two percent, high enough to be brought up, but low enough to impact the class average."

"Why would you do that?" I ask. "Are you insane?"

Arthur shrugs. "To get to know you. Why else? I was a ninth grader in pre-cal. I could've done that math with my eyes closed."

"God," I say. "You are crazy."

"Yes," Arthur says, shuffling Gwen's new tarot deck. "Crazy about you."

When he leans over to kiss me, I let him. No one's around, and I don't really care if Gwen is spying on us through the kitchen window. Let her assume what she wants. He drops the cards onto the patio table and places his hands on the sides of my head. His kiss is gentle and soft, like he's restraining himself.

Honestly, I'm still recovering from the shock of learning Arthur's hidden feelings. He has a fairly established reputation of being a ladies' man, and I've always just sat back in the shadows, watching him flirt with girls—and guys sometimes, I guess—never once thinking he was serious about being with me. I'd always thought us making out that one time had been a fluke, a lapse in his judgment.

"I meant what I said the other day," Arthur whispers. "I've been in love with you...forever. But I don't want to force you to rush into anything, or make you uncomfortable by talking about it."

"Arthur."

"Just let me finish before you say anything, please," he replies.

I sigh and bob my head. "All right."

"You said we have the whole summer, but I already know how I feel about you, and I don't need two and a half months to sort out my feelings. Fuck, I don't need two seconds. And if you could just tell me how you feel, even a little, I think it would stop eating at me."

I swallow and look off to the side, intentionally avoiding his gaze. "When you first moved here," I begin, "I was still getting over that bastard Todd and everything he did to me. Those wounds were still fresh and raw. So I never thought for one second that you would want to talk to me, let alone hang out with me. But I knew." I turn my head to face him, and we lock eyes. "The second I heard you laugh, that I loved you, and you're the reason, the main reason anyway, that I'm still single. I don't need the whole summer to sort out my feelings, either. I'm just really scared, you know."

Arthur leans back in his chair and exhales like a balloon deflating. It's the first time I've admitted to myself just how I feel about him, about me, about the whole fucking situation. The look on his face is unreadable, and I'm not sure if I should say something or just let him be, so I decide to reach into my bag and pull out two oatmeal cream pies.

"I'm sorry," Arthur says, his eyes still closed. "I don't know why I waited all this time to say something."

I throw one small plastic-wrapped cake at his chest. His eyes fly open and he looks down at his lap.

"It's not like we're in our eighties," I say. I fumble with the package before ultimately tearing it open with my teeth. "Or on our deathbeds, or something."

Arthur sighs. "Yes," he says. "But I'm sure it hasn't been easy seeing me with all of these girls and shit." He's angry now, and I'm not sure if it's something I've said or done.

"Look," I say. "I know I'm not the only one in love with you. You've had the whole school after you ever since you moved here. I'm not a dummy. I always thought you were straight, that you saw me as a friend only. Until that day when you let me kiss you."

His eyes meet mine, his look now very readable.

Idiots. We're both idiots. For the past few years we have been dancing alone because we were too afraid of stepping on each other's toes, and all it would've taken was a five-minute discussion. I sigh again and open another pie. *Eating my feelings seems like a good idea at the moment.*

"I'm not here to give you a lecture on sleeping with half of Avalon, Arthur."

"Two girls," he corrects me. "I've only ever slept with two girls, and I haven't been with anyone since last summer. Since my dad found us."

Thankfully I don't have to respond to this because Gwen and her co-worker burst out of the front door, the screen barely moving fast enough to allow their hasty departure.

"Jesus fucking Christ," Gwen says. "I hate working in the evenings." She stretches her arms and pops her neck. I cringe at the sound. Her co-worker bumps Gwen's fist with their own, and they leave. I think their name is Jo, but I'm not sure, because I've seen them only once.

"Well," she says, smiling at the both of us. "Did you like the cards? What did the reading say?"

Arthur laughs and picks one up. "I definitely did." Then Gwen looks at me.

"And what about you?" she asks. "I mean, it looked like you had your hands full out here, so..."

I realize that I had been too caught up in my feelings to even look at the deck, so I wipe the cream off my hands and reach for the first card. I turn it over.

On the card are the words TWO OF CUPS, and below the writing is a picture of two men giving each other sixty-nine. I place it down on the table and roll my eyes.

"Well?" Gwen asks. "Which card did you draw?"

Arthur reaches for it, and I cover his hand with mine before he can turn the card over. "Nuh-uh," I say. "Bad luck to let someone see the cards you've drawn for yourself."

Arthur slides his fingers into mine, and Gwen watches us with anticipation, like she's critiquing a performance or something.

"Okay," she says, finally. Even though she's practically shouting. "What fuckin' card was it?"

"Two of cups," I say.

"Two of cups, eh?" Gwen shoots me a look and folds her arms. "It's about fuckin' time. That's all I'll say."

I roll my eyes, ignoring her optimistic jab. "What about you, Arthur? What card did you draw?"

"Death," he says. The words printed on the card are as plain as day. "What does that mean? Am I going to die?" The humor in his voice indicates that either he doesn't believe in the cards, or that he doesn't care.

Because tarot isn't an exact science, there's no way to be sure if the card means actual death, spiritual death or rebirth. Regardless, a hushed silence falls over the table, and Gwen and I exchange worried glances.

"No, silly," Gwen says. "It rarely ever means literal death. You're probably going to see a big change some time this year. That's all."

"Yeah," I say. "We weren't doing a spread or anything, and you just picked a random card. We didn't even ask the cards anything. Don't get hung up on it."

Arthur laughs and runs a hand through his hair. "You know most of this shit goes over my head."

He hands me the card and I place it on the stack in the middle of the table.

This will be Arthur's last summer in Avalon, I just know it. I can feel it in my teeth.

Chapter Five

Mordred

The next morning, I wake up to a text from Mordy. Something's come up and he can't make our coffee date, and he wants to hang out on my next day off instead, so that we're not rushed. I send him a text agreeing to this, and check Facebook to see if the store's gotten any new messages. But before I can log out of my personal account, I receive a friend request from Mordy — which I accept — and begin scrolling through his personal feed. It doesn't take me very long to see that Mordy is passionate about his multicultural heritage, Cuban food and trans rights. Photos from various pride marches and Cuban restaurants litter his page. I begin to wonder if he or his sister is transgender, or both, because there are several tagged photos of them where they're both posing in front of a pink-, white- and blue-striped flag.

My excitement grows with every tagged picture, and I see a comment left by a relative, where Mordy handles being dead-named with grace. *So, he is trans, or at the very least, non-binary.* I wish I had that kind of patience and composure. Blowing up at friends and family members is not my idea of being mentally healthy. I know it's something I need to work on, because I love these people and need them in my life.

I lay my phone down on the coffee table and think about what I've just learned. If what I suspect is true, Mordy is trans and proud of it, black and proud of it. Crushing wouldn't be an appropriate term to use, because I don't feel that way toward him, but I do admire him, deeply. And he's becoming a Santería priest. *God, he and Morgan are so cool.*

When I shift my shoulder beneath Arthur's chest and arms, he makes a noise and tightens his embrace around my body. He must've fallen asleep on the futon after I did, because I remember starting an episode of *Charmed* — in preparation for the reboot — and that's it.

"Hey," I say. "Don't you have to work this morning? It's almost six-thirty."

Arthur's body jerks and he scrambles to get up off the futon.

"Fuck! I have like fifteen minutes to get ready."

After he jumps into the shower, I head to the kitchen and begin making us breakfast. He must have gone to the store, because he has a bunch of odd stuff in his fridge, like veggie sausages, baby spinach and egg whites. Now, I've been a vegetarian since I was fifteen, so the food itself is not weird to me per se, but I didn't expect to find it in his fridge.

When Arthur returns to the kitchen, I've already made us omelets and half a pot of coffee. His hair is still damp, pulled into a sloppy ponytail, and his shirt is covered in tiny wet spots from where he didn't dry off completely. I hand him a plate, and he sits down on the futon.

"Damn, this looks good," he says. "Thanks."

We don't really have much time, so we focus on eating and drinking our coffee. After Arthur's finished, he puts his plate in the sink and grabs the pan off the stove.

"Hey," I say, "I can wash those dishes when I wash mine. You'd better get your boots on. You're gonna be late if you don't get going."

Arthur walks over to me and tilts my head back slightly. His lips are warm and inviting, and if I had any sense at all, I would tell him to call in sick and spend the morning with me. But I don't, and I lightly push his chest away.

"Do you need me to drop you off before I head to work? I can come back on my lunch break if needed."

I shake my head and take another sip of coffee. "No," I reply. "Gwen doesn't have to work today. I'll just get a ride from her or Lena."

"Okay," he says and heads to the front door to get his boots. "You know, I wasn't joking about that toothbrush thing last night. I wouldn't mind if you stayed here with me until you have to go back to school."

"You looking for a roommate?" I ask. "You that hard up for rent?"

"No, but I am that hard up for you."

After Arthur puts on his boots, he walks back over to me and kisses me again, licking my top lip as we pull apart.

"I love you," he says. "And I'll see you this evening. Text me when you get off work and I'll come get ya, okay?"

"I will. Now get your ass outta here."

A lot just happened in the past fifteen minutes, and honestly, I'm glad that I'm alone to process it. Arthur basically just asked me to move in with him and casually told me that he loved me, like it's the easiest phrase in the world to say to someone. I get up from where I'm sitting and head to the bathroom, to look for the green toothbrush he mentioned. I open the cabinet and stare at it. If I open the package, it'll be an indirect acceptance of everything he just suggested, but if I leave it alone, he might return home and misinterpret my feelings. I decide to open the package and use the damn thing, before eventually placing it in my side bag. That way, if I get too freaked out or distressed over something, I can always just leave.

We're not even officially seeing each other yet, and here Arthur wants me to move in with him. What is he thinking? Last night we had both been too tired to do anything, but what if we hadn't been? What would have happened if we'd started messing around? *I'm not ready for that. I'm barely ready for this.*

I walk back to Arthur's bedroom and stare into a sliding mirror that's attached to the closet door, then remove my shirt and toss it on the bed. I look at myself. My scars aren't nearly as red as they once were, and they aren't as bumpy, either. I run my thumb across them.

When I look at myself, I see a man, but is that what Arthur would see? There's no way to know without asking someone to intrude on his thoughts, and I won't allow Gwen to do that, despite her repeated offers to do so. I reach for my shirt, and it suddenly moves to my left like a skipping stone, until eventually landing on the floor.

Arthur had never mentioned a ghost in his house, but it wouldn't be the first time something like this happened to me—and only me. Spirits and my connection with the dead are two of the main reasons why I'm drawn to brujería—death doesn't scare me, never has.

The shirt is folded neatly and sitting on the floor when I grab for it a second time. Being in Arthur's room like this feels very invasive and I don't like it. *I shouldn't have come in here.* Something catches my eye right as I slip my head through the neck of my shirt, though.

Two picture frames.

A picture of us, the three of us—Gwen, Arthur and me—waiting in line at Kings Island. I remember the day well. We'd waited in line for like two hours to ride the Diamondback, and it hadn't even been that scary. We had all been sunburned and exhausted, Gwen had thrown up on herself during the ride, but I didn't think it lived up to the hype, while Arthur had seemed content just being there with us.

The other picture is just the two of us, Arthur and me. I still have really long hair and breasts—even though I'm wearing a binder—but he's smiling and has his arm around me. I take the picture frame into my hands and look at it more closely. I remember the day this photograph was taken—the day right before I moved into my dorm. Leaving Gwen and Arthur for the first time like that had easily been the hardest thing I've ever had to do. *My freshman year of college really sucked.*

I bend down to place the frame back on the side table and am struck with an overwhelming sensation of grief and mourning, the feeling familiar and somehow oddly welcoming. My knees buckle underneath the weight of it all and I fall onto Arthur's bed, still clutching the picture frame.

What the fuck is happening?

Visions, or memories that are not mine, swarm my mind, pushing out any thoughts that belong to me. From the scenery, I gather that these are Arthur's memories. Memories from the past two years or so. Most of them involve Arthur sobbing, or getting into fights with his father. The hardest one to watch is his father slapping Arthur during a heated argument over me. Other memories include Arthur smoking weed until he passes out by himself, and drinking and falling asleep in an empty bathtub.

"Why are you showing this to me?" I shout, trying to gain purchase on my consciousness. "What do you want me to say? It's not like I know what I'm doing here. I'm in pain, too!"

The final memory I'm shown must be a recent one because Arthur is here, in the trailer, pacing back and forth, talking to himself. I'm concerned at first, but then realize he's repeating himself over and over again, possibly rehearsing something he's about to say. When I hear my name, I listen and watch him intently. When his tone changes abruptly, I can tell that he's getting frustrated with himself because he doesn't know how I'll take his confession that he loves me—he's terrified, actually. I know this not because I know what he's thinking, but because of the way he's gripping the sides of the sink and shaking his head.

Tears run down my face, and when I blink, I find myself sprawled out on his bed, gasping for air. The middle of his mattress is soaked with my tears. Who knows how long I've been here, lost in Arthur's thoughts?

I sit up and look at the picture once more. Arthur's suffered so much more than I could have ever thought. Underneath his easy-going, delightful personality is a relatively fragile human being, someone who has struggled with self-imposed isolation and loneliness.

When I get to the front of the trailer, I find my bag and retrieve the green toothbrush. I walk to the bathroom and sit it next to his in the porcelain holder. I have no idea if what I'm doing is the right thing, or what just happened back in that bedroom, but I need to stop hiding behind this wall that I've erected all around me. *It's time.*

Arthur and I will be connected regardless of what happens this summer. The bards sang about it hundreds of years ago, and they'll sing about it again.

* * * *

Mordy and I hang out the next day. His sister has to help their uncle with another ceremony, so she doesn't join us. We have lunch together at a coffee shop a few blocks away from the craft store. Emmett ignored me most of the day yesterday, and I was thankful for it, if I'm being honest with myself. Hopefully Mordy will clarify some things for me today, because the broken-glass-everywhere scene was rattling, to say the least.

"I'll have the veggie burger," I say. "Extra pickles, please."

The waiter takes our menus and informs us the soda machine is broken.

"So you're a vegetarian?" Mordy asks, his chin propped up on two fists. He's wearing a pair of eyeglasses today, and his dreads are wild, like eels trying to swim away from a net or something. His T-shirt, overalls and high-top Converse are blindingly white as usual.

"Yeah, since I was fifteen, I think." I take a sip of jasmine tea, mentally noting just how delicious it is with a slice of lime.

"Don't you miss meat, though?"

The conversation we're about to have is one I've had about a thousand times before and don't really care to have again. My cheek twitches in response, and I wait for him to ask more questions about my dietary habits.

"I mean, I dig it," Mordy says. "Don't get me wrong. I think it's totally admirable. I just like my *ropa vieja* too much to ever give it up, you know?"

"Trust me, I do know. I miss tacos al pastor, but it's a moral thing that I can't shake no matter how hard I try. It's just a personal thing. I don't care about what other people do."

Mordy nods and takes a sip of coffee. "It's cool. I'm not here to harsh your mellow."

After our food arrives, we talk briefly about life in Avalon. Mordy has lots of questions about Gwen and my family, about magick and about my personal feelings on destiny. Most of the questions are easy to navigate, and the conversation flows as effortlessly as water, but then Mordy asks me about Arthur, and I have trouble describing our friendship, a dam suddenly appearing.

"Is he your boyfriend?"

"Not exactly," I say. It feels like a lie, like I'm betraying Arthur by saying this, but we haven't made any formal commitments to each other. Not yet. "Though he is my best friend, and I am staying with him at the moment."

Mordy's eyebrow arches and a smirk forms in the corners of his mouth. "So what you're saying is that he's ready to be your boyfriend, you're just not sure."

I don't want Mordy getting the wrong idea here. I am sure about being Arthur's boyfriend, I'm just afraid of what obstacles we'll face in the future, of what it will mean when we're finally allowed to love each other openly, of the expectations Arthur will have of me once it's finalized. But mostly I am deeply afraid of fucking everything up.

"Are you into girls at all?"

I shake my head. "No," I say. "I once dated an eighth grader when I was in the sixth grade, but it ended after three straight months of her trying to get into my pants. I guess I just didn't know how to describe the way I felt inside."

Mordy nods, as though he understands what I've been through.

"I didn't know the words yet, you know?"

"So, no pride demonstrations in here Avalon this summer? No drag queen story hour?" Mordy asks.

I laugh. "Only if hell freezes over within the next two weeks. And it's pronounced Ay-va-lone, not Avalon."

"Well, *excuse* me. How long have you lived in Ay-va-lone?"

The waiter comes and removes the dishes from our table, and brings me a small pot of fresh tea. I pour myself a cup before answering Mordy, because it's a short, but complicated story.

"I was born here, and then I was placed in foster care after my parents overdosed on heroin. I think I bounced around Kentucky until I was like eight or nine, then I came back here."

"Damn. H? That's hard as fuck. I'm sorry to hear that."

"Oh," I reply. "It was literally over fifteen years ago when that happened. I don't remember Juan or Sherry, but I'm sure they loved me as well as they could, given the circumstances."

"Well, I'm glad to see that you've managed to come out on top. You're strong, and I respect those struggles."

"Thanks," I say. I guess I had never really thought of it as a struggle, or something worth dwelling over. At least, not my parents' deaths.

"And now? Your Facebook says that you no longer go by Gonzales." Mordy says this in a way that is less of a statement, and more like an accusation. "What happened there?" *My name is no longer Gonzales, but I asked for the name change – not Gwen, not my mom, not my dad.*

Fred Lotte, the patriarch of the family, our dad, had insisted that I think carefully about changing my last name, always maintaining that it was a part of my heritage. But after I'd lived with Gwen and our parents for longer than I had lived with my biological family, I asked them if I could become an official part of their family. They had argued that it wasn't necessary, that I was already a Lotte.

What's funny is that I've chosen both my first and last name, and I have no regrets.

Even though I don't know him that well, I assume that Mordy probably grew up surrounded by people who shared his ethnicity and culture, whereas I had not. If his presence on social media is any indication of his past, our upbringings were different. I don't have any pictures with my biological family, no connection to anyone other than the Lottes. My identity hadn't fully developed until after I had been adopted by Fred and Anna, and even now I have difficulty from time to time. But I'm proud to share a last name with Gwen, and I wouldn't give up Fred and Anna for the world. Like so many things in my life, it's complicated.

I choose my words carefully, but say them as firmly as I can. "Things are different here. I mean, do you have any idea what it's like to grow up in a town where most everyone is white? I have really had to overcome some serious shit in order to accept any kind of love from anyone."

Mordy puts down his cup of coffee and makes a fist, then hovers it over my tea.

"Go on, tap it," he says. So I do, and when our skin touches it feels electric, scorching even. "You're real peoples out here, you know that? You say what's on your mind, and I can see that when I talk to you, you're listening to me. Not thinking about how I look or sound, or what I'm going to do next."

I nod to him and pour myself another cup of tea. "So, enough about my messy-ass life. What about you? Why are you here? And don't say 'visiting my uncle', because your sister and uncle are practicing sorcery in his barn right now."

Mordy's laughter fills the empty cafe, and the barista glances at us.

"Yes," he says. "They are doing just that. But I am here visiting him and his family."

"Right," I say. "Why?"

"Morgan was originally sent here by our *abuelo* to gather information about some incidents that happened right before he moved to California back in the day, and then I got into an argument with my *abuelo* about it, and drove out here myself."

"What kind of incidents?"

Mordy looks around to make sure no one is listening to our conversation.

"Do you remember when those kids from that day care went missing? I think it was called Debbie's Daycare, something really generic like that. You were probably nine—"

"Ten," I say, cutting him off. "Yeah, I remember when that happened, because Gwen and I were pulled out of day care after the second round of abductions occurred. Damn, that was years ago. I had forgotten all about that."

"Right, from a different day care. So you remember how crazy things got once the media got a hold of the story. It was all over the damn news for weeks. How the Feds and state police tore this place up. Child protective services shut down three in-home day cares. Everyone was terrified to go to work because when they got off, their children might be missing."

"I do remember hearing about that," I say. Something black flashes in my peripheral vision, and I look out of the window to my left. A large blue jay lands on a light post and very pointedly stares at us.

"Fuck him," Mordy says, now looking in the same direction. He pulls out a necklace—or rather, a braided string of small animal bones—from within his white shirt, and shakes them at the animal. "Come at me, you little pissant. I will add to you to my collection."

The bird doesn't move, instead keeping its glossy, beady eyes glued to Mordy.

"Emrys would not dare enter this place, because there are two powerful black magicians in here. Let him watch us convene. Little fucker."

The barista and waiter don't seem to mind us, the enormous blue and white bird now perched outside or the lack of customers, instead flirting with each other, talking about how it's supposed to rain this evening, and how they're looking forward to seeing a movie together tonight. How they are oblivious to the overwhelmingly dark manifestation outside, I do not know.

"Who is Emrys?" I ask, then snap my fingers in Mordy's face, trying to get his attention. "Mordy! Earth to Mordy! Hey, Mordred!"

Somehow the blue bird rotates its head in a complete circle, then spreads its wings as if in response to hearing Mordy's full name, and flaps them three times before crowing and flying away. Mordy seems entranced by the whole situation, and shoots me a dangerous look once the bird leaves our sight.

"Fuck, not Emrys himself, but possibly a spy." His voice is as dark as the coffee in his hand. "Lance, please do not call me Mordred in front of others."

"Okay," I say. "I only did it because I wanted to get your attention."

"I'm sorry," he replies. "But Morgan is the only one who calls me Mordred."

Mordy excuses himself and heads to the restroom. I turn my phone over on the table, and see several texts from Arthur. I'm trying to be better about answering his messages, because I want him to know that I care about him and the things he says, but he sends me one every thirty minutes, and I have trouble keeping up with them. Some of them aren't important, but others are, and I try my best to address those.

Last night we fell asleep on the couch again, and when I woke up, I could feel his cock pressed against my side. The desire must have traveled from his body into mine, because I had to get up immediately and hop into the shower, afraid of what I might do if I lingered there any longer. Arthur would never pressure me into having sex, or being intimate with him in any way, but my brain and body have never gotten along, and I know they would betray each other if given the chance.

When I finish responding to Arthur's texts, he tells me he loves me, that he'll see me later tonight. I still haven't told him that I love him, and I'm not sure if it bothers him or not, but I'm not ready to actually say those words to him.

"Before that asshole shit-eater out there arrived, what were we talking about?" Mordy asks, returning to the table. His glasses are hooked on his shirt and his face looks wet, like he's been splashed with water. "Cops?"

"Cops and CPS," I say. I slide my phone back into my side bag and focus on what Mordy's saying. "Them in-home day cares."

"Those kids that returned, I read somewhere that they were never the same again, as if their very life force had been stolen from them. My Aunt Jessie was one of those kids."

I gasp. "What? You actually know one of them?"

"Know one of them? Hell, I was practically raised by her."

"Raised?" I ask. "But how, if they never went back to being normal?"

"Santería is a healing practice. My *abuelo* fled this town with my mother and her sister. My aunt did not speak until she was seventeen, and that was after years of intense prayer, meditation and sacrifice. *Tío* Myrddin has stayed here though, fighting the good fight, protecting children from the evil lurking underneath Avalon."

Now, I believe in magick, and I believe that anything is possible, but Mordy is suggesting a conspiracy, or a subterranean barbarity of some kind. I can't do anything but look at him stupidly.

"Earlier you said that there were two black magicians here. Were you talking about the two of us?" I move my index finger back and forth, pointing at our chests.

Mordy reaches for my free hand and takes it in his own, electricity or something similar to it passing between the two of us. "I was," he replies. "Lance, when you walk into a room, the light bends, submits to your darkness. I've seen it. I'm seeing it. Surely you feel it inside."

When I first started getting into magick, I'd thought it was all herbs and charms, candles and meditation, that kind of stuff, but then something inside had changed while I was learning about witches who were incinerated at the stake, famous witches throughout history like Lilith, Medea and the Witch of Endor. The treatment and exile they'd endured. Then a weird sort of vengeance, combined with a profound longing and sorrow as deep as the ocean, had started seeping into my prayers at night, and had often overshadowed the spells I would cast with Gwen. We'd practiced Gwen's folk magick for a few years, a form of seemingly harmless white magick—until I'd moved away—

because enchantments would have gone haywire if I hadn't repressed the rage I felt toward certain groups of people in town.

Fast-forward to my freshman year of college, and my little world is rocked when I learn about brujería through school. Three pages into the textbook and I'm Googling everything under the sun that has to do with Mexican witchcraft — *hechizos*, shape-shifting, corn shuck dolls, hexes, bone divination. Stuff I had always assumed was too dark, too black for my soul.

I must have blown through half of my student loans on those books alone.

But it had been worth it.

Looking into Mordy's eyes, seeing that same rage reflected in them, tells me it was worth it.

"Okay," he says. "I get it. So practicing black magick and calling yourself an actual sorcerer sounds kinda weird. I feel you, I do. But tell me this…if you had the power to stop those old white ladies out there on the street from straight staring at you for no fuckin' reason, you wouldn't do it? If you could produce an evil eye at a moment's notice when some asshole in blue pulls you over when you weren't speeding, you wouldn't do it?"

His words make sense. Of course they do. Like pieces of a puzzle, they align perfectly with the injustice that witches have endured since the advent of monotheism. Prejudice and discrimination have been a plague on society for far too long, and when you add racism in there, it's like a pot on the stove just waiting to boil over.

"I'm not talking black magick like poisoning people, bro. I'm talking about justice. The line that lies in between right and wrong, that gray area."

I wag my head. "You're right," I say, finally. "But how do we make things better without hurting people? I ain't into violence, man."

A light, similar to the one Arthur gets in his eyes, appears in Mordy's. "Neither am I," he says. "But violence isn't necessarily the opposite of healing, bro. What if I told you that there was a way to hurt someone without actually hurting them?"

His line of thinking is sort of confusing, but I decide to go along with it anyway. Mordy must see this in my face, because he excitedly scoots his chair closer to me and brushes his shoulder against mine.

"All right," he says. "Now we're talking. So, I have some questions that you can hopefully help me with."

"What do you want to know?" I ask.

"The first thing I want to know is if you know that Emmett Crabtree used to go by the name Emrys Caerwyn."

Chapter Six

Morgana Le Fay

For the next week or so, Mordy and I are inseparable.

Before work, after work and during work, Mordy and I spend most of our time discussing Avalon and Emrys through texts. Most of it seems unbelievable to me, because I've known Emmett since I was a child and have never had any problems with him—he's always been a sweet, kind, old man. Vacant, yes. Vicious, never.

But ever since Mordy and his sister arrived in Avalon a few weeks ago, Emmett has been in a foul mood, even lashing out at Caspian for small, insignificant things, like not emptying the wastebasket in Emmett's office—something I've never done, or seen *anyone* do, not even Emmett.

Today I was supposed to have lunch with Arthur, but he'd had to cancel because of some mix-up at work. He's been acting weird around me, too, going silent anytime I talk about Mordy, or mention that we're hanging out. I'm not sure if something has happened at work, or if his family has been harping on him about not starting school in August, and I'm too afraid to ask him because he's been in such a dark mood.

During my short morning shift, I receive a text from Mordy, asking if I would be interested in having lunch at his house. Since Arthur canceled our plans, I agree to it, because I'm eager to meet *Tío* Myrddin, and because I'm curious as to what their farmhouse looks like. From the way Mordy talks about his uncle's home, my imagination is leaning toward something grand and showy, like something from a gothic romance novel. The anticipation is killing me.

Mordy and Morgan show up, and Morgan waves at me with enthusiasm through the tempered glass window out front. Emmett must have sensed their presence, because he emerges from his office in the back immediately and stands behind the counter, folding his arms. Pacing back and forth like wildcats watching their prey, the twins occupy the sidewalk, never breaking eye contact with my boss.

"Lance," he says, startling me, his voice sharp and almost menacing.

I stop counting the change in the cash register and look up, afraid he's going to tell me to never come back, or ask me to call the cops, ultimately forcing me to quit.

"Those kids out there are a bad bunch. Mark my word, they will bring this town nothing but despair."

The twins must know he's talking about them, because they stop walking and turn to face him. I don't really want to involve myself in their drama, so I chuckle and place a hand on Emmett's shoulder, hoping to lighten the situation, but my stomach lurches as soon as my hand makes contact with his shirt, and I stumble backward a few steps. Emmett tilts his head slightly, and rests his eyes on me for a split second before returning them to Mordy and Morgan.

"Caspian tells me you've been reading a book about Santería. Careful now, better not dabble in the dark arts like that. Voodoo is not for children."

From the way Emmett says it, it sounds like Caspian has been keeping tabs on me. *Snively asshat.*

Clutching my sides, I respond, "With all due respect, voodoo and Santería are not the same thing, Mr. Caerwyn." Using his former alias like this is dangerous, I know, but he's pissed me off, and possibly even hurt me somehow, because the burning sensation in my stomach won't go away. Morgan bangs on the window, and I hold up a hand. We don't need a repeat of two weeks ago, but I'm aware that I need to get out of the shop ASAP.

"I'll be out in a second," I say. "I just have to get my bag."

After I turn around, Emmett pushes my bag into my chest like it repulses him to touch it. There's no way he could have gone to the break room to retrieve it and returned in the mere seconds it took for me to talk to Morgan. My hand burns now and feels like it's blistering — the hand I'd used to touch Emmett.

"Are you scheduled to work tomorrow?" he asks. "I can't remember."

"Yes," I reply. "In the morning."

"Take the day off," he says. "Caspian has been asking for more hours. He can cover it." Now's not the time to argue with my boss about cutting my hours for no good reason, so I nod and punch out my time card. He doesn't respond to me when I tell him goodbye, and I try not to take it personally, because I have no idea what the fuck is even happening.

On the way to their uncle's house, I debate whether I should tell Mordy and Morgan about my short but bizarre interaction with Emmett—how my hand burns like I've just taken an iron to it, how my bag appeared out of thin air or how he didn't seem to mind when I called him Caerwyn. My mental state is still pretty frazzled, so I decide to tell them later, when we're closer to the old farmhouse and farther away from the store.

When we pull up to their house, the scenery does not disappoint. With an enormous yard full of scattered, blooming white and pink dogwood trees, the house looks like it was wrenched straight from a fairy tale. The cracking blue paint and missing side paneling add to its ethereal ambiance. Their uncle comes out to greet us, his hands and green shirt covered in a powdery substance, flour maybe.

"You must be Lance!" he shouts, walking over toward Mordy's Escalade. "How do!"

I take his coated hand and shake it with vigor. How I could have missed this man all of these years is beyond me. Never in my life have I laid eyes on him—not at the grocery store, not at one of the two gas stations here in town, or even at the post office. Standing beside his niece and nephew, their likeness is uncanny, and I wonder if he looked like them at their age.

"Well," he says, with a thick country accent. "Come on inside. Them beans and cornbread ain't gonna eat themselves. And, Lance, I didn't put no ham in the pot and used Crisco in the bread, so you'd better eat as much as you can...seeing as how my kinfolk are too good for their uncle's cookin'."

After lunch, Mordy and *Tío* Myrddin insist on cleaning the dishes and the kitchen, so Morgan shows me around the farm while we snack on sour blackberries from vines growing alongside the house. The sun bathes the spacious green fields in a delicious white light, and birds fill the air with their song. An enormous honeysuckle shrub lends us its fresh, saccharine scent, making the scenery even more storybook-like with every deep inhale. The farmhouse, Morgan explains, is where they live, but the two barn-like structures out back are off limits to anyone outside of their family.

"But since you're with me," she says, her hands on the barn door, a hint of mischief in her tone, "you should be fine. Oh, real quick—do you have any amulets or talismans or anything like that on you?"

I shove my hands into my jeans pockets, feeling for anything that might contain magickal properties, and come up empty-handed. The only necklace I'm wearing is tucked underneath my shirt, the plastic charm that I never take off, the one Arthur gave me, and when I produce it, Morgan shields her eyes like she's staring into the sun.

"Fuck, that'll do it!" she screams. "Take it off, or cover it up. Do something, quick!"

I grab the black ball suddenly, protectively cupping it in one hand.

"N-no," I stammer. "I can't take it off."

Morgan removes one hand, and peeks at me through her middle and ring fingers.

"What?" she asks. "Why not? Who gave it to you?"

For some reason, just thinking about Arthur around Morgan makes me uncomfortable.

"A friend of mine," I manage to finally say. "A close friend."

"Step away from the barn." Morgan's voice is strange, commanding. "Stand here."

I do as she says, and she takes my hand into hers, gently prying my fingers from the charm.

"Can I at least check it out?"

I drop my hand and allow her to fondle the necklace with slender, delicate fingers. Her white nail polish is perfect, not a chip or blemish in sight, like the rest of her hair and body. When she moves in closer to examine the cheap piece of plastic, I can smell the onion that she had for lunch on her breath.

"Ah," she coos. "I see now." Our eyes meet and I feel trapped, frozen from a mixture of cycling emotions. *"Him."* Her eyes narrow and she takes a step forward, stomping on my shoes. "Do I scare you, Lance?"

I throw my hands up and try to put some distance between us. "Uh, I think maybe we should head back to your uncle's house." *This is bad. Really bad.*

A bellow escapes from somewhere deep within Morgan as she places her hands around my neck. "I can take him from you. He belongs to me." Whoever is choking me, *whatever* is choking me, has taken over Morgan's body and is controlling her movements.

There's no way she's the one steering this ship at the moment.

I don't know what else to do, so I sweep my foot underneath hers and bring us both crashing down onto the ground. Her legs coil around my torso, and I struggle beneath her crushing weight, my stupid genes failing me once again. *I hate being so fucking small.*

"Pretty little knight," she taunts, her voice distorted, no longer recognizable. "Where is your king now? Is his castle nearby?" Morgan slides her hand up my shirt and caresses my chest, her wandering fingers soon finding their way to my necklace. "Not that it matters, of course, because you'll do. What was it you said the last we met? Ah yes, a life for a life?"

"Morgan!" I shout. "Morgan!" I writhe in between her thighs, trying to escape.

Morgan—or Morgan's body that's possibly being controlled by another entity—rams her fist into my nose hard, and blood spurts out of my nostrils, soon blanketing my chin and cheeks. I don't know what else to do, because I'm not a large man and there's no one else around, so I try to reason with the visiting phantom, or whatever the fuck it is.

"Morgan. Morgana," I gurgle. "Morgana le Fay." The last word barely breaks through the steady brook now occupying half of my face. *Please work.* "Beneath the hallowed moon, we shall meet, free of malice, and twice as sweet. Please accept this blessing with a smile, and free yourself, from whatever ails you, for a while." It's an old folk spell of Gwen's. I hope it works.

Magick swallows the both of us, swirling around Morgan like a black, misty cyclone, eventually releasing her from the spiritual hold, then lifts our bodies several feet into the air and drops us with as much force as the Hellevator.

When my breathing finally steadies and I roll onto my side, I see Morgan sprawled out, spread eagle, her white pantsuit covered in my blood. I crawl over to her and check her pulse. She's breathing heavily, and not moving, but at least she isn't dead. My nose is throbbing now, and I may have sprained my ankle in the fall. *God, I hope it's a sprain, and not something worse.* A brief moment later I bend down and scoop Morgan into my arms. I don't know how far I'll be able to carry her on my bum ankle, but I'm still going to try.

Thankfully, Mordy sees me dragging her body across the field a few minutes later, and rushes to help.

"What's happened?" Mordy's eyes are focused on his sister. "Where did all of this blood come from?" he asks, his voice manic.

"Don't worry," I croak. My knees buckle beneath my weight, and I crumple onto the ground like a piece of paper. "It isn't hers."

"*Dios mío!*" Mordy's uncle shouts from the porch. "Mordy, you get your sister, and I'll get Lance."

* * * *

Outside, a veil of darkness has fallen by the time I regain consciousness, and moonlight pours through a pair of sheer scarlet curtains. The twins and their uncle are positioned around me in a triangular manner, one family member near my head and two near my feet. When I try to raise my head, Morgan reaches out to help steady me, but I can't stop from flinching at her touch. *Tío* Myrddin places his hand on Morgan's shoulder and she slumps forward, letting go of my hand.

"I am so sorry." Her words spill out of her mouth, pooling at her knees. "I don't know what happened out there. But Mordy tells me I did this to you. Oh, I'm so sorry, Lance." She puts her head in her hands and starts sobbing, the force of each sob shaking the floor beneath my body. That thing—whatever it was—had very little to do with the sad and broken woman sitting next to me.

"Morgan," I say, calmly. "Has this happened before?"

"Do you mean blacking out and assaulting people, or just the blacking out?" Mordy asks. "Because yes, the latter happens all the time."

"I see." I ease back down onto the pillow and gaze up at the ceiling, slightly turning my head to the left and to the right. We must be inside of *Tío* Myrddin's farmhouse. The ceilings are high and beautiful, just as I had expected, with Christmas lights nailed all over the walls, and strands of what appear to be garland hanging from the chandelier in the center of the room.

To our right is an enormous, painted mural of the *Virgen de Regla*, and to our left is an altar covered in glass candles, flowers, dried fruit, feathers, coins and incense, dedicated to Elegua, a spirit who aids in protection and blocking negative energy. Mordy *was* right, I realize—it does somewhat resemble the *Santisma Muerte* shrines in Mexico.

"Why do you have garland hanging from that light fixture?"

"Defense," Myrddin replies. "From psychic attacks. And to bring good luck."

"Plus *Tío* Myrddin loves Christmas," Morgan adds, obviously pleased with my question. "Don't let him tell you otherwise."

Morgan and I barely know each other. We've met a few times, and nearly every time, violence has played a role in our meetings. I glance at her. Sitting next to her uncle and twin brother, she seems small, demure, meek even, not at all like the overpowering, colossal presence I encountered out by the barns. When our eyes meet, I think about what she said, about Arthur. Now I know I'm all wrapped up in this myth shit, and I've only ever toyed with the possibility of it being real, but after today, denial isn't an option any longer, especially since Arthur pulled that fucking death card the other day.

I rub my arms and close my eyes again. Morgana had said something else that really bothered me, something about taking Arthur away. This is a piercing thought that I don't ever allow myself to have—the idea that someone could steal Arthur from me, that he will eventually get tired of my self-absorbed, heady bullshit and find comfort in someone else's arms. The emotion this thought provokes is unlike anything I've ever experienced. Devastation, despair, isolation—all of it could be made true if Arthur decides that I'm not worth the wait. *I have to tell him before it's too late.*

"Hey," Mordy says, looking down at me, a black stone dangling from his neck. "Why don't you go upstairs and clean off? I'll get your bag and you can borrow a shirt of mine."

After I clean the crusted blood from my mouth, I inspect my nose in the bathroom mirror. No swelling or enlargement of any kind. This amazes me because Morgana was a jackhammer and I was the road beneath her fucking rage. My ankle doesn't hurt anymore, either. *Weird.*

"Here you go." Mordy brings me a shirt and I switch it out with the one I'm currently wearing. When I rejoin him, he's sitting cross-legged at a coffee table in the middle of the room. His bedroom is small like my dorm, and basic, austere. No posters, no calendars, only a huge cross hanging above his bed. Since he's only staying here for the summer, it makes sense.

When I get closer, I see that he is wearing a binder underneath a white, ribbed tank top. His muscles are well-defined, and his shirt accentuates their shape. I stare at them with envy.

"Have a seat," he says, patting the floor next to him. So I do.

On the coffee table is a mound of red and black stones, beautiful and smooth. I take one into my hand and turn it over, only to discover symbols on the stones.

"Are these runes? Are you making runes?" I ask.

"Sort of," Mordy replies. "These carvings symbolize the Orichás."

"Oh yeah," I say. "The gods from Santería, right? Aren't there like four hundred of them, or something like that, though?"

"Four hundred plus one," Mordy corrects me. "And I can't afford that many stones, so I am going to make twenty or so, and hope the spirits have mercy on my wretched soul for reducing their numbers, or whatever."

I laugh. Here we are talking about gods and runes and spiritual mercy, but there's no need for awkward laughing or full explanations, because we both believe in magick, and it flows through our bodies like blood.

"I hope I'm not bothering you by being here," I say. "I probably need to leave soon anyway."

Mordy hands me a red stone. "Here," he says. "Why don't you carve one for yourself?"

It takes me longer to carve a skull into the stone than Mordy, and honestly, I'm almost too embarrassed to show it to him because it looks more like a red monkey than anything, but he forces me to place it in with his stones.

"Let us pray for protection, and a favorable outcome. I think it's clear that something is out to get us, or at least you and my sister."

After Mordy cleanses each stone with fire from a green plastic lighter, he places them down on the glass coffee table and waits for them to cool.

"So," I say, finally mustering enough courage, "I think it's awesome that your family is so cool with you being trans or gender-nonconforming, or whatever it is you call yourself."

Mordy chuckles. "They weren't always so accepting. Except for Morgan. I feel like she knew before I knew, and I'm not even talking about her visions, either."

"Gwen is the only person in my family who even makes an attempt to call me Lance, and to use the correct pronouns."

"Wait, what?" Mordy turns to me, baffled. "You're transgender, too?"

His surprise is genuinely shocking to me. "Yes, I am a trans man."

"Are you kidding me? I thought you were just short, or like, younger or something." Mordy slaps his leg and yells. "Holy shit! In this little ass town, there's not one, but two Brown trans dudes sitting in a fucking farmhouse. Get out of here!"

With all of his hooting and hollering, I can't help but share his excitement, even if I don't want to.

For the next thirty minutes or so we let the stones cool and talk about testosterone, my top surgery, and if I plan on coming back to Avalon after I graduate. The conversation leaves me elated, the heavy feeling in my chest slowly but surely exiting my body.

"I graduated this past May," Mordy says. "BA in fine arts. Not sure what I'm going to do with it, just kinda playing it by ear. Might go to San Fran for grad school—probably not though, seeing as how it's expensive as fuck and gentrified as all get out. Who even knows anymore?"

When Mordy talks I'm automatically hypnotized by his words, like he's casting a spell over my mind and body, and I'm willfully accepting of it. Embracing it with open arms, even.

"I hope Morgan didn't scare you off with that forest-spirit-witch-shit."

I shake my head. "Nah, we're cool."

"Okay, awesome," Mordy replies, then reaches for his phone. "Are you free at all tomorrow?"

The prospect of hanging out with Mordy, someone who can empathize with me, with what I go through, with what I've gone through, is exhilarating. I have a hard time concealing my joy and excitement, and feel a smile forming in the creases of my mouth.

"Yeah, of course." I pick up my stone and blow on it, trying to expel some of this new crazy energy that I'm now feeling. Mordy is watching me like a fly on the wall.

When I turn and smile at him, he leans in to kiss me, and I'm so confused and discombobulated that I place my hands around his neck. I assume he takes this for a sign, because he pulls me close and kisses me deeply, parting my teeth with his tongue. But after a few seconds of concentration and intentional focus, I pull away from him. He leans in again and tries to kiss me for a second time, but I put my hand on his chest, and gently tell him no.

"I'm sorry," I say. "But I can't do this."

"Ah, that's right," Mordy says. "Your boyfriend-that's-not-really-a-boyfriend."

"I hope you're not mad at me, because I'm very flattered, and very honored. Like for real."

Mordy leans back on his elbows and says, "But you dig me, right? I mean, it isn't all in my head, is it?"

The answer Mordy wants is not the one I can give him, and I have to be mindful of this when telling him how I feel, because I don't want to lose or fuck up our friendship.

"You and Morgan are the two coolest people in Avalon at the moment," I say. "Your style is on point. You drive a cool fucking car. And you're both initiates. I would be lying if I said I wasn't immediately drawn to you, but what you're looking for in this friendship is not the same as what I'm looking for. I'm sorry if I was giving off mixed signals."

Mordy runs his tongue across his silver tooth and clicks his teeth. "So he is your boyfriend."

"Yes," I finally admit to Mordy—and myself. "Arthur is my boyfriend."

Mordy balls his hand into a fist and taps mine with it. "You're all right, you know that?"

Gaining Mordy's acceptance means a lot to me, so I'm relieved when he says this and changes the subject.

"What kinds of shit is there to do around here?"

"Well," I say, "I guess that depends on what you like to do. There's a lake nearby where folks drink and party and swim. And there's a joke of a mall fifteen miles away. It's not much, but it has a pretty cool bookstore."

"What about sex shops?"

I laugh. "You mean like a Hustler, or something?"

"Yeah," he replies. "Or something similar, I guess."

"Hmm. There's a Lion's Den on the way to Monticello. About fifty miles from here, I think. I've never been there, though."

"Dope. You interested in a mini-road trip next weekend?" he asks in all seriousness. "I'm drivin'."

Chapter Seven

The Promise

Later that night, Mordy drives me home, asking me all kinds of questions about Arthur and Gwen along the way. Morgan stays behind because she used all of her energy healing my busted nose, ignoring my pleas and insistence that it wasn't that big of a deal because you couldn't really see any swelling. Besides, it made me look kind of tough. When she was through with the healing ritual, my face was back to normal, though, no bruising, no blood, no deviated septum—my disappointment is obvious.

"You're telling me," Mordy says, pulling into Arthur's neighborhood, "that a reincarnation of the greatest warrior-king that's ever lived is now some teenaged, redneck construction worker that lives here, in a trailer park?"

"Hey," I object. "I never said that he's a redneck. And he's really sweet. I think you'd like him. I know he'd like you."

"You sure about that, smalls? I mean, if my sister is channeling some aggro medieval witch spirit who harbors ill-will toward your man, *and* I'm a possible reincarnation of their supposed *love child*, I think we should hold off on meeting each other. For a while, anyway. Until we know more about what the hell is happening in this town."

After we make plans to hang out this coming weekend, we tap fists, and I climb out of his enormous vehicle. The door to the trailer is unlocked, which seems kind of weird to me, so I open the screen door cautiously, only to find Arthur sleeping on the pulled-out futon, some movie still playing on the TV.

Yin and Yang come to greet me when I enter the kitchen. They are by far the sweetest, gentlest, most perfect angel babies I've ever seen, so I scoop both of their little vibrating bellies into my arm and creep over to Arthur. I turn off the TV with my free hand and carefully place the kittens on the mattress. Arthur could sleep during a hurricane, so I'm not surprised that he doesn't stir or move when the floor creaks beside and behind him.

My phone battery had drained within minutes of our arrival at Mordy's uncle's house despite being fully charged, and I didn't have a charger in my bag because I hadn't known I was walking into some weird energy vortex. Gwen had told me she would call me earlier in the evening to see about possibly going to the lake on Sunday, but my phone has been dead for several hours, so I have no idea who else could have texted or called me.

After I wash my face and brush my teeth, I climb into Arthur's bed, somewhat leery of what might be lurking in the shadows of the trailer. But I close my eyes anyway, and try to fight the red and black images that eventually lure me to sleep and haunt my dreams until I wake.

* * * *

In the morning I get up and walk into the living room, only to find the futon upright, a blanket folded on the coffee table and a few dishes drying in the dish rack. A lukewarm pot of coffee that was made a few hours ago beckons me, and I help myself to a cup.

My phone is fully charged now, and I'm not prepared for the amount of texts I received from both Gwen and Arthur. The last text is from Arthur, and I can tell from the words he has chosen that he's upset about something. He knew I was hanging out with Morgan and Mordy yesterday, and while I hadn't anticipated being there until well past midnight, I honestly hadn't thought it would be such a big deal if I came home late.

Arthur and I don't normally fight, because he's so calm and collected most of the time, that I usually just hope for a peaceful reconciliation. Something about this feels different, though. Arthur has been grumpy lately, and I haven't been able to cheer him up, no matter what I do. Maybe my shitty personality is finally rubbing off on him. I hope not—there's not enough room in the world for two Lance Lottes. Hell, there's barely enough room for one.

After I step out of the shower, I hear the front door spring open. Arthur didn't mention his landlord stopping by, and I hope to god that it's not another *otherworldly visit*, not after last night. I need a break. So when I see Arthur standing in front of the open refrigerator, my heart thrums with relief and something else, and I want to wrap my arms around his torso.

"Hey," I say. "What are you doing home so early? You could have texted me and I would have made us some lunch."

He laughs, head still basking in the artificial fridge light. "Gettin' you to answer a text these days is nearly impossible."

"What's that supposed to mean?" I ask. "I answer texts. Sometimes."

Something about my comment digs at him, because he spins around with an exasperated look on his face, and replies, "Did you get my texts last night? Any of them?"

I sit down on the futon and remove the towel from my damp hair. "My phone died," I say. "And I forgot my charger. The last thing I read from you was about canceling lunch."

When he shuts the refrigerator door and turns around again, I see that he's gotten a haircut. Most of his long, sun-bleached blond hair is gone. I point at what little hair he has left in awe.

"Wow," I say. "I've never seen you with short hair."

Arthur runs a hand over his new buzzcut and says, "Yeah, I know. I'm still getting used to it myself."

"It looks good, though. I really like it." The brown freckles splattered across his nose and cheeks are darker today, too, probably because he doesn't wear sunblock when he's out working. I'm not sure if I've actually looked at him like this in a while. Arthur is the most beautiful person I've ever seen or met, and at times, his presence can be intimidating.

"Are you datin' that Mordy guy?" he finally asks, his tone an odd mixture of agitation and sorrow. "Because if you are, you can just tell me."

"What? No," I say. "Why would you even think that?"

"I dunno. Why wouldn't I? You hang out with him every day, and now you're coming home during the middle of the night. What else could I possibly think?"

Now, Arthur has been with a lot of girls, so many girls that I stopped trying to keep a tab on them years ago.

During his freshman year, he dated two girls, one during the spring semester and the other during the summer. Their names were Jenna and Ashleigh. After that, Arthur had been surrounded by girls. His voice had dropped, he'd continued to gain inches on everyone, and his popularity had grown among the students. I'd witnessed only two years of this lunacy while in high school with him, but his ability to instruct and influence others was uncanny and unmatched. Even the teachers had gotten tired of his bizarre leadership skills.

But I've never mentioned any of this to him. Not once. Nothing about how seeing him holding hands with Ashleigh had all but broken my heart in two. Nothing about how I'd cried when I'd seen his prom pictures that year. I'd just sat back and watched girls cycle through his life these past few years, and said nothing. Dates, dances, prom, everything and anything involving school spirit, or the fencing team. Cheerleaders. Dance team. None of it. All static, no deejays.

I stand up, fists balled at my sides. "Arthur Pendragon, are you telling me who I can and can't hang out with?" I ask.

"What?" Arthur's hostility cracks, along with his voice, and he says, "No, I would never do that."

I pick up the wet towel and do my best not to stomp into the bathroom, but the trailer is so small that any movement other than tiptoeing rattles the damn thing like an aluminum can full of rocks. When I return to the living room Arthur is fumbling through his wallet, looking for something. He slings a key down onto the coffee table and looks up at me, eyes brimming with tears.

"I got a key made for you yesterday. I sent you a text about it, but you never responded, so I left the door unlocked last night. Why did you sleep in my bed?"

I rub my eyes. "Because you have to get up in the morning and I didn't want to disturb you." Now I'm on the verge of crying, and I hate it. "You can believe what you want, but I'm not dating Mordy. He's just a friend. A good friend."

"Well, that key is yours. You can have it if you still want to stay here."

Things are not going as I had imagined they would. Arthur and I were going have dinner tonight, and we would possibly watch the latest episode of *Sabrina*, and I would tell him how I've been desperately in love with him since the first day we met. Ideally, we would then make out for a few hours and fall asleep contently on the futon.

Voilà — happily ever after.
Nothing at all like this.

"No," I say. "I know you can't stay, and that you have to go back to work, but I don't want things to end like this."

"End?" Arthur looks at me, his eyes full of wild shock. "What do you mean?"

I rush to his side and throw my arms around his waist. "Mordy is trans, Arthur." My eyes search his for a visual response, anything. "Like me."

"What?" he asks, sinking into my embrace. "What are you talkin' about?"

"I'm sorry." I bury my head into his side. "I should have said something earlier, but it's not easy for me to talk to about this kind of stuff. And he's also into witchcraft, it's called Santería. I may have already mentioned that, I don't know. It's a mixture of Cuban and African witchcraft, and he's been teaching me stuff, things." The words plummeting from my mouth are barely comprehensible, I know this, but I don't want Arthur to get the wrong idea about us, and I'm terrible at conveying how I feel.

Arthur puts his hands around my shoulders and squeezes them. "I am a fucking jerk." I shake my head, rubbing my wet hair against his T-shirt. "No," he says, "I am. I'm the world's biggest ass." I pull away from him and wipe my eyes. "Oh fuck, Lance. God, don't cry. Forget I said anything, okay?"

Now's not the proper time to tell him how I feel, not when there's so much anger and confusion in the air, so much negativity, but I have to do something, so I take his hand and kiss the back of it, brushing my lips across coarse spots of skin.

"I need you to know that I am not romantically involved with Mordy. The only person I care about right now is standing in this room."

Arthur pulls his phone from his jeans pocket and starts dialing a number.

"Who are you callin'?" I ask. "When do you have to be back there? Oh shit, I didn't mean to make you late."

"Hey, Tater," he says, after a man's muffled voice comes through the speaker. "Let me talk to Chuck." A few seconds later, he says, "Hey, Chuck, some asshole busted a goddamn bottle in my driveway and I just now got a flat pullin' out. No, that's okay. I'll just come in super early tomorrow and stay late if that's cool with you. All right. I know, I know — Bud runs a mad two-for-one tire deal. I'll see you tomorrow. Bye."

"You shouldn't have done that," I say. "I don't want you to get fired because of me."

"Well, I'm not going to get fired. I've worked for that company for a while now and have never taken any additional time off, and I ain't never been sick. Besides, Chuck has a nasty hangover, and I'm fairly certain he won't make it through the whole shift. I'm really sorry for being a douche."

Thoroughly deflated from our previous argument, I lean into Arthur, my muscles unwinding, and when he lifts me into his arms, I am wholly surprised. Our eyes meet and he kisses me ferociously, his mouth engulfing mine in a fury. I barely have time to breathe in between the swift movements.

With our lips still locked, Arthur kissing me like we're trying to win some kind of contest, he carries me into his bedroom and gently lays me down on the bed. His shirt comes off, and his belt. I swallow, registering every single move that Arthur's body makes. When he joins me on the mattress, he kisses me tenderly and deeply, a sharp contrast from his earlier madness, his seemingly insatiable appetite.

I run my hands through the blond hair on his sweeping chest, then caress his arms and back, taking note of every freckle, mole and dimple. His body is a flawless canvas, free from scars or blemishes, not a single imperfection in sight. A truly Herculean beauty.

But it's not the shape of his muscles, or the dimples above his posterior, that excites me.

The way he always looks at me like I'm center of the universe is what ignites the flame within.

The fantasies I've had regarding Arthur didn't prepare me for the actual wanting, or the desire now throbbing in every limb, and I know he shares my desire because I can feel the eagerness through his jeans as he presses against my thigh.

Arthur's fingers trace the stubborn curves of my figure, fanning the heatwave that's now traveling up and down my body like an unhinged see-saw. When they land on the button of my pants, I gasp and trap his hands with my own.

"Don't get me wrong—I want to make love to you. Oh, God, I do," he says breathlessly. "But I know you're not ready. I just want to feel your skin against mine. I'm not going to rush into anything and hurt you."

I move my hand and watch with bated breath while his fingers fumble with the top button of my pants. "Yes, you will," I whisper, anticipating a future heartbreak. Surely nothing that feels this good and right can last.

The soft kisses he plants on my inner thigh send shudders throughout my body, and I find myself alternating between gasping and moaning, clutching at the flannel sheets underneath our bodies. Arthur pauses briefly to remove his pants, wiggling out of the blue denim, and crawls back into bed with me. Other than his briefs, he's practically naked, and the sight of his body frightens me a little, because it means that we're actually in his bedroom, on his bed, doing what I thought was impossible.

After Arthur rolls on top of me, he pushes away from the mattress, and peers down at my face.

"I've wanted you like this for a long time now," he confesses. "And I mean a long time. I guess that sounds kinda creepy, doesn't it?"

"Liar." I bite my lip and follow his eyes as they wander across my face and body. "Why didn't you say somethin'? You could have had me like this a long time ago."

He laughs and leans in to kiss me again. "Yeah, right," he replies. "If I had tried kissin' you back when we were kids, you would have shut me down immediately."

"No, I wouldn't," I lie.

What Arthur says is devastatingly true, because I stopped trusting myself and others after Todd broke up with me, but I don't want to think about those times or him ever again, so I push his ugly name out of my head and pull Arthur's face into mine. His tongue lashes at me wildly, like I've just released something fierce and feral into my mouth. I seize his back and dig my fingernails into his skin, his soft moans stoking the fire burning between my legs. *I want him so bad.*

When our mouths finally separate, I slide my hand down his chest and reach into his underwear, tugging at the curls inside. I grab his cock and marvel at how good it feels in my hand. He gasps and lets me play with it until my hand is lightly covered in sticky fluid.

"Hey, that's not fair," he says in a half-whisper, half-moan. "Lance, wait." His hand wraps around my wrist and he pushes me back onto the mattress. "I want you to feel good, too."

"I do feel good," I say. Arthur kisses my neck then pulls back, the desire in his eyes now unrestrained and savage.

"Can I watch you touch yourself?" Arthur asks shyly. "You don't have to take your clothes off."

"Okay," I whisper. I slide my hand into my boxers and touch myself. My clit is engorged, and I'm positive that it won't take much stimulation to orgasm. "As long as I can watch you," I say, never taking my eyes off him.

Watching Arthur masturbate and gush cum into his hand is single-handedly the most erotic, arousing thing I have ever witnessed. After he's finished, he gets into bed with me and kisses my mouth, neck and collarbone until orgasmic waves of relief surge throughout my body, leaving me completely drained and euphoric.

Afterward, we both roll over onto our backs and stare up at the ceiling.

The last time we'd tried this sort of thing, I had gotten kicked out of the Pendragon home and had been permanently banned from stepping foot in their house ever again. It's hard to believe that it's been nearly a year since my exile was set in motion.

"Do you want me to make us something to eat?" Arthur asks, sliding his hand into mine.

I crane my neck to look up at him. "Nah, let's just stay here for a little while longer."

He squeezes my hand and bobs his head in agreement.

The truth is that I've waited so long for this moment, and now that it's happening, I want to savor it for as long as I can. Part of me still can't believe we're in his room, free from harm or violence, able to do whatever we want, whenever we want.

"You know," he says, rubbing his thumb against my palm, "when you go back to Lexington, it's gonna kill me."

"Don't say that. Why would it kill you?"

"Do you even have to ask that question?" Arthur's tone is suddenly very sad. "Last summer you left and I didn't see you for an entire year. My heart can't take you doin' that again."

I sit up, but don't let go of his hand. "That's not going to happen. I'll come back as often as I can."

Arthur pulls his hand away and positions himself on the edge of the bed, his legs hanging off the side of the mattress. "You say that now, but what if—"

I push two pillows out of my way, crawl over to him and slide my arms around his neck. How my feelings aren't blatantly obvious by this point, I don't know.

"There's no buts," I say. "Not this time around. I'll come back every break, and we can FaceTime and stuff. That's how long-distance relationships work, or at least, I think so."

Arthur seizes my arms and swings me onto his lap. "Relationship? You mean like boyfriends?"

I reach up and run my hand through his freshly cut hair. "Yes, silly, that's exactly what I mean."

Seeing excitement replace the sadness in his eyes is too much for me, and I bury my head into his shoulder. "God," I say. "Stop looking at me like that."

"Lance Lotte," he whispers into my hair. "I know that I am just a big dumb country boy, but I promise that I will love you for as long as you let me."

Chapter Eight

The Lady of the Lake

Arthur leaves for work the next morning, and I message Gwen, asking her to bring over a box of my shit. She doesn't know the status of our relationship yet, and I know that I can lure her here by texting her something like *Oh, his bed is really soft*, or *It's weird, but Arthur wears tighty-whities like a grandpa*. Her long-time ship has finally sailed, and she will want to know every dirty detail. Not that I'll give her every dirty detail, of course. Some things aren't shareable, but I know how her brain works, and I want to see her. *So bait her I shall.*

While I wait on Gwen, I make a fresh pot of coffee and some toast. Arthur has been buying everything lately, and I feel guilty, so I plan on walking to the gas station and replacing the bread and toilet paper. Earlier, when I suggested this to Arthur, he argued with me, insisting that he made enough money, that I didn't need to spend what little I got from Camelot Crafts, that I needed to save it for when I returned to school. He's stubborn and myopic at times, but if I'm going to stay here the whole summer, I'm going to contribute whatever I can.

Once my toast is ready, I walk over to the fridge and pull on the handle, only for it to not open. It's been doing this lately — sticking, that is — and when I'd asked Arthur about it, he'd said it was probably the ghost. *The ghost.* I hadn't mentioned what had happened to me a few days ago in his bedroom, because the visions still freak me out a little, but he did say that the shower will turn on occasionally, and that one night the lights had flickered on and off until he'd finally gotten out of bed, only to find Yin scratching at the front door. Receiving this bit of information had been somewhat jarring, but Arthur had reassured me that he believed Yin had gone outside while he'd been getting groceries from his truck, and that the ghost had been warning him. I'm not afraid of ghosts, but ghosts, demons and entities are all completely different beings, and we don't know what we're dealing with here in this trailer.

Arthur doesn't practice magick, and knows very little about it, other than the stuff he hears Gwen and me discuss. If something evil wanted to attack him, he would be defenseless, which is partly why I'm having Gwen bring over some of my belongings.

"Hello?" Gwen says through the screen door. "Arthur, if you're in there, you'd better put it back in your pants!"

The door opens and Gwen steps through the doorway wearing a pair of Daisy Dukes and a tank top without a bra, the shape of her breasts conspicuous. I rush to help her with the box she's carrying in one hand.

"Please take it," she exclaims, loosening her grip on the cardboard. "Jesus. What the fuck do you have in here? A treasure trunk?"

"Close," I say. "Mostly books. Want a cup of coffee?"

"Sure," she replies. "You know, I'm surprised by Arthur's ability to turn such a dump into an actual home." She plants her hands on her hips and continues, "It's surprisingly really nice in here. Do you have any half-n-half?"

Gwen then kicks off her sandals and bends down to pick up Yang. Spring is the season I always associate with Arthur, because of his delightful disposition and his ability to turn any cloud into sunshine, but summer is without a doubt Gwen's season. Sunny and easy-going, she is a living embodiment of the solstice, the longest day of the year in perpetuity. *I love her.*

"Why did you need me to bring over a box of shit anyway?" she asks, taking a seat on the futon. "Thanks. Ooh, that's hotter 'n hell."

I hand her a carton of milk and sit down next to her. "Sorry, it looks like we're out of half-n-half. Hope soy is okay."

Gwen looks around the small room. "So, Mom said you never come home anymore. That you haven't been home in like three weeks. Are you pretty much staying here now?"

"I am," I admit. "Until he gets tired of me."

Gwen laughs. "Yeah, like that'll happen. I mean, unless you're torturing him with self-inflicted chastity. I see how he looks at you — *all the time now* — like you'll disappear if he blinks."

Gwen is not only my sister and best friend, but she's also my biggest cheerleader. Ever since she figured out my feelings toward Arthur, she's tried setting us up, only to fail every time, because I used to struggle being alone with him once I realized how I felt. My senior year was absolute fucking hell.

Botched attempt after botched attempt.

During my year away from Avalon, Arthur and Gwen had grown closer, because he knew I would tell her everything, about classes, about my body healing, whether I had snagged a boyfriend — a question that he'd asked her more than once. Gwen made sure to tell me every detail of their conversations, too. Thinking back on it, maybe our botched attempt at intimacy happened for a reason — maybe Gwen and Arthur were meant to become better friends, and my absence had acted as a catalyst for this. Whatever the reason, she is totally invested in a 'Larthur' pairing now.

"You haven't slept with him," she says, suddenly pulling the cup away from her bottom lip. "But you have done *something*. I can tell by how chill you are. I bet it's huge, isn't it?"

Some things aren't shareable. "I'm not telling you shit about his body, you creep."

"You have seen him naked, though. Haven't you?" Gwen sucks her teeth. "Okay, so maybe he won't end up gushing like a geyser and dying from blue balls after all."

"You are disgusting."

"And y'all are gonna end up fuckin' like rabbits by the end of the summer. Don't fight it, Lance. I might not know how big his dick is, but he has big lips and I can tell he's itchin' to use them."

On that note, I take our cups back to the kitchen and place them in the sink, hoping to God that the ghost isn't listening to our conversation, and that I can talk to her about Emmett and Camelot Crafts.

"Do you have to work today?" I ask when I return to the living room.

"Yes, but only for two hours because someone needs to leave early, and Olivia asked me to close. Why? Don't you? I thought you usually worked Fridays. Are you wearing Arthur's shirt?"

My phone buzzes and I pick it up from the coffee table. Mordy has sent a text instructing me to turn on the local news, stating that it's urgent.

"I normally do," I reply. "And yes, I am."

I get up from the couch and turn on the TV. Arthur doesn't have cable so I have to mess with the DIY coat hanger bunny ears that he made for a signal.

"But Emmett gave me yesterday and today off. Told me Caspian was lookin' fer more hours, at least that's what he said."

"That old man is fucking weird, dude," Gwen says. "Do you know that he and Olivia used to be married? That they still share a lake house somewhere along Neve Lake? He's always creeped me out."

"Really?" I ask. The signal is shitty, but I manage to get the channel to come through, at least mostly. The blurry words on the screen are enough to make me choke on air—LOCAL GIRL MISSING SINCE TUESDAY – TAMMY DIXON, AGE 18.

"Holy shit. Tammy?" Gwen says, edging closer to the TV screen. "I just talked to her on Monday night. I ran into her walking out of the library. She said that she was in a hurry, that she was meeting someone. I wonder what happened?"

Why, at this very moment, I remember of all things that I did not send her an apology through Facebook I'll never know, and now I have a sneaking suspicion that I'll never get the chance. It's not a good feeling.

"Tammy Dixon was last seen leaving Baubles & Books late Tuesday evening. Her current whereabouts are unknown. If you have any information that could help the police in their search, please call eight-five-nine-one-one-seven-nine-six-three-two for non-emergency police-related matters."

Gwen and I sit in silence for the next few minutes. Mordy sent me that text because, I assume, he thinks Emmett had something to do with the disappearance, but I haven't spoken to Gwen about any of Mordy's theories, simply because I don't think she'd believe me.

When I glance at Gwen, tears are streaming down her face, and she's fighting a meltdown. Normally, she would say something stupid about a bad hook-up and someone struggling to find their way home, but I think she can feel it, too—that the disappearance was deliberate and dangerous. That Tammy is not coming back. I scoot over to her and put my arm around her shoulders.

"Tammy could be a cunt," she says. "And she stole my girlfriend in the eighth grade, but goddess, I would never want something terrible to happen to her. I know you don't really like her, but she isn't a bad person."

"No," I reply, squeezing her softly. "I don't know her. She always just catches me on a bad day, I think. I guess you could say that our stars are never in alignment."

Gwen puts her arms around me and buries her face in my shirt.

"I need to tell you something." I stroke her hair. "Something that you're gonna find weird, but you have to listen to all of it before you say anything, 'cause there's a lot. Here, let me fetch you a glass of water first."

When I return from the kitchen, Gwen is standing by the screen door, watching a couple of kids fight over a bicycle that doesn't even have a seat. I hand her the glass of water and lean up against the door frame.

"Do you remember when you first came to live with us?" she asks. "I think you had just turned nine."

"Yes, I do remember. You were very disappointed to discover that I wasn't from Mexico, and that I couldn't speak Spanish. And you refused to let me play with your Barbies."

Gwen takes a drink of water. "That's because you kept giving all of them mustaches and cutting their hair, even though I had plenty of Ken dolls."

We both laugh.

"I guess that was a sign of things to come, huh?"

She nods. "I always knew, you know. Even when you told me your name, it didn't sit right with me. I would think, this kid's a boy, not a tomboy, but a boy, because there ain't nothin' female about him."

I say, "Well, I'm glad one of us knew, because it felt like hell for a long time there. Still does, sometimes, but not as bad, I guess."

"Last year, Arthur and I would meet up every week and talk about school, but I know he was hanging out with me because he knew you and I talked daily."

I groan and fold my arms. "Yeah, even my therapist told me that I needed to talk things out with him, but depression is a bitch, you know?"

"I do know. Arthur certainly knows." Her words twist at my insides like dough being pulled apart. "Anyway, he first saw you at the pool. Has he told you this yet?"

"No," I say. "The pool? What pool? When?"

"According to Arthur, you were probably twelve or so, and it was just you and me. We were hanging out over by the concession stand getting ice cream, and Mom had let you get your hair cut, like really short. Not even a bob, but like super short."

We walk over to the futon. "Oh shit," I say. "I remember that haircut. It was the first time she let me cut my hair. It was a sick 'do."

"Arthur said that he was here visiting his mamaw for the summer, and that he was with his family at the pool. He said you were dressed in a baggy black T-shirt and a pair of basketball shorts."

"Ah, I remember those days. I don't think I've ever actually owned a real bathing suit."

"Another sign that we overlooked, I guess." We both laugh again. "Anyway, he said he watched us for like a hour playing Marco Polo and getting into a fight with squirt guns, or some shit."

"Weird," I say. "That's a pretty thorough memory."

"I say 'us', but Arthur told me that he was more interested in you. That you were his first crush. He remembers the details because it was you, Lance, not me."

I scoff. "What? You're lying to me."

Gwen shakes her head. "No, I'm not. He said that he talked his mamaw into getting a pool pass just so that he could come to the pool, and hopefully muster enough courage to talk to you."

"You're a goddamn liar."

"And how he never did," she continues. "Because he was still too shy to talk to people. That when he came back every summer to see his mamaw, he would hope to run into you, so that he could finally introduce himself."

I sink back into the black cushion. "I never knew any of this. Why didn't he tell me?"

Gwen looks at me like I'm the dumbest person in the world. "He also told me when his family moved here to help take care of his mamaw, he was relieved to find out that there was only one high school, because that meant he might actually get to talk to you."

"But that's like crazy," I say. "He didn't even know me. Dude, that was literally almost ten years ago."

"Sometimes the only logical explanation out there is illogical."

Here's my opportunity — a perfect segue into what I need to tell Gwen.

"I know you think all of this Arthur shit — er, King Arthur shit — is ridiculous and fantastical. But I need to tell you about some things, about some kids I've been hanging out with, about Emmett and Camelot Crafts, about what happened to me a few days ago. You're not going to believe me, or at least, you won't want to believe me, because it's all so fucked."

For the next few hours Gwen and I talk about everything — the text from Mordy at the party, running into Morgan and Mordy at the party, Emmett threatening the twins when they were in the store, Morgan shattering glass everywhere afterward, Emmett Crabtree answering to Emrys Caerwyn, Morgan attacking me at the farmhouse and the bizarre abductions of several children years ago.

At first Gwen argues with me, stating facts and rational explanations as if I hadn't already thoroughly explored those avenues. But then we discuss how her powers had begun manifesting themselves after she'd started working at Baubles & Books, how Olivia had started asking Gwen to help her with morning blessings, how Olivia had given her a black crystal to wear for protection and how adamant Olivia is about always having two people close the store at night, even coming in if someone has to leave early.

"Does Emmett ever come into the store?" I ask.

My books are scattered all over the floor now, and I've located a scrying bowl, a five-pound bag of sea salt, two white candles, a bottle of holy water, a green crystal and several sticks of Palo Santo.

"No, but he's always looking in when I'm working, watching me like it's the first time he's seen me *every time*. I don't know anything about that old fucker, but I bet he's a pedo or something. And he's like twenty-five years older than Olivia. That's fuckin' nasty, dude."

I open a cabinet over the sink and grab a bag of pretzels, then get us some juice. Arthur will be home soon, and Gwen has to leave for work in forty-five minutes, so we have to squeeze in as much cleansing as possible.

"Here," I say. "Eat this while you read."

Gwen takes the glass of juice and says, "What exactly are we looking for? I don't see how we can do anything without knowin' the full story."

I shove a couple of pretzels in my mouth. "Arthur," I say, crunching loudly. "The other day he pulled that Death card." Gwen rolls her eyes at me. "And no, he probably isn't going to drive his car off a bridge or have a heart attack any time soon, but that doesn't mean he isn't being sought after by God knows what." I think back on the incident in his bedroom and choose my next words carefully, in case something — or someone — is listening to our conversation. "If there's a demon here, or if someone has put a curse on Arthur, or hasn't yet, but will attempt to, we need to fortify his home and his truck."

"Okay," Gwen says, slowly. "But what about that bitch who attacked you at her uncle's house? She *was* possessed, and you still agreed to hang out with Mordy this weekend. Don't you think it's about time to consider protectin' your ass as well?"

A large Celtic cross on the wall behind us, the one Arthur's mamaw gave to him, begins to shake violently. I see Gwen's eyes dart across the room as if trying to materialize whatever it is that's pulling the cross.

"L-lance," she stammers. "What the fuck is happening?"

When I don't answer her immediately, the cross swings back and forth until it's nothing but a big gray blur, as if it's trying to communicate with me, trying to agree with Gwen.

"Hopefully, cleansing the house and truck will do the trick!" I practically shout at the cross. "Besides, I never take my amulet off, and tonight I can leave the rune that I made at Mordy's outside, to absorb energy from the moon. I'll keep it in my pocket at all times!"

The heavy cross stills a moment later.

"What was that?" Gwen asks, her voice shaky. Gwen doesn't deal with ghosts or spirits very well. How she's able to hold drunken séances every other weekend, I'll never know. Blacked out on frozen daiquiris, probably.

"A ghost, I think. But not a demon." My eyes return to the cross, which is now slightly tilted to one side. "What are you reading?"

Gwen puts her hand on mine, never moving her eyes from the book now resting in her lap. "What about this? *Limpia de Huevos*? Have you ever tried it?"

"An egg cleansing? That sounds really familiar. Here, let me see what it says."

The book states that an egg *limpia* can be helpful in removing negative energy and impurities from the mind, body and soul, among many other things. Arthur just bought a carton of eggs yesterday, and while I've never tried to cleanse anything with an egg, there's a first time for everything. The book also states that only a powerful shaman should attempt the ritual—I'm not a shaman and I'm not powerful, so we'll have to be very careful and just hope for the best.

"We'll do me first, and then I can do you," I say. "If that works." She nods.

Gwen and I repeat different prayers during the cleansing, but the rituals are similar in every other aspect. She takes an unopened egg and touches my forehead with it, making a pentagram on the skin, and continues to do this on my neck, shoulders, hands, hips, knees and feet. Afterward, she cracks the egg into a bowl of holy water that I have left over from a Christmas Mass I attended earlier this year. I'm not a practicing Catholic, but that's neither here nor there. *Magick is magick, regardless of the channel or source.*

We deviated from the ritual slightly because we were pressed for time, but like all spells and forms of witchery, intention is key. I hope ancient shamanic magick operates on a similar philosophy, anyway.

After the cleansing is complete, Gwen and I take handfuls of salt and sprinkle it around the outside of the trailer. Children outside stop playing basketball to come over and watch us perform this spell, but I'm more concerned about the group of teenage boys marveling over the fact that my sister isn't wearing a bra.

Gwen leaves a few minutes before Arthur gets home, and when he walks into the living room, the trailer smells like I've been burning funky incense. Palo Santo has a very strong, particular scent, and while I love it, I know it can give people headaches.

Arthur doesn't mention it though, instead spotting a stack of my clothes on the kitchen counter and pointing at it.

"Those are mine. I had Gwen drop off some of my stuff earlier today."

"I know those are yours," he says. "I couldn't fit into that shirt if I tried."

"I just figured that if I'm going to be staying here, I should have a change of clothes, or something." I haven't figured out if *staying here* means *living here*, and I don't want to freak Arthur out, so I don't say it.

"Oh," I say. "Here."

The green crystal in my hand will bring the person wearing it protection, luck, prosperity, wealth, all kinds of shit—it's what we in the magick world refer to as a catch-all crystal. Arthur stares at the gemstone, and after I drop it into his hand, rolls it in his palm several times.

"Jewelry already?" The humor in his tone makes me want to kiss him, because I haven't seen him all day, and because his freckles are just so damn cute, but I can't get caught up in my feelings, not now, not when I have so much research to do. "You sure move fast." He laughs.

"Well, you are my boyfriend now. And this is a crystal, dummy, not jewelry."

"Say that again." He closes the distance between us and kisses my hand.

"What? Dummy?" I ask, savoring the scent of his sweat mixed with the smoke in the air. "Crystal? Jewelry?"

"Boyfriend."

"You *are* my boyfriend," I say. "Now go take a shower. You smell like a bologna sandwich." Arthur bites his bottom lip, and I know he wants to kiss me, because I've seen that look a hundred times now, but I have so much to do at the moment that I can't let his twinkling brown eyes enamor me.

"Why don't you join me?" He grabs my waist and pulls me into embrace, leaving a trail of feathery kisses all along my neck and collarbone.

"In your dreams, Pendragon."

"You have no idea," he whispers into my ear, then he kisses the side of my head.

Flirting with Arthur like this feels so weird and foreign, because I've spent so much time wrestling with my feelings that having him reciprocate them makes me uneasy. I'm still not sure what to make of everything Gwen said, about the pool, high school, and hoping to run into me every summer. That adds a layer to our relationship I hadn't even considered — the possibility that Arthur has been infatuated with me since we first met, maybe even longer than that.

Insane.

"Hey," he calls from the shower. "Can you bring me a towel? I think there's a couple folded up on the bed. The scratchy red one please — if it's clean!"

When I enter the bathroom I can make out Arthur's shape behind the frosted sliding shower door. Something about his movements and the sound of running water hypnotizes me, and I watch his hands go up and down his body. I'd said *'in your dreams'* like I don't share those same dreams, the freedom and confidence to be naked in front of another person. Not just another person, but him.

"Is that for me?" he asks, breaking the spell. Water drips off the tip of his nose.

Our eyes meet, and even though I'm sure I look extremely stupid, he says nothing when I hand him the towel, smirking at me instead. The truth is that I'm so afraid of being hurt by Arthur that every time I remove a brick, another one takes its place within seconds, and the wall becomes even greater, even stronger.

I turn around and leave the bathroom, closing the door behind me. The last, and therefore most annoying, barrier that I will have to overcome is also the most difficult. Arthur keeps reassuring me that he doesn't want to rush into anything, that I don't have to share a bed with him, that he's content with what we have, but goddamn, I want to his body, too.

The struggle is real.

Maybe if I set goals for myself I can push past the veil, destroying any last vestige of Linda for good — and finally accepting who I am — while hopefully welcoming Arthur's love *as Lance*. The person he's loved all along, or so I hope.

Right before bed, I take my phone into the living room and look for the charger. It has less than five percent of its battery left, but still manages to vibrate in my hand before I can plug it into the wall. The screen lights up and I see that Mordy has texted me, asking if I'm still up for the morning trip to Monticello tomorrow.

Thanks to Emmett's last-minute changes, my next shift isn't until Sunday afternoon, and Arthur is doing something with Gwen all day tomorrow. Besides, hanging out with Mordy is refreshing, a break from the usual, and we have much to discuss since the last time we hung out.

I tell him *yes*, that I will see him tomorrow, and mentally set my first goal.

Buy a dildo.

Chapter Nine

The Plan

Mordy and I get back from the Lion's Den right around lunchtime. We'd left super early in the morning because he'd said it might make me more comfortable if it wasn't so crowded and busy. Seeing as how there were like a hundred truckers in there buying all kinds of interesting things, I'd decided it didn't matter in the end, and paid for my purchases with ease.

On the way back, Mordy and I had discussed my fears and hopes about having sex with Arthur. Talking to another trans man about sex is like drinking a glass of water after a hardy jog — you don't know how much you need it until you need it. Morgan is lucky to have such an open, chill brother. I wouldn't trade Gwen for the world, but I wouldn't mind adding Mordy and Morgan, if she allowed it, to my family.

We decide to have a light lunch at Baubles because Gwen is working today, and we need to discuss meeting up later. Gwen has never met Mordy before, and I know how Morgan feels about white witches. I hope he doesn't share her sentiment.

"You must be Gwen!" Mordy shakes Gwen's hand with vigor. "My name is Mordy, Mordy Lafayette. Ooh, girl, that looks like it hurt." He points at the fresh cheek piercings she must have gotten earlier today.

"Oh, they fucking hurt all right. Not so bad right now, but when I smile, it's like this puffy, tight feeling. My face feels like it's on fire."

I groan. "Please tell me you paid someone to shove needles in your face, that you didn't do them yourself."

"Wouldn't you like to know?"

Gwen takes our order and leaves.

"I made something for you." Mordy reaches into his bag and pulls out a black velvet pouch. "You can choose to accept it or not. I understand completely if it goes against your beliefs. Here. Take it."

I accept the little velvet bag with drawstrings, and peer inside.

"I don't know if it will bring you any joy or comfort to hear me say this, but I killed the chicken myself. I fed her a good meal, bathed her, sang to her, let her sleep in my lap while I stroked her feathers and then slit her throat in one swift move. Her death was instant. Afterward I offered a prayer and deboned her myself."

I swallow and gape at the string of chicken bones now dangling from my fingers.

"My God, dude," I say. "This is the nicest gift anyone has ever given to me."

Mordy leans back into his chair and releases a deep sigh. "Okay, so you like it," he replies. "Dope. I thought you might kick my ass and send PETA after me."

We laugh, and Gwen surprises us by setting down three plates of food.

"I'll be free in like five minutes," she says. "Don't eat my fucking pickle, Lance. I mean it."

Mordy picks up his grilled cheese and begins eating, while I admire my new gift with unabashed awe.

"Is this for protection?" I ask.

He nods, and wipes off his mouth. "Yes," he says, after taking a drink of soda. "Something is trying to fuck with you, man. I'm not sure what it is, or why, but I've never seen Morgan lash out at *anyone* like that. And until we get to the bottom of things, you need all of the extra help you can get." I'm silently thankful Gwen isn't around to hear Mordy's warnings, because her head is already too big and we wouldn't be able to carry it out the door.

"Gwen and I cleansed each other yesterday, and I cleansed the house and truck. To be honest, I'm more worried about Arthur."

"Ooh," Gwen says. "Arthur? Are we talking about sex?"

"No, dumbass. We're talking about how he pulled the fucking Death card. What is with you?"

Mordy sets his glass on the table. "A tarot reading?"

I shake my head. "Worse. Just a single card. I was too freaked out to even consider having him shuffle the deck again and get another one, because I already knew what the card would be."

During our lunch, Mordy launches into his Emmett-is-the-antichrist tirade, and I send Arthur pictures of the bone talisman he made for me. In response Arthur sends me a picture of himself wearing nothing but a pair of golden Speedos. I have no idea where he is or what the hell he's doing, but my laughter causes a disturbance at the table, and Gwen snatches the phone from my hand.

"Hey, asshole, that's my property."

"Yeah," she says, "but you're family, so we share everything."

"No." I grab the phone out of her hand. "Not everything."

"Did Arthur tell you someone asked him to be Rocky tonight at a showing of *Rocky Horror Picture Show*? We're supposed to rehearse some of the moves at y'all's trailer this afternoon."

"You have got to be kidding me," I reply. "You know how I feel about that movie."

"Are you saying that you're not going?" Gwen asks.

I shake my head. "Hell no."

"Not even to see your man Arthur dance around in a pair of golden underwear?" Mordy asks. "What's the point of setting sequential goals if you can't get past the first one?"

Gwen has no idea what we're talking about, and I don't care to explain Lance Lotte's Plan for Sexual Healing with her. Mordy understands the awkward silence between the both of us and quickly changes the subject, asking Gwen what type of magick she practices.

I stare down at the picture on my phone. Arthur never says no to anyone — he's the life of the party, the first one to skinny-dip, the first one to strip if he loses at Jenga, the first one to enter a haunted house. He moves so fast sometimes that I don't know if I'll ever be able to catch him.

I never have been a very fast runner.

"All right," I proclaim. "We'll go see that dumpster fire of a movie. But I am not dressin' up, you hear me?"

After lunch, Gwen, Mordy and I agree to meet up with Morgan at the library to discuss Tammy's disappearance. The library is the most accessible, neutral, non-magickal place in town, and it has a quiet room for studying. Gwen and I decide to walk the two miles it takes to get there while Mordy fetches Morgan.

"I like him," Gwen says as we round a corner. "He's really funny. And sweet."

"You'll like Morgan, too, then." *I just hope she likes you.* "I know you're not a fan because of what happened a few days ago, but she's really nice. I honestly don't think she'd go out of her way to hurt me."

Gwen scowls at me. "You seem awfully trusting of these two people that you just met…who can possibly summon demons."

When the library comes into focus, I breathe a sigh of relief. At some point the weather had started feeling more like summer and less like spring, and every time I open a door, I'm afraid I might turn into a black-and-brown puddle as soon as my foot hits the sidewalk.

Maybe I shouldn't wear so much black all the time.

I hold the door for Gwen and a woman with a baby stroller. The AC hits my sweaty face and limbs, replacing the scorching heat with arctic pins and needles — that I prefer, if we're being honest.

"You weren't there," I say. "The stuff Morgan, or possibly Morgana, I'm not sure, was saying, wasn't necessarily terrible or frightening."

"What exactly did she say?" Gwen asks. "And don't forget she knocked you out, dude."

Telling Gwen *exactly* what Morgan said doesn't particularly appeal to me at this moment, but I promised myself this morning that I wouldn't keep anything from her — not if we're going to find Tammy.

I hesitate, then reply, "She told me that Arthur belonged to her. That she could take him from me." The words don't sound good, I already know this, but I refuse to hate Morgan, or think ill of her because of something that was said during a possible demonic possession.

Thankfully Morgan and Mordy haven't arrived yet, because the look in Gwen's eyes could wilt an entire bed of flowers. I know what she's thinking—that I'm a fool, putting myself in unnecessary danger and possibly jeopardizing my relationship with Arthur. But she's wrong. Deep down, I know Morgan isn't a bad person, that Morgana wasn't a bad person—the realization sends me stumbling into a table and chairs.

"Lance!" Gwen shouts, reaching for my arm. "Are you okay?"

"I'm all right," I reply. "It's probably just the heat. It feels like the fucking Sahara out there."

"Did she say anything else?"

"Yes," I say. "She said that I once told her 'a life for a life'."

The library is quiet and empty, save for the librarian and two pages stocking the back shelves. Saturdays and Sundays are pretty chill. In fact, this library is always chill—I rarely see anyone here.

Gwen bristles. "What the hell does 'a life for a life' mean?"

We enter the study room and take a seat at the table. I remove my side bag and hang it on the back of the chair. Gwen is still wearing a scowl, and now I'm thinking that maybe this meeting will be a disaster.

"I'm not sure. Neither is Morgan."

Gwen folds her arms. "Or so she says."

"Come on, give her a chance before you start in on her."

"Give her a chance? That's fresh comin' from you. Do you hear yourself?" she barks. "You never give anyone a chance. You immediately hate them from the beginning, and then they have to grow on you. I don't know how Arthur puts up with your bullshit."

"Queenie," I say, "what do you want me to say? I'm sorry. I'm working on myself. You think I like being like this? Fuck, I'm trying my best here."

A gentle tap on the window interrupts our bickering, and I turn to see Morgan and Mordy standing on the other side of the door. I wave them in, and Mordy opens the door.

"We intruding on something?" Mordy asks, his smile a welcome change from the scowl plastered across Gwen's face.

Morgan rushes to my side and envelops me in one large bear hug. I squeeze her in return, and we all take a seat at the table.

"Morgan," I say, "this is my sister, Gwen."

Morgan removes her sunglasses, and Gwen shifts uncomfortably in her seat, trying to maintain her anger, but she seemingly fails to do so when her expression softens.

"Hello, Gwen," Morgan says. "I'm pleased to finally meet you. Lance never stops talking about you."

Gwen's glower slowly morphs into a thin smile. "Nice to meet you." Her response is short, but more pleasant than I had expected. Morgan looks like a goddess today, even more so than usual, dressed in a sheer, strapless summer dress, the light fabric clinging to her curves. Gwen is as transparent as Morgan's dress—a pretty face is the easiest way to get in her good graces, and Morgan isn't just pretty, she's positively nymph-like. Gwen's fortress will be in shambles within the hour.

After the dust settles, I produce a notebook, and we discuss everything we already know. Gwen shares her experiences with Emmett and her thoughts on Tammy's disappearance. The twins air their concerns about Emmett as well, providing us with new information that Morgan learned this morning from their uncle. The conversation ends with us assembling a list of possible magickal sites here in Avalon, anything that might account for the darksome energy now accumulating in town.

"Do you think we should talk to Arthur about this?" Mordy asks. "I mean, because of his reading and shit."

"As well as some other things," Gwen adds, her voice icy again.

I don't have to look at her to know that she's glaring at the side of my head. Bringing Arthur into our current situation isn't ideal, not when we're still trying to figure out if it's just *him* that's in danger, or if it's the whole group, but Gwen won't take no for an answer. Getting Arthur to believe that he, or we, are in danger will be a grand task in and of itself, and I can't shoulder that burden alone.

"If it makes you more comfortable, Lance, you three can talk to him. I don't have to be there."

"No," I say, eyes darting across the round table. "We're all in this together now. It's too late to turn back. So if you've got anything else to say, any secrets at all, you'd better get them out of your system, because this is it. No more man-behind-the-curtain shit."

Mordy holds out his fist and we all tap it, one by one.

"What do we do next?" Gwen asks.

The four of us push out our chairs, then stand.

"You mean besides checking out these places?" I slip my side bag over my shoulder. "I'm not sure. Summer solstice is in a week and a half. Do you think we should do something for it?"

Morgan and Gwen both say, "That's a great idea!" then turn to look at each other. They don't see it, but I do—that fate brought us together, that it brought *them* together. Mordy clears his throat, locks his arm with his sister's, and walks to the door.

"So, summer solstice is a thing we're gonna do," he says. "Check. But what about in the meantime?"

My phone buzzes and I pull it out of my pocket. Arthur's just sent me a text asking what I'm doing tonight, if I'm free.

"*Rocky Horror Picture Show*," I blurt out before I can stop myself. "Let's go."

All three turn their faces toward me. "Excuse me?"

"Tonight. There's a midnight showing down at the MLK theater. Why don't we all go?"

"Do people dress up or...?" Morgan asks. Her excitement is as clear as the skylight above.

We exit the study room and make our way toward the front of the library.

"Word." Mordy grins and high-fives me. "Let's do it. I can drive."

"Yeah, you can dress up," I say, answering Morgan. "But I'm not."

"Good." Morgan laughs and puts her hands together. "Because Columbia is my favorite character. I can't wait!"

Gwen looks at me askance.

Because Columbia is her favorite, too.

Chapter Ten

Litha

The day before the solstice, Gwen asks me to help her clean the lake house Olivia is letting her borrow for the weekend. Their boss-employee setup is weird, *super weird*, but I'm not here to judge their relationship, or to make a big deal out of something that doesn't concern me, so I agree to help without offering my opinion. They're both adults, and what they do is their business, I guess.

When we pull up to the lake, I can hardly believe my eyes.

Three stories tall and made of yellow brick, Olivia's house is humongous and magnificent. The first floor is more window than brick, and there are flowering magnolia trees everywhere. We get out of Gwen's car and begin our walk up the dirt road that leads to the big, fancy house.

The front of the building is engulfed in wildflowers and purple bushes. There are no neighbors in sight and not a single boat on the lake. If seclusion is what Olivia's going for, she's got it down.

Leading out to the lake is a long wooden dock, a dock that will undoubtedly be used as a launch pad into the water at some point during the weekend.

I know how Arthur thinks.

Inside, the house is just as nice and well-maintained. Other than dusting and possibly making beds, there's not much to do. I wonder why we were even asked to come out here to clean.

What is else is there left to do?

By noon, we've already emptied the trash cans, thrown away the food in the refrigerator and sanitized the doors, wiped down the counters and swept the floor. Gwen is in cleaning mode, though, which is weird, because she hates to clean.

"Hey," I say. "Slow down. Do you want to order a pizza or something? Do you think we could even get delivery out here?"

Gwen drops the broom in her hands and starts babbling. I get up from the couch and go to her. She's obviously not okay, and I know how irritated she gets when someone states the obvious. When she turns around, her face is covered in tears and snot. I pull her into an embrace and stroke her hair, carefully avoiding her cheek piercings, which aren't fully healed. *I bet it hurts to cry.*

"Jesus," I say. "Tell me what's wrong."

"Lena." Her response is muffled by my T-shirt. "Lena broke up with me," she says. "Can you fucking believe it? I wasted two years on that bitch."

"Oh no. I'm sorry."

Gwen wipes her nose with the back of her hand. "Left me for some dick named Ryan. *Ryan*. A man, Lance. A goddamn man. I've already cleansed my phone and deleted all remnants of her off my social media. But I loved her. We were supposed to move in together after she finished college. Guess she didn't want to hang around a loser anymore."

"Hey," I chide. "You are not a loser. Don't call yourself that."

"Yeah," she replies. "That's easy for you to say, Mr. Astronomer."

"I'm not an astronomer yet. And none of that shit means anything anyway."

"No," she says. "But you will be. And now I'm gonna be stuck in this fucking hellhole of a town with no one. What am I gonna do when Arthur leaves?"

Arthur hasn't mentioned, anything to me about moving or going to college. If he has plans to do either, that's news to me.

"I need to burn something tonight," she says. "And get really shit-faced."

There it is. I'm glad I agreed to come, because the idea of Gwen drinking next to a lake when she's depressed freaks me out, and someone will need to keep their wits about them.

After I've made us each a cup of tea, Arthur pulls up to the house in his truck. You can tell before he even arrives because the truck is making a weird knocking sound and you can hear it from a mile away. I walk down the driveway and help him carry bags of groceries up to the house. Gwen stays inside and finishes her tea.

"Holy shit. This place is nice as hell. Are we really supposed to be here?"

I shrug. "According to Gwen, Olivia's cool with it. I dunno, but don't ask her anything right now. Lena broke up with her, and she's super pissed at the moment."

Arthur and I leave Gwen to process her feelings, and walk along the banks of the lake. Morgan and Mordy are supposed to join us later this evening, because Myrddin needs them for another early-afternoon ritual. We make it halfway down the dock before Arthur starts taking off his shoes.

"You're as bad as Gwen, you know?"

He laughs. "I'm just taking my shoes off. It's hotter 'n hell out here, don't you think?"

Arthur's not kidding. It *is* hot. And I wish I had brought a bottle of water with me. Too late now, seeing as how Arthur's stripped down to his tank top and rolled up his blue jeans. When he submerges his feet into the water, I know I'll be forced to do the same, because if not, my blood will boil inside my skin.

"So, what happened?" Arthur asks, leaning back on his elbows. "To Gwen, I mean?"

"I guess Lena broke up with her, said she's seein' another boy. Lena's been away at Eastern for over a year now. I bet she's been seeing that boy all this time."

"Jesus," he says. "What a fuckin' way to spend the solstice."

I run my hand through the warm water, admiring the spreading ripples. "Yeah, there's a lot of fucked-up shit happenin' right now."

"What do you mean?"

Arthur doesn't know about any of it. I haven't told him any of our theories, or about the time when Morgan attacked me, or talked to him about Tammy's disappearance. None of it. I'm not withholding the information on purpose. I just need support, someone to tell him—and me, I guess—that I'm not crazy, that I'm not making it all up. One of my goals is to be honest with Arthur, to get everything off my chest once and for all, but I'm not ready to do it, not yet.

"I have some stuff that I need to talk to you about later." A car horn blares in the distance, and Arthur shields his eyes with his forearm. "But not right now," I say.

"What kind of stuff?" Worry lines form on his brow. "Bad stuff?"

"Stuff that we don't have to worry about for a while," I reply. "Don't get your undies in a bunch."

Arthur stands up and wipes his hands off, then removes his shirt in one swift motion and starts undoing his pants. I survey the area, shocked and disoriented by what he's doing. It's only twelve-thirty, and I have no idea if there are children within viewing distance. He drops his jeans and jumps into the water, splashing me in the process.

"Arthur! You ass!" I shout as he dips in and out of the water like a cottonmouth. "I'm soaked."

Two hands plunge out of the water and grab my ankles. "Arthur, no!" I say, trying my best not to fall face first into the water. "Don't do it! Don't you fuckin' dare! Arthur!"

One minute I'm standing under a beautiful open, blue sky, and the next I'm holding my breath, clawing at Arthur's arms, surrounded by brown water.

"You had plenty of time to brace yourself," he teases, spitting water at me.

"What if my phone was in my pocket? What then? Would you have bought me a new phone?"

"Yes," he replies. "Of course I would."

That's not the point! I want to shout at him, but he's having too much fun, and I let it go. I'm not in a foul mood, and I'm not even that upset about being unexpectedly thrown into the lake because it's so freaking blistering out here.

We swim around for a few minutes, and race each other to arbitrary spots in the lake—which Arthur sets several times. I never win. Then I swim over to him and wrap my arms around his neck, keenly aware of my chest pressing against his bare back. Arthur and I wade in the water like this for a moment, without speaking.

"Do you ever think about leavin' this place?" I ask, my cheek propped up against his.

"Where? Avalon? Yeah, sometimes."

I kiss his ear, then his jaw. "What keeps you here?"

"My mamaw," he replies immediately. My legs wrap around his back and hips, and he grabs my thighs. "Why?"

"Gwen just mentioned it today, that once you leave she'll be all alone."

Arthur steals me to his front, his hands now gripping my backside. "Why are you asking me this?" His voice sounds weird, like I've said or done something to upset him.

"I'm just curious, is all. Are you actually able to touch down at this depth? Just how tall are you?"

"Six foot four and a half, I think. Why are you curious?" he asks. "What do you plan on doin' after you graduate? Move a thousand miles away from here?" *From me* is what he means, but doesn't say.

I tighten my arms around his neck. "Arthur Pendragon, I'm sorry, but it looks like you're stuck with me. We're a pair."

Being with Arthur means experiencing a lot of *firsts*—first love, first time living with a boy, first time making out with a boy in a lake. His mouth is hot and his touch urgent, like I'm a present that he's trying unwrap—and I'm allowing myself to enjoy every moment of it. Arthur slides his hands up my shirt and tugs at my stomach. I know he's afraid that if he goes up any farther I'll pull away from him, so I squeeze his hips with my legs, hoping he'll get the message.

"I don't know what adjective to use," he says, finally resting his hands in between my shoulder blades. "So don't get mad at me for sayin' this. But you are the most beautiful person I've ever seen." Accepting compliments is not a skill I claim to have. Accepting compliments from the boy I love? Out of the question. "Or handsome," he continues. "I don't really know if what I'm saying is politically correct, or whatever."

"Gwen told me that you saw us at a pool once when you were a kid."

Arthur blushes—I've never seen him blush. "Oh, Christ, she told you that? I am never telling her a goddamn thing ever again."

I laugh and kiss his pouting mouth. "Was it love at first sight?" I bat my lashes for dramatic effect and prop my chin on my fist.

"Yes," he says in all seriousness. "It was."

"You've got to watch out for Brown boys in baggy T-shirts and basketball shorts. We'll steal your heart every time."

Arthur shifts his hips underneath my legs and I can feel his cock rub against my shorts. We're still the only two people outside at the moment, and I can't hear anyone or anything, so I reach my hand down into his briefs and take hold of him. He gasps and moans. Seeing him squirm in pleasure like this adds to my own mounting desires.

"Lance, no," he whispers. I let go of him instantly and remove my hand. He grabs my wrist and kisses the tips of my finger before I can back away. "I wasn't kidding when I said I think it's unfair to you. I'll wait until you're ready, so that we're *both* ready."

"I don't mind, really." My protest is barely a squeak. "Because if you want—"

"I'm not sure what that fucker Todd did to you, and to be honest, things are better that way, especially while he's still in town."

"Oh, God, we don't have to talk about this."

Arthur drops my hand. "But I promise you that I will give you as much time as you need. Because I love you, and I respect you, and I already know that I'm gonna to fuck up a bunch in the future, but I want us to be together. I've wanted it for a long time now. I mean, I can't believe you never caught me starin' at you like a freak during tutoring."

At some point, the universe had decided that, for better or for worse, our paths would cross, and things would never be the same again. Floods? Overdone. Fires? Too brutal. Earthquakes? Too messy. But Arthur and Lance? Just right.

I put a few feet between us, because I don't want him to see the tears in my eyes, and say, "I'm in love with you, too." My body then drops into the water like the jerk I am, and I wait until I'm ready to stop hiding—maybe thirty seconds—because I'm a coward who can't hold their breath that long.

Arthur's already putting on his jeans by the time I come up for air. He doesn't mention the fact that I just told him that I'm in love with him for the first time ever, instead extending his hand and helping me up out of the water. Before my feet can hit the dock, he's gathered me into his arms, his fingers interlaced in my wet, stringy hair.

"Just hearing you say those four words is better than any sex I've ever had, and well worth the wait," he says, our lips meeting one last time. "I love you too, Lance."

Mordy's SUV pulls up to the lake house in a frenzy, a cloud of dirt trailing behind the vehicle. Morgan hops out of the car once it stops, and waves at us. Arthur takes my hand, and we walk up the hill to greet them. I'd be lying if I said I wasn't nervous about the meeting. I want him to like Mordy and Morgan— hell, I want everyone to like one another, to get along—but Gwen's already in a mood, and there's all of this history that we may or may not share with one another. A possible nightmare lurking on the horizon.

"Hey, guys," I say. "I'm glad y'all were able to make it."

Mordy shakes Arthur's hand, and I see Morgan look Arthur up and down behind her sunglasses.

"You must be Morgan." Arthur extends his hand and Morgan takes it reluctantly. A visible spark occurs between the two of them when their fingers touch. Arthur laughs and shakes his hand. "Shit," he says. "Fuckin' static electricity!"

Mordy, Morgan and I exchange glances.

This weekend might actually be the two longest days of my life.

"Come on," I say, taking Morgan's arm. "I'll show you around the house."

"Is Gwen here yet?" Morgan already likes Gwen, I can tell. "Do I have anything in my teeth?" she asks.

Even though the solstice celebration doesn't technically begin until tomorrow, when day breaks, Gwen and I start preparations for the day-long ritual by making little sachet bags of herbs for tea and blessing sticks to burn in the fire. I brought some copal for the purification ceremony, and even though I've never used it, I'm eager to add it to my practice.

Morgan and Mordy spend most of the day and early evening making tamales and fritters for tomorrow's brunch, while Arthur gathers kindling and wood for tonight's fire. Then, after a short discussion, we all decide on going to bed early this evening and waking before sunrise, to soak up as many sunrays as possible. Gwen's already started drinking. I hope she doesn't ruin things for herself by waking up with a hangover, or by not waking until noon. That happened last year, and it wasn't fun.

By the time night falls, all of the food is stored neatly and nicely in the refrigerator, and all of our herbs have been rationed and wrapped. Coming to the lake house a day early was a good idea. Normally, any time Gwen, Arthur, and I try to plan a getaway or a camping trip someone ends up forgetting something, or we run out of something crucial on the first night. But not this time around — things feel good, serene even, given the circumstances with Emmett, and Gwen's unfortunate breakup. Despite it all, I'm glad we're spending the weekend together. *Rocky Horror* was fun — and Mordy was correct, seeing Arthur in a pair of tight, golden underwear was a need that I hadn't realized I had — but something about the five of us celebrating the-season-to-come just feels right, like we've done it before.

After Mordy gets the fire going, we all form a circle around it and dig our bare feet into the sand. Morgan claims she and Mordy are breaking initiation rules by being outside at night, and that they could face serious spiritual repercussions, but ends her monologue by saying it's worth it — while staring straight at my sister, who is already drunk and oblivious to the comment.

Gwen has brought an acoustic guitar with her to the fire, even though I told her to leave it at home, because who wants to listen to a bunch of drunk people singing off-key and strumming an out-of-tune guitar? She plays a few Beatles songs, then bends over to throw up into the grass. Arthur grabs the guitar from her and hands it to me. When she's finished retching, I strum the guitar a few times and set the tuners, adjusting the pegs to the best of my ability.

"Do you play?" Mordy asks, leaning back on his elbows. His silver tooth shimmers in the firelight, and I'm reminded of just how cool he is. "How 'bout some Cardi B? Post Malone? Or old-school Bone Thugs?"

"He knows the first Taylor Swift album by heart," Arthur says. He gets up and pokes the fire with a big stick. I glare at the back of his head.

Morgan giggles. "What? Do you really? You mean that country album, like *Fearless*, or whatever?"

Arthur replies before I can, "Yeah, he knows the whole fuckin' album. Start to finish. You should ask him to play."

Two summers ago, right after I graduated, Arthur and I had learned to play the guitar at the same time. YouTube was a great resource, and it hadn't taken either of us long to learn a few songs. By the end of July — that summer — we were pretty good, because all we had done was play video games and watch YouTube tutorials. It had been the best possible way to spend our vacation, actually. But I learned the songs for him, because she's his favorite singer, problematic guilty pleasure or no.

"Oh yeah," I say, trying my best to deflect his comment. "You know all the words to all the songs."

Our dirty secret is out in the open, and all anyone can do is laugh to the point of tears and gasp for air while Arthur and I are staring at each other like we've just enacted the biggest betrayal in the world.

Mordy eventually talks both of us into performing the entire album. Arthur can't sing to save his life, and Gwen's guitar is a cheap piece of shit, so the tuning keeps slipping, but we *do the damn thing* anyway. I know that when Gwen's head pops up after we're finished, she's going to ask one of us to go get more booze because she drank the last wine cooler, and because we're out of Popsicles.

"I'm not going to jail for you," I say. "Why don't you get Mordy to do it?" I realize just how foolish I sound as soon as the words leave my mouth—Mordy isn't from these parts, and the hills can be onerous to navigate at night. The only way to the gas station is by walking half a mile down the road, and three-quarters of a mile after you make a right turn. There's no way he could walk there without getting lost.

"Pretty please," Gwen says. "With sugar on top?" If her heart hadn't been completely shattered from losing Lena, there was no way I would do this for her. She drinks too much for someone her size, and one day it's going to catch up with her.

"I'm not going to jail for you."

"Don't be such a jerk." Gwen tugs on my arm and lifts me from the ground. "Just get two bottles of the pink stuff that tastes like Kool-Aid. Here's twenty-five dollars. You can keep the change. Come on, you know that old dude never checks your ID."

"I'm serious, Queenie." I point my finger at her chest. "If I end up getting busted for this shit, I'm putting a hex on you, your children, their children, their children's children."

"Yes, yes. We get the fuckin' picture. You'll curse my uterus until the end of time. Now get out of here before the store closes."

When Arthur and I return from the gas station — unscathed, thank God — Gwen and Morgan are both in their underwear, sitting across from each other, staring into a dark blue basin made of glass or ceramic — I can't be sure because it's full of water. *A tool for scrying.* It's not mine, and if it's Gwen's it must be new, because she's never mentioned it to me.

"Olivia's bowl," Gwen says, before I can ask, her face a speckled mosaic from the water's reflection. "Mordy found it in a closet when he was looking for a towel, and you're just in time because we haven't started. Come on, put that shit away and join us."

The last thing we should be doing on the eve of Litha is playing with Olivia's fucking scrying bowl, especially since we don't know what the hell is lurking inside of Morgan, but Gwen will go apeshit if I try to intervene or stop her, and it's not worth it.

"Nah, I'm good." Arthur opens a beer and hands it to me. "But don't say I didn't warn you against using someone else's scrying bowl."

"Well, you're no fun." Gwen's tone is mocking but playful. "If I see somethin' about you, I'm not going to tell you."

"Good," I reply. "I don't need to know anything about the future."

Gwen sticks out her tongue. "Not even if I see a hand-fasting ceremony." Her eyes dart to Arthur, who has returned to putting away groceries.

"What's a hand-fasting ceremony?" Arthur asks. I had hoped he wasn't listening to my sister's drunken ramblings.

"A witch thing," I say. "Just Google it." My go-to response anytime he asks something I don't have the energy — or don't want — to explain.

Mordy walks in from outside with a joint. "What kinds of ice cream did you get?" I'm thankful for the interruption. "Something fruity, I hope." His eyebrow arches and a smile spreads across his face. *High as a kite.* "Do you want some?"

Arthur accepts Mordy's offer to share his smoke, and I walk over to the door leading out to the side deck.

"Lance," Arthur says. "Do you want any?"

I shake my head and push back the light chiffon curtain with my free hand. "No thanks." I lift the glass bottle in my grip. "This beer is enough."

Mordy howls. "That's because weed makes your lil' man horny!"

I choke on my beer and slowly turn my head, only to find Mordy on the floor, about to cackle himself to death.

Gwen erupts. "Thank you!" She points at me, then at Arthur. "Thank you! I'm glad someone else had the balls to say it!"

I want to die.

Meanwhile, Arthur is looking befuddled and very concerned, seated on the couch to my left. Something tells me I'm going to regret having told Mordy some of my secrets on the way to Monticello.

"I hate you all," I reply, opening the door. "Every last one of you."

Several minutes pass, and when I walk back inside to recycle my beer bottle, Morgan starts shrieking and tearing at her arms like something's crawling on her skin. Gwen places her palms on Morgan's shoulders, trying to wrench her out of the trance, or whatever it is she's experiencing.

"Help me, Lance!"

The ceramic bowl smashes into the wall after I send it across the room with my foot, and Gwen locks her arms underneath Morgan's armpits, dragging her away seconds later. Morgan is still thrashing and yelling at the top of her lungs, demanding someone 'stop him'. Mordy takes a seat next to his sister and envelops her and Gwen in his arms, the three of them a human chain.

"Shh," he whispers. "*Recuerda quién eres.*" *Remember who you are.* "*Yu nombre es Morgan Lafayette.*" *Your name is Morgan Lafayette.* My Spanish is fairly limited, and I'm by no means fluent in the language, but I took it in high school and college and am able to follow their conversations somewhat.

Mordy rocks the two women in his arms for several minutes, until Morgan finally goes limp in Gwen's arms and collapses onto the floor. Not only do we need to find out what Emmett Crabtree is up to, we have to find a way to rid Morgan of whatever this is.

Arthur is fast asleep on the couch, and somehow slept through the entire episode. I wish I could do that.

"How long has this been happening?" I ask.

Mordy bends down and takes his sister into his arms. "Since she was a baby. The doctors diagnosed her with colic, but my grandfather knew better. We've tried everything—exorcisms, baptisms and dark shit like animal sacrifices, but nothing works. I even had to stop Morgan from killing herself once."

Gwen gets up and goes in search of something to clean the water now covering half of the floor. When she returns, she's wearing a baggy T-shirt and a pair of shorts, her arms full of paper towels. We don't talk while we remove pieces of the broken basin from the floor, instead focusing our attention on collecting the scattered shards.

"You already love them," she says finally. "Mordy and Morgan."

"I do," I admit. "Give it time, you will too."

Then she and I walk out onto the patio. "I wasn't lying the other day. When I said you had changed. I feel like I barely know you anymore. You're a completely different person now."

I slide my hand around her shoulder. "I love you. That will never change. No matter what happens. You are my sister, and I will love you until my very last sunset."

"Me too." Gwen leans into my embrace. "Morgan's pretty fucked up, huh?"

"Yes, completely and totally, I think."

"Well, you know it's a sign from the universe," she says. "We have to help her. We have to rid her of whatever the fuck is in there."

"I know," I agree. "And soon."

* * * *

The next morning, I wake to Mordy tiptoeing across the floor, doing his best to not agitate Arthur and Gwen, who are still asleep. The couch is too small for two people to share, so I fell asleep on the floor next to Gwen. When she rolls over, her arm moves from my chest and flops onto the wooden surface beneath our bodies, and I get up to join Mordy outside.

A thick fog fell last night and settled on the lake and fields surrounding the house. When I take a seat next to Mordy, I can see ghostly fingers still playing with the normally steady water.

"You okay?" I ask. Mordy stretches his arms and cracks his neck. "Morgan still sleeping like a baby?"

"Oh yeah," he replies. "If I let her, she'll sleep for the next sixteen hours."

"Damn," I reply. "That's crazy."

Mordy nods. "Yes, visions like that take a lot out of her. Her body usually requires a few days to recuperate. The whole process is a nightmare."

"You're so good with her." I nudge him with my shoulder. "You're such a good brother."

Mordy doesn't respond to my comment, his eyes following the movement of the lake.

"Arthur is really cool. So is Gwen. They're both like you. Honest and genuinely themselves."

We haven't spoken about Arthur since our drive to Monticello, and I had been worried that Mordy wouldn't like him, given his attraction to me. "Yeah," I say. "They are amazing people."

"You know, when Morgan first told me about Gwen's get-together, I didn't want to go. I had a feeling that we were walking into some redneck barn party, and I was prepared to throw down if needed." I laugh, and his eyes dart from the lake to me. "But then I met you, and realized I was being a judgmental jerk. Look, I'm not going to sit here and lie to you and say that my feelings for you have changed, Lance."

"I'm sorry," I reply, taking his hand. "If things were—"

"Don't you dare say 'different', because you know as well as I do," he says, "things have never been different. That man sleeping in there has been, and will continue to be, the center of your universe. We can't change the course of things, not this course."

"Why do I get the feeling we've had this conversation before?"

"Fuck, Lance, have you met you? You've probably had this exact conversation with hundreds of men over the course of a thousand years. I swear, Arthur had better treat you right." Mordy lets go of my hand and touches the side of my cheek. "You think you're not good enough for him or some shit, and that's absolutely, completely false." He kisses my jaw, his lips lingering. "It would never work between the both of us anyway, because I don't do long-term relationships. Or at least that's what I'm going to tell myself for the next month—whatever I need to tell myself to make it through this shit."

My heart is broken by everything Mordy's just said, and I don't know what I should say or do, so when he gets up and leaves me on the porch I don't follow or call out to him. We both need time to process everything that just happened.

A few minutes later Arthur opens the door, alerting me to his presence, and steps out onto the creaky wooden floor.

"Hey," I say. "Mornin'." When he doesn't respond, I look up at him and watch him descend the side stairs. "Hello, Earth to Arthur. Are you sleepwalking?"

"I'm just going to come out and say it, because we both know I'm a big baby and that I don't know how to keep anything to myself. And I don't want to make a big deal out of nothin'."

I get up from the floor. "What do you mean? What are you talkin' about?"

"I guess I'm just trying to figure out why you and Mordy were out here holdin' hands, and why he kissed you. Is he into you, or am I missing something?"

"No, you're not missing anything," I finally admit. "And it's not the first time he's kissed me, either. I'm sorry, I should have told you earlier."

Arthur turns around and raises his hands in the air, then lets them drop to his sides. "I don't understand," he says. "I thought you said there was nothin' to worry about, that you two were just friends? Are you lyin' to me?"

"You've kissed plenty of girls. In front of me!"

"Yes," he responds. "I know I have, and I can't change that. I would if I could, but I can't. But that doesn't change the fact that we weren't together then. We are now, or I thought we were anyway, and I would never dream of touchin' another girl or guy, or whatever."

Arthur's right — we *weren't* together back then, and I can't hold that against him. Not if we're going to get past this. I have to let things go, because jealousy is not a good look.

"And I can't change the fact that Mordy has feelings for me. It's not like I'm over here, trying to attract men or something. It's not like I can help it. I'm not actually doing anything."

"Maybe I haven't done a good job of showing you how much you mean to me." Arthur runs a hand through his hair. "How absolutely fucking scared I am of losing you, of pushing you to the point of not coming back. For good."

I sigh. *Why do things have to be this messy? It's now or never.*

"Arthur," I say, trying to maintain composure, "I've been in love with you ever since you moved here. The entire goddamn time, but I didn't want to be a creep because you were in the ninth grade, and because Todd had convinced me that no one would ever want me, not as I am. I know that I'm a trash heap, and that I'm hard to be around most of the time, but when you told me you loved me last year, I reread the text over a hundred times. I still have it. I never deleted it."

"You never said anything, though. Were you even going to mention it?"

I shrug. "I don't really know what I'm doing here. If we're being honest, I have no idea. I thought maybe, I dunno, maybe you would have moved on after a year, or whatever. You were always hangin' out with girls. I didn't know if you loved me as friend, and I didn't want to hope for anything more."

Arthur stalks over to me. "Move on? Yeah, real love can change, but it never ends. What would you have done if I never said anything?"

The sun is completely overhead now, I notice. The lake is a gleaming cobalt blue, and across the way, someone is pushing a paddleboat into the water.

"I guess deep down, I figured it would all just work itself out. I never considered the possibility that our friendship would end over this."

Arthur closes in on me, his arms big and warm. "Todd Butcher is literal human garbage," he says. "Sometimes it scares the absolute fuck outta me, the intensity of my feelings. And I don't know how long I've felt like this, but it feels like forever, like it's always been there."

Because it has, I realize now. There are many versions of our story out there, and not a single one has a happy ending, but we're here, together, and we have the opportunity to change things. I'm not going to tell Arthur that our love is nearly a thousand years old, because that would probably freak him out, but I am going to tell him about Emrys, Morgana and our theory that something bad has happened to Tammy. Maybe not right at this very moment, but definitely sometime this weekend. I just hope the others are ready, because I am.

After lunch we decide to light the morning fires and say our prayers. Gwen and I have been doing this for the past three years now, and even though Arthur's watched us do it before, having Morgan and Mordy present makes me feel self-conscious. Maybe it's because I haven't officiated any ceremonies or rituals in their company, or because this is a purely pagan celebration being held per Gwen's request, but it's a little embarrassing. Then, after the last of the copal burns, Mordy and Morgan sing songs in Spanish, offering their blessing as well, and I take this as a sign that they're accepting of our personal blend of witchcraft. *Our holler magick.*

Once the fire dies down, Arthur removes his shirt and beckons for me to come swim with him. Mordy and Morgan are already dressed for the occasion— Mordy in a white binder and a pair of white swim trunks and Morgan in a white one-piece that has Gwen practically swimming in a puddle of her own drool.

Mordy is already in the water by the time I reach for the sunblock. I'm wearing a pair of swim trunks and a tank top, my usual summer outfit, but today I've decided to try something different. Seeing Mordy swim in his binder has given me the confidence to remove my shirt. Arthur watches me with great interest as I do this, and when I hand the sunblock to Gwen, she throws it to Arthur and tells him to do it.

His hands fumble with the cap, and suddenly he's awkward and shy, not at all the self-assured man who picked me up from the store a few weeks ago, but the silly, dorky boy I remember leaving here last summer. When he finally removes the cap, too much lotion catapults itself out of the bottle all over his hands, and I wait for him to lather it on my body. Even though his hands glide across my back and chest methodically, I can tell he's nervous.

"Don't you think that's enough sunblock on my chest?" I ask. "Jesus Christ, dude!"

Arthur answers with a shake of his head. "Nope," he says. "Oops, look, I think I missed a spot. Oh, there's another one. And another. Shit! I hate to break it to ya, but this might take all day."

I arch an eyebrow. "You sure seem to be enjoying yourself."

With a swallow, he replies, "You have no idea."

I laugh. *Oh, but I do.*

I do.

Chapter Eleven

Excalibur

And just like that—the weekend is over.

The Wheel of the Year has turned again, with Flora and Minerva switching places, and my return trip to Lexington looms in the near distance.

But I don't want to go back to school, not yet. I don't want the twins to return to California, either, to end their year-in-white. I don't want to leave the lake house. I want to be selfish and keep everyone to myself. For things to remain as they are—perfect, in sync.

Before we head home the next morning, to prepare for our confrontation with Emrys, Mordy and Arthur decide to go for one last swim. Gwen and I finish loading her car and join Morgan, who is eating a raisin bagel like it's a chore, not a pleasure.

Last night, things had felt somewhat tense after we'd finished swimming and come inside to make dinner. When Mordy had asked Arthur to go for a walk, I'd thought things were going to come to a head, and that our perfect weekend was going to end in Band-Aids and bruises—but then they'd come back from the walk laughing and chatting about music, and a heavy weight had lifted from my shoulders. *From* our *shoulders.*

This morning, they'd both gotten up and made breakfast for everyone. Arthur taught Mordy how to make grits, and Mordy taught Arthur how to make café con leche. We'd had our final meal on the patio, and made plans to hang out this coming week. When Morgan had asked Gwen to have coffee with her in front of everyone, I'd thought Gwen was going to die from embarrassment. She likes to talk a big game, but at the end of the day she's just as awkward as the rest of us. Morgan wouldn't take no for an answer, either, so that made things worse for her — and better for us.

"Do you think he'll believe us?" Gwen asks.

"Who?" I say. "Arthur?"

Gwen removes her sandals and places them beside Morgan's beach towel. "Yes."

"Probably not? I mean, who the fuck in their right mind would believe they're a reincarnation of a dead king? We don't really have any proof of this, either. Just a hunch."

Gwen takes the bagel from Morgan's hand and takes a bite from it. "Do we really have any proof of anything? What have we seen that he hasn't?"

"Are you kidding me?" I ask. "Morgana le Fay literally attacked me." Morgan leans forward, looking at me sheepishly, and I continue, "I'm not blaming you. I'm just saying, I've seen and heard things that Arthur hasn't. So have you, Gwen. We will just have to make him believe. Somehow."

"And how exactly are we going to do that?" she snaps. "Unless Morgan wants to demonstrate her powers by turning into a werewitch again, and I'm not sure anyone wants that, no offense, Morgan."

"None taken."

Gwen adjusts her sunhat. "I don't know how the hell we're going to convince him, because all it sounds straight-up insane."

For the next few moments we sit in silence, the heat from the sun boring into our exposed skin. Arthur and Mordy are taking turns running and jumping off the dock, trying to out-cannonball each other. I'm not sure if they're doing it for my sake, or if they truly want to be friends, but watching them splash around in the lake like children warms my heart.

Gwen is right — I have changed, or maybe I'm finally allowing myself to open up to others. I'm not sure.

"Look at those two," Morgan says. "My brother is a goddamn idiot. He's going to break his neck doing backflips like that. Mordy! Mordred! Fuckin' Christ!"

Morgan gets up from her towel and marches toward her brother, who might actually break his neck doing jumps, because the water is shallow in that area of the lake. Arthur swims farther out, until eventually he's nothing but a bobbing golden head in the distance. If I weren't so invested in trying to figure out a way to convince Arthur that he's actually *King* Arthur, I would swim out to join him.

"You know," Gwen says, "one day, that boy is gonna ask you to marry him."

I turn to her, surprised by her sudden change in tone. Her eyes don't leave the lake, though, and she continues, "And you'll hee-haw for the next several years, like you always do because you're a stubborn ass, but then you'll eventually say yes, and pop out two of the most beautiful babies we ever saw. And I'll finally be an aunt, who spoils them rotten."

I laugh at the outlandish idea of Arthur and me being dads. "I'm glad you seem to think so."

"There's no thinking involved," she replies flatly. "Morgan saw it that night in the scrying bowl. Plain as day."

Gwen turns to face me, no hint of a joking smile anywhere, and looks at me fixedly, until shouting draws our collective curiosity toward the lake. Mordy's screaming and waving his hands in the water, calling Arthur's name. I hop to my feet as fast as I can and run to the shore, slipping on sand twice before reaching the water.

The reading. The card. Oh God.

"I told him not to swim that far out," Mordy says, after coming up from the lake, his mouth full of water and his voice hoarse from shouting. "That we don't know how deep the lake is! I don't know where the fuck he went! Can you see him anywhere?"

Without thinking, I dive into the warm water and swim past the dock, past Mordy, past the neon orange signs that read *Danger*. Mordy's and Gwen's voices overlap as they urge me to stop.

Everything's a blur. I dunk my head under the water and open my eyes, but I can't see anything other than brown water and fallen debris from trees. I try to hold my breath as long as I can, diving deeper and swimming farther into the dark abyss that rests at the bottom of the lake.

Arthur. Not yet. Please, God, not now. Our songs haven't had time to be written.

After my lungs start to burn and panic sets in, I realize that if I push any harder, I might actually die, and begin battering the heavy waves with my fists. I open my eyes in the murky lake once more and drive my body as hard as I can, struggling to follow the rays of sunlight penetrating the surface.

"Lance!" is the first word I hear when my head breaks through the top layer, followed by, "Oh God, there he is!"

Air violently shakes the insides of my chest, flooding my deprived lungs, and I flail my arms, emerging from the water like a fish on a hook, the sound of Gwen's voice to my left immediately demanding my attention. I whip my head around, still desperate for oxygen, my eyes chasing her voice.

"What the fuck is that?"

I follow Gwen's gaze to a spot in the lake that appears to now be on fire, and I kick my feet frantically, trying to distance myself from the dazzling phenomenon. Then a flash of lightning strikes the now boiling water, and a glittering sword thrusts upward, momentarily mesmerizing me with its presence, followed by a resplendent golden hilt and Arthur's head. I choke back a bizarre mixture of sobs and laughter and propel my body toward his.

"Dude," he says, completely unfazed by the fact he was underwater for so long. "You are not going to believe me when I tell you what I just saw."

"Try me," I say, staring at the sword with trepidation.

Faces are long and patience is thin by the time we return to the beach. Mordy looks like he wants to throttle Arthur, and Gwen is wearing a similar look. Morgan appears more interested in the sword than anything, and doesn't remove her eyes from the long, shiny blade.

Nobody wants to say it, but my best friend, Arthur Pendragon, just drew an untarnished sword from a flaming lake—and not just any lake, but Neve Lake. The realization sends me to my knees down on the sandy bank. There's no turning back now, not when we have a magickal sword, an impending battle to fight and a goddamn wizard to destroy.

Chapter Twelve

Two of Cups

For the next week or so, everybody lies low. I go back to work—only two days a week now, because that's all Emmett can stand, I guess, even though I've never been rude or cross with him, but whatever—and try to gather as much intel as I can, which isn't much. Caspian never leaves me alone now, is always ready to turn the corner when I am, trying his best to act nonchalant but possibly serving as another set of eyes for Emrys. If I didn't think he might be helpful in the future, I would have busted his ass for going through my bag the other day. I really had to restrain myself when I saw Caspian shaking half of the contents onto the floor and just leaving them there. *Was he raised in a fucking barn?* The scene played out during my first full shift after returning from the lake house, further solidifying my suspicions that Caspian was not only a dick, but a snoop as well.

Mordy hasn't been messaging me nearly as much since we came back from the lake house, and I'm honoring his feelings by leaving him alone, but fuck if

I don't miss him. I suspect he has some internal shit he needs to process before we can reform and forge an actual plan. Our friendship is important, but then again, so is saving his sister and stopping Emrys, or the Merlin, as Mordy has taken to calling him.

His heart is in pieces, and I can't put it back together. That's not something I can help with at all.

Gwen, Morgan and I had coffee yesterday, speaking in depth about the list of sacred places we'd assembled the last time we were at the library. So far we've decided on our local town cemetery, a structure in Avalon known as the Little Henge, and possibly an abandoned cathedral on the outskirts of town. I hope Mordy is able to come with us. His participation is crucial, especially if we're going to exorcise whatever it is living inside of his sister, and because I'll have an excuse to talk to him. *God, how I miss him.*

When the clock strikes twelve, I clock out and walk over to the door. Avalon is an oven during the summertime, and I hate the heat so much that I'll suffer through Caspian's awkward attempts at small talk. *But seriously, who the hell wants to talk about what carrion eats with their co-worker? A fucking psycho.*

Arthur's truck pulls up to the front of the store, and I nearly tear the door off its hinges. When I step into his truck, I take note of his clothes immediately – a black tie and a blue button-down shirt, tucked into a pair of khakis. These are his nice clothes, the clothes he wore to his graduation last month. I slam the truck door and reach for my seat belt.

"Where the hell did you just come from?" I ask, poking him in the shoulder. "You sure are dressed up."

I'm covered in sweat and I haven't washed my hair in two days. Who knows if I remembered to change my shirt when I got up this morning. I don't even want to think about what Arthur sees when he looks at me.

"I thought I told you about the sermon my mamaw was asked to give today."

"Oh, shit," I say. "I forgot all about that. How was it? Was she nervous?"

"Nervous, yes, but eager. She did really well."

Arthur's grandmother is a Sunday school teacher at the Baptist church here in Avalon, and occasionally the preacher will ask her to give guest sermons. His mamaw is his closest relative, and one of the nicest old ladies I've ever met. But I'm surprised he still goes to church, given that his parents and siblings go every Sunday as well.

"Was your dad there?" I ask. "Did he say anything to you?"

"He was." Arthur bridles. "And he didn't so much as look in my direction. Cassidy was there, Mom too, but they sat in the back. Cassie waved, but my mom just sat there."

"I'm sorry," I say. *This is all my fault.*

Arthur's truck hits a pothole and everything on his dashboard flies onto the floor. I bend down to gather a handful of assorted mail, unopened letters mostly, and he places a hand on my thigh. "Leave it. I'll get it later. And I'm not sorry."

We haven't spoken about him moving out, other than his act of doing it. Gwen claims he did it because of me, but she loves to romanticize things, sensationalizing them to the point of being unrecognizable.

"Don't you miss Gary and Cassidy?" I ask, not knowing how to navigate the conversation. "Your mamaw?"

"Gary and Cassidy will understand someday soon. I'm sure Cassie is already feeling the heat. I remember one time last year when my dad shouted at her for painting her nails, and threw the nail polish into the trash. I pray for them at night, but my dad is a lost cause."

Arthur pulls his truck into the trailer park. "My mamaw was the one who suggested moving out. I told her what Dad did to you and she said it was unacceptable, that I didn't need to be around that anymore."

"What do you mean you told your mamaw about what he did to me?"

Arthur unbuckles his seat belt and takes the keys out of the ignition, then stops moving. "I simply told her that I loved you," he says. "And that Dad yanked you off my bed. And how I was this close"—he makes a gesture with his thumb and pointer finger—"to putting my own father in the hospital." As Arthur says this, he keeps his eyes on the steering wheel. "I don't think I've ever felt so angry in all my life, Lance. I've never put my hands on another human being, but if Gary hadn't come into the room, I'm not sure what I would have done to my dad."

Arthur has every right to be pissed off, to be angry at his dad, but I'm not sure it's good for him to hang on to spite like this. I reach for his hand and caress it with mine.

"It was either me or him," he says. "If I had stayed in that house for a minute longer, I would have ended up killing that man, or myself. I thought if I moved out, I could smooth things over with you, make them better somehow, and you would come back. Living on my own has been weird, you know? My mamaw is the only one who has come over, besides you and Gwen, of course. It's one of the reasons why I brought Yin and Yang home."

I smile. "A wise choice."

"I agree. Let's go inside. These clothes are hotter 'n hell."

"Arthur." I tug on his hand. "I love you. And I'm here now. So you don't have to think about that stuff with your dad anymore. He can't do anything to me. He can't keep us apart."

His chest heaves, and he exhales deeply when his back hits the leather interior. "I thought he ruined everything. That you didn't want anything to do with me because my dad's an asshole and a homophobe."

Gwen was right. He did move out because of me. I let go of his hand and reach for the car door. *I hope I'm worth it.*

The inside of the trailer isn't as hot as it has been these past few weeks. Arthur has installed an AC unit in the kitchen above the sink, and while we can't run it all the time, because it freezes, it does help a little. I plop my side bag down onto the counter and go in search of some cold water. Arthur joins me in the kitchen, checking his phone, his backside leaned up against the counter.

Now, I've seen him dressed up for church before, but it's been a while. I've never seen him in a tie, though, and my hungry gaze consumes every bit, every crumb of his being, as though he'll disappear if I blink. Seeing him like this has left me spellbound, for some bizarre reason. *He looks so good, his aura so white.* The blue shirt brings out his brown eyes, and he's wearing my favorite cologne.

I reach for his phone—he looks down at me, caught off guard—and place it on the counter. Then I slide my hands up the cotton shirt, my fingers tracing the contours of his body, and undo his tie, his chest quivering underneath my touch. I know he's fixated on my every movement right now, because his muscles tense every time I fidget with a button, but I don't dare look at him.

A brief moment later, he bends forward, his lips finding mine, and he kisses me softly. When I lean into the kiss, he grabs at the back of my shirt, knotting it in his hands, his restraint clearly waning. The urgency in his kisses tells me that he needs—*no, wants*—this as much as I do. Arthur's guarded exploration of my body begins once he finds the hem of my shirt and forces it out of the way. I relish the sensation of skin against skin as he cautiously navigates his way across my stomach and over the scars on my chest.

When he finally removes my T-shirt, it's as much of a shock to me as it is him, like I'm just now seeing my chest for the first time. We stare at each other, trying to figure out what we should do next, where we should go.

So I lead him over to the futon and sit next to him, my mind unbuttoning his shirt faster than my fingers are capable of doing. *I never once thought we'd make it this far.* I push his shirt off his shoulders and crawl onto his lap, mounting him between my thighs.

"Lance," he murmurs in between moans.

My body is screaming for his, but I'm not sure if it's the right time to be heard. If I remove his undershirt, I know I won't be able to stop myself, and I'm not sure I want to anymore. Confusion is bleeding into my wanting. *I have no idea what I'm doing.*

Then suddenly, his heavy frame is on top of me, his hands everywhere, leaving no spot untouched, like he's feeling around in the darkness. When he traces the waistline of my pants with trembling fingers, I gasp, my breath caught somewhere in between denial and desire. *Are we really doing this?*

"Are we really doing this?" he whispers, as if he's just read my mind, his lips grazing my neck. "Because it doesn't feel real."

'*It doesn't feel real.'* He removes my pants and presses his knee between my legs, never taking his eyes off mine, my own desire reflected in big brown irises. His hands clamp onto my hips and he pushes himself into me, grinding his cock into my swollen labia, all traces of sweetness gone, replaced by a vicious hunger.

"Arthur," I finally say, somewhat disoriented from the last several minutes of rubbing and prodding and kissing.

"Right," he says shakily, suddenly withdrawing from my arms. "I'm sorry. I'm gonna go take a shower."

"No." I reach for his hand. "Don't go."

"Look, you have to let me walk away if we're going to do this, because I want you so bad right now that I can't see straight."

"Okay," I whimper. He gets up from the futon then heads toward the bathroom. I flop my head back into the cushion, my skin still ablaze from his scorching touch. He acts like I don't want him as badly as he wants me. If only he knew how many times I've touched myself thinking about his lips, his chest, the body underneath those jeans.

"Will you bring me a towel?" he calls from the shower. "Lance?"

When I walk into the hot, steam-filled room, I notice a folded towel sitting on the edge of the sink, and he opens the sliding door, giving me a look that nearly brings me to my knees.

"Why don't you get in here with me?" he asks, then closes the glass door. "You don't have to take your boxers off."

I turn around, hang the towel on the back of the door and lay my hand against the warm glass. *I want this. I deserve this. I deserve to be happy.*

As soon as my foot hits the shower floor, Arthur's body presses against mine and our desire springs to life again, blooming open like a garden under the sun. His mouth is a cyclone, spiraling kisses landing haphazardly across my neck and chest. I can't tell if I'm breathing anymore because I'm getting so caught up in his body, in his movements, in our shared desire.

When I curl my fingers around his erection, Arthur places his palms on the wall above my head, this time allowing me to do what I want with his body. I get on my knees and fill my mouth with the length of his cock, his hips thrusting into my face with so much force I have to brace myself, using his thighs to steady my balance. When I finally feel the backs of his legs become taut, I look up at him expectantly through the falling water, and his hands gently lift me from the floor of the tub, seconds before his jism spills onto my thigh.

One minute he's standing next to me, the next he's on his knees, splashing handfuls of water on my leg. He stops once it's clean and kisses my calves, his mouth eventually moving upward along my inner thigh, stopping at the hem of my shorts. I dig my hands into his hair, now thinking I should have taken them off.

"I would never ask you to do anything you're uncomfortable doing, I hope you know that."

I nod, almost too enraptured to speak. "I know."

"But I want to make love to you." I don't say anything, too stunned by his words, by the dizzying effect they have over me. "You can follow me into the bedroom if you want, but I'll understand if you don't, and I won't ask you again."

Arthur leaves the bathroom and I stay in the shower until the water runs cold. When I get out, I see a pair of dry shorts resting on the sink, next to the towel. I remove my wet shorts and wrap the towel sitting on the sink around my waist. I don't know what the hell I'm doing, or what the hell I should do. But I leave the bathroom anyway.

I rest my hand on the bedroom door and pause briefly, trying to think of a single reason why I shouldn't do this.

But I can't.

When I open the door, Arthur turns around, still wearing a towel.

Without thinking I chuck mine out of the way, onto the floor, and say, "I'll get that later."

Arthur is by my side in a matter of seconds, dropping to his knees immediately.

"Wait, what?" I ask.

He positions himself in front of me, grabbing my ass for balance, and shoves his mouth into my bush, his tongue lapping at my clit slowly and deliberately. I'm already past the point of being overripe, moist and ready to rupture at any moment—it won't take much for me to climax if he keeps doing this. He sucks the soft flesh between my legs, and I can't help but rock back and forth against his chin. My nails dig into his shoulders, and the insides of my body explode, a mixture of spit and cum running down my thighs.

When I extract his mouth from my cunt, his lips are red and puckered and he's flushed with desire. I help him to his feet and lure him toward the bed. He props himself up against a pillow and I run my hands across his stomach, absorbing all of the splendor of the moment. His cock is ready for me again, and I go to put it in my mouth, but he stops me before I reach him.

"I don't want to make things awkward or ruin the mood," he says, his voice husky. "But would you put this on me?"

Morgan's vision at the lake house, the one about babies and Gwen being an aunt, pops into my head, and I greedily accept the circular piece of latex.

"You're not making things awkward. Safe sex is hot sex, dude."

This isn't the first condom I've put on someone, either—or the second, or the third—so I unroll it with ease, pinch it and slide it down his shaft. His breathing has gotten haggard, and I know by the way he's shivering that he wants me as much as I want him. When that's done, I spit in my hand, even though I'm plenty wet down there, and make my way toward him.

"Wait, are you sure? Do you need me to—"

I shake my head. "No, I've been practicing with…something. It should be fine."

"You mean a vibrator, or something like that?" he asks, his eyes now brimming with curiosity.

"Yes," I say, sliding closer to him. "Something like that."

"God, that's so fuckin' hot. Is it here?" Arthur is really interested in my dildo all of a sudden. "You have it here, somewhere?"

"In a makeup bag, under the futon," I answer him. "But I'm more interested in you at the moment."

Arthur nods. "I don't know how big your toy is, but this might hurt a little. I'll be gentle."

"This isn't my first time being with a man," I reply. "But it has been a few years, so slow at first is probably best."

I didn't tell Gwen everything *that happened with Todd. She's my sister, for God's sake.*

Arthur stops talking after that, kissing me instead, and I climb on top of him, inserting his cock into my front hole. Going slow isn't even an option, I decide a few seconds in, because it doesn't hurt at all. All pleasure, no pain. I kiss his half-open mouth and grab his shoulders. His moans and the way he keeps his eyes glued to me heighten my arousal, and I come within minutes of riding him. He must have been really pent-up, too, because shortly after my second orgasm he arches his back, and I slide up and down his cock until it's too sensitive to touch. We roll over, lying on our backs for a moment, and I get up to use the bathroom.

Making love to Arthur was everything I'd dreamed it would be, and then some. I feel like I'm walking on clouds.

When I return to his room, Arthur's pulling on a pair of jeans, and this makes me very aware that I'm walking around the house naked. I look down at my body and cross my arms, then turn to leave his room. He gets up suddenly and rushes to block the only way out.

"What are you doing?" I ask. "Move."

His eyes wander up and down my body. "Just looking at my insanely sexy boyfriend."

"Shut up," I mumble, now feeling thoroughly self-conscious. "Move."

"I'm being serious, Lance. That was the best sex I've ever had. I'm just sorry it didn't last that long."

"Me too." I sigh. "But I came like three times, so it didn't bother me."

His eyes widen. "Jesus. Three times?"

"Yes," I reply. "Three."

He wraps his arms around my neck and kisses the side of my head. "God, your body *is* incredible."

* * * *

A couple of hours later, Arthur and I make supper together.

As weird as it sounds, we haven't really discussed the sword that's now propped up against a bookshelf in the living room. My hope is that during our meal I can broach the topic with caution. Gwen and I were supposed to do it yesterday, but she'd gotten called into work for a double, and it hadn't happened.

"So," I say. Arthur turns around, hands full of bits of tomato and lettuce. "I've been meaning to ask. When did you get that tattoo?"

Arthur's gaze shifts from mine toward the ink on his arm. "Oh, this? A few months ago, I guess. Right after my last fencing tournament. A few of us went out one night, and everyone was supposed to get one, but only Tiffany and I actually went through with it. Fuckin' hurt like hell."

Right after moving here from Indiana, his freshman year of high school, Arthur had joined the fencing team and had begun making a name for himself almost immediately. The coaches had seemed annoyed by this at times, but everyone else on the team had admired his ability to fly and lunge at the same time. Now that he has a magickal sword sitting in his trailer, it all makes perfect sense — his talent is another piece to this cosmic puzzle.

"Why?" he asks, setting a plate down on the coffee table. "Is it because you think it's a sick tat?"

"Don't call your tattoos 'tats', please. You sound like a frat boy. And I'm asking because we need to talk about something. Here, let me get that for you." I take the pitcher of iced tea from his hands. "But we can talk about it after we eat."

"Okay. Do you want the rest of this arugula? I think it probably needs to get eaten, and you know how I feel about wasting food."

"Absolutely not. It tastes straight up like grass. You should just pitch it. Why do you have so much weird food in the fridge anyway? Are you on a diet or something?"

Arthur huffs. "Why? Do I need to lose weight?" he asks. "Are you calling me fat?"

"No," I reply, wounded. "You know I would never say that. But you have soy milk in there and veggie dogs."

Arthur hands me a plate and takes a seat next to me. "Yeah, because I don't eat real hot dogs anymore. Can you scoot over a little? I don't want to spill this on your lap." He then reaches across the table for a bottle of ranch. "I don't eat pork or beef, man. I don't eat any of it anymore, not since you posted that goddamn video of those pigs in that crate thing."

I stare at him. "How long?"

"I dunno. Eight, nine months? The boys at work used to give me shit about it at first." He laughs. "But now when we go out they won't eat anywhere that doesn't serve at least a grilled cheese sandwich or a salad." My eyes don't leave his. "What? I like pigs." I don't ask him if he's doing this for me or for himself, and take a bite of my taco instead. "But I'll tell you...I fuckin' hate arugula, and I had to learn how to cook tofu real fast."

After dinner Arthur washes the dishes and I read through my notebook. Gwen and I have made a list of things that I could say to open the conversation, things that might make it less awkward, but at this point, I think I'm just going to take the plunge. He found a fucking sword in a flaming body of water, for God's sake.

I walk over to the bookshelf and take the sword into my hands. Nausea hits my stomach as soon as the hilt touches my palm, forcing me to stumble backward into the wooden shelves, knocking an entire row of books onto the floor. When my eyes return to the sword that didn't just slip out of my hand, but struggled to get away from me, it's standing upright as if being held by an invisible hand, and the tip of the sword is pointing toward the old Celtic cross on the wall. The one that had freaked out when I said I didn't need to protect myself.

"Lance!" Arthur shouts. "Are you okay?"

"I'm fine," I say. "But look." I gesture at the dangling sword and that cross that's now swinging with abandon, and by the look on Arthur's face, I'm guessing I won't need a list after all.

Chapter Thirteen

The Holy Sites

Kusanagi-no-Tsurugi. Gram. Durendal. Hauteclere. Thuận Thiên. Excalibur.

Swords have been on my mind ever since the incident at the lake house, and I've spent most of my free time lately researching them, so much that it's become a slight obsession.

Thanks to the Internet and role-playing games such as Dungeons & Dragons, most folks interested in legends and mythology are aware of magical weapons and the implications of their lore. Not to mention, mythical swords containing great power have been sung about in ballads and honored in epic poems throughout the ages, from Japan to France to Vietnam. Finding information on this stuff has been easy — processing it, not so much. These swords capable of leveling entire cities, swords that liberated the oppressed, swords that drew their power from thunder and lightning, the heavens themselves — all were awesome weapons that supposedly brought the person wielding them valor and victory. Invincibility and notoriety. How my best friend fits into any of this, I still don't know.

Among the many magickal swords that I've researched over these past few days, one stands out as being the sword that brought both light and damnation into the world — *Excalibur*. The very sword sitting in Arthur's trailer, the very sword that he drew from a goddamn lake. While there are numerous tales out there regarding this specific sword, they all end with Arthur Pendragon, King of the Britons, dying. The bards of old left us with one ultimate, unmistakable message — once discovered, there's little hope of keeping Arthur alive.

When Arthur and I discuss the possibility of such a sword existing, we don't explore that aspect of its mythos, for one simple reason — because I don't want to think about it. The discussion ends with Arthur telling me he'd had a vision underwater — or 'hallucination', in his words — of a long-haired woman dressed in a white cloak handing him the weapon, and further claiming that once the sword was in his hands, the undertow had released his body and his desperate need to breathe had disappeared.

During the several-hour-long conversation, I'd had to gloss over other details, like Morgan sleeping with Arthur and Mordred being the one who kills him in nearly every iteration, because I didn't want to overload him with information, and because everything was starting to get to me. Arthur means so much to me, and the thought of him dying tears me in two. I can't think about it. I won't allow myself to think about it, to even consider it as a possible outcome.

Our lives are already messy, and now this.

* * * *

When Mordy finally texts me, I nearly drop the phone from excitement. It's been over two weeks since our last interaction and I have so much to tell him. His responses seem muted, so I do my best to keep my emotions in check.

Mordy and I agree to meet at the café where we'd met for lunch last month.

Neither of us have much of an appetite, and I'm not in the mood for coffee, so when Mordy suggests we go for a ride, I readily accept. The inside of his SUV is neat and trim, and it smells like he just wiped down the seats with rubbing alcohol. The abrasive odor immediately aggravates the insides of my nostrils. I'm not sure where he's taking us, and I struggle to find the right words to say. *Why do things have to be so difficult?*

As his black vehicle climbs the deserted hillside, a light drizzle falls from the sky, and the sound of thunder calls my attention toward the wild, now-gray yonder. The bright sun was shining not five minutes ago, without a cloud in sight for miles, and now it's nowhere to be found, hidden somewhere in the dark, swollen canopy above. I roll down the window and stick out my hand to see if the ambience is as ominous as it appears, and soon discover that the temperature has decreased significantly, too.

When the small stone structure comes into focus, I turn to Mordy. *Little Henge.* How Mordy was able to navigate through these hills without a GPS is beyond me. The terrain isn't the absolute worst or anything, but one wrong turn and you could easily find yourself with a blown-out tire. He unbuckles his seat belt and removes his phone from its holder on the dash, and returns my stare.

"Come on," he says finally. "A little rain never hurt anyone." His tone is unexpectedly playful, light. *I'm glad.*

"Except for the Wicked Witch of the West," I reply. Mordy smiles and bites his bottom lip. "All it took was a bucket of the stuff to destroy her entire gig."

"She was green, we're Brown. And made of tougher stuff than smoke. Now get out."

The ground sags beneath our weight, and pools of water collect in our footprints as we slosh through the wet grass. My canvas high-tops are soaked within seconds, and for once in my life, I'm glad I had the sense to don a hoodie during the middle of summer.

When we come to the hill where Little Henge sits, Mordy is the first to discover a set of wooden boards that have been nailed into the side of the mound. He insists I go first, making a basket with his hands because the top step is still too high for me to reach, as if someone is trying to keep outsiders from visiting the man-made marvel.

Once we're both over the hill, we slog through the muddy grass in silence, the rainfall more violent and aggressive against my black hood. Mordy's wearing a pair of glasses today, which seems like a bad decision, because the lenses are completely spattered with water. There's no way he can see anything, so I take his hand in mine and we make our way to the stone replica.

Despite having lived in Avalon for several years, I've never actually been up here. Beer cans and discarded plastic wrappers litter the tall green grass surrounding the stone arrangement. I let go of Mordy's hand and begin collecting the trash to put in my hoodie pocket.

"Lance," he says, the wind now playing with his sopping-wet dreadlocks. "Hey!"

There's so much trash everywhere that it looks like someone used this hill as their personal landfill. The thought sends me into a rage, and I frenetically fill my pockets with the garbage until there's so much shit stuffed in there that I can't fit any more.

"Lance!" he shouts again. "Lance, listen to me!" I turn around. Mordy's on his knees, completely drenched, his once-white outfit now covered in grass and mud. "There's no use. It doesn't matter what you do. You'll never be able to clean it all."

"What do you mean?" I ask. "I can take my hoodie off and use it as a bag. This is fucked-up, man." I shake a handful of discarded candy bar wrappers at him. "Just look at all of this shit!"

"No, you can't," he replies, rainwater filling his mouth as he speaks. He spits. "Because the trash belongs here. It belongs to the Henge, yo."

I remove my hood and gawk at him. "What the hell are you even talking about?"

The rain is hammering down on us like little fists, and I can barely stand, the pressure is so great.

"Listen to me! The trash...it's part of the Henge," he repeats. "It belongs here. The more you clean, the more it generates. There's some invisible fucked-up trash factory pumpin' this shit out."

"Do you know how insane you sound right now?"

Mordy hoots. "Your boyfriend literally found a sword in a lake! This is the only logical explanation there could be. The Henge wants to keep people out. It knows trash and shit makes it unattractive or whatever. Trust me."

I look at the contents in my hands. A two-liter, an empty box of tampons, some shoestrings. He's right. Why the fuck would anybody come up here just to throw this kind of shit away?

"But why?" I ask, the rain no longer waging an all-out attack on my sweatshirt.

"Look around, dawg. We're up on this hill alone, man. No one around for miles. I'm not even sure how I got out here. I just drove with no knowledge of anything, and bam, my car ended up here. Something compelled me. I don't know where the fuck I am."

"Why would it make trash, though? That makes no fuckin' sense. This is a sacred spot."

"Like I said, maybe it makes the trash to keep people away. Dude, this grass is tall as fuck. Ain't nobody been up here in months. Who knows what the hell is living in here? But one thing's for sure... Little Henge is protecting itself."

When I survey the sky overhead, I can see where the clouds begin and where the sun ends. Darkness has settled on this part of the mountain, and this part only. We aren't even that high above the ground where Mordy's car is parked, but down below, a blanket of silvery mist has fallen on the grass. From this far away it looks like an enormous, glistening spiderweb.

I take a giant step toward the ground clouds, and Mordy grabs my arm. "Whoa, easy there. You tryin' to break your neck?"

"What?" I ask, the glamour wearing off. "What are we doing?"

"Uh... You were trying to walk straight off this fuckin' hill, I think."

"Why are we here?" I shout at the stones. "Why have you brought us here? What do you want from us? I'm not here to fuck around, not when my friend's life is in danger." Mordy places his hand on my shoulder to comfort me, but I shrug it off. "I'm being serious here! If you have something to say to us, you can come out and fuckin' say it because you're wasting my time."

"Lance."

My eyes dart to Mordy's. "No, now's not the time for patience. You know about the card, and now we have a fuckin' sword. Arthur's time on Earth grows short, and here we are bein' dicked around by some ancient Lego set."

Thunder cracks directly above our heads, followed by three flashes of lightning that strike the center of the stones, and Mordy shields my head with his arms, the both of us cowering on the ground. The grass is on fire now, engulfed in alternating flames of silver and gold like an elaborate display of holiday lights. A figure materializes within the smoke — a tall, raven-haired woman wearing a headdress made of feathers, adorned in a shimmering, fluid gown that seems forged from the fire itself. When she steps through the flames I can see that her face is painted white, and that she is accompanied by two large flying bats, one hovering above each shoulder.

A white face, two bats, surrounded by a flurry of flames. Why does she look so familiar?

"Holy shit. I think that's Mictēcacihuātl," I say. One of the few goddesses I remember from my research. The Aztec Goddess of Death. *Why is she here? Of all places?*

"What? Who is *that*?"

For a second, I'd forgotten that Mordy is sitting right next to me, clearly taken aback by whatever it is we're now seeing.

"The Queen of Mictlān, an Aztec Underworld deity. It just has to be her."

"Oh, her!" Mordy says sarcastically. "Why didn't ya just say so in the first place? Why is she here?"

The queen stops before us and secures a strong hand on my head, flames still roaring behind her.

"Are you the one known as Lance A. Lotte?" she asks, her voice somewhere in between gentle and demanding. "The one who has summoned me here today?"

I have no fucking idea if I was the one who summoned her here today, but have no intention of letting her know that, so I shrug and say, "Yes, my name is Lance. And maybe?" Not daring to meet her burning gaze.

"Arise, young warrior." Her voice booms across the hill, and I do as she says, because she is the Goddess of the Underworld, and probably not one to be fucked with. I'm not a warrior, but this might not be the best time to discuss that bit of info.

She produces a dagger from within her long, bell-shaped sleeve. A short blade made from a black crystal, attached to a hilt that is decorated in snake carvings, made from gold.

"W-whoa!" I stammer. "I'm not a warrior, and trust me, you don't want my heart. It's very weak and not courageous at all. Also, I'm kinda attached to it, seeing as how I need it to live."

The bats screech loudly behind her, and I have to cover my ears to muffle the terrible sound. From what little I've read on the subject matter, Aztec priests seem like they were a brutal bunch, known for human sacrifices and ritualistic cannibalism. Eating hearts, drinking blood, that kind of shit. She points the dagger at my chest, where the scars from my surgery are.

"Your heart is strong and plenty courageous," she says. "Not many are brave enough to call on me these days. I feel like I have been asleep for centuries."

That's because you have. Things have taken a weird turn. An Aztec death goddess is talking to me because I shouted at a bunch of rocks, and now she's telling me I'm a brave warrior—a first, for sure.

"Your highness," I say, "I must admit that I had no intention of calling you here today, and if I did, I apologize, because it was an accident. I don't want you to think I am some powerful shaman or anything like that. This has got to be a mistake."

Mictēcacihuātl laughs. "Who determines what is powerful and what is not? Is there a test, or perhaps a battle of wills? How does one know if they are powerful if they never have the chance to prove it?"

Mordy is still sitting in silence, clearly shaken by whatever is happening. He won't even look at me, his eyes set on the fire behind Mictēcacihuātl.

"Listen to me, little warrior, for I must return to Mictlān soon. Your heart spoke to me, awakened me from a great slumber because you prepare for battle, am I right?"

"Yes," I reply weakly. "You are."

"Take this blade, the Xiuhcoatl. It is my brother's, but you must do your deed soon, because he will realize it is gone and return for it if you are not swift, and he *will* eat your heart if he finds it missing."

Mordy stirs and acknowledges the fire. "Wait, are those the flames of hell? Or is this all one big fuckin' hallucination?"

The Aztec queen looks at him for the first time. "That all depends... Are you interested in returning with me? I do enjoy a man in white."

I'm not sure, but I think the queen is hitting on Mordy, which could be good or bad depending upon his reaction. *She is married to the King of the Underworld, after all.*

When Mordy looks at her, clearly beguiled by the syrupy words she's speaking, I place a foot in between their bodies. "What am I supposed to do with this?"

"Kill the oathbreaker," they both say, at the same time.

"Emrys," Mordy says, the effects of her spell wearing off. "We must kill Emrys, Lance."

"I thought you said there were ways to hurt him that didn't involve causing him physical pain!"

Mordy shakes his head. "That was before the girl went missing. Now he must be stopped. We can't do that with evil eyes or dolls, man. The only way to do it is by sticking that fucking thing through his black heart!"

Mordy and I argue like this for a few minutes, until I realize the crackling flames beside us have gone out. The rain has stopped as well, and the sky is clearing. When I search for the Aztec Death Goddess, she's nowhere to be found. She's taken with her the bats, and possibly the trash, as the circle is wholly free from garbage now.

As Mordy and I walk to the car, my thoughts are soon joined by another voice — *her* voice.

"Lance, you have the heart of a warrior and the spirit of a panther. Don't be afraid to listen to both if you find yourself in danger. When the time comes, you must look deep inside to unleash your true might. The blade will help you end the warlock's life, but you will have to give something in return. How far you are willing to go to make this trade is up to you."

"She talkin' to you, ain't she?" Mordy shakes his head, placing a hand on the hood of his car. "Ask her if she like a man in black? Because my year-in-white is about to end, and I'm going to burn every last fuckin' piece of white clothing I have."

Mordy and I don't speak on the way back to town — the sound of hip-hop blaring from his stereo speakers fills the uneasy air instead. I'm not sure I'd know what to say even if he did want to talk.

There's no use in denying anything Mictēcacihuātl said, because even though most gods and goddesses spend much of their time tricking humans, or manipulating them to further some kind of fucked-up agenda, nothing she'd said could be misconstrued to mean anything other than the truth. In order to kill the warlock, free Morgana and save the king, I will have to trade something precious, dear to me. *The plan is that simple, but is it, really?*

It's not quite eight o'clock when we pull up to the front of Baubles & Books. Gwen and Morgan are already sitting outside, eating ice cream, when we get out of the car. Since the encounter with Mictēcacihuātl, I've had a killer migraine, and no amount of Tylenol has helped, either. Gwen picks up on my sour mood immediately, and hounds me about eating better, hydrating myself. I don't have the energy to argue with her, so I allow her to force a half-eaten sundae on me while Morgan's eyes follow my movements like an owl watching a mouse.

"Where the hell have you two been?" Gwen asks. "Because y'all look real fucked-up."

Mordy speaks up before I have the chance. "We were visited by this ancient Aztec chick and her flying bats at Little Henge. Walking through flames, pulling a straight-up Galadriel on us. She gave Lance here a snake knife and instructed him to kill the Merlin with it."

The Merlin aka Emrys Caerwyn aka Emmett Crabtree aka the owner of Camelot Crafts aka my boss.

It's the first time anyone's actually said his real name in our circle.

How the fuck I'm supposed to actually go back to work after receiving this dagger, *and* being told how to kill him, I don't know. Working two nights a week has been strenuous enough, but I don't want to quit just yet because I still owe Arthur money for my portion of the rent and bills, and because we don't know everything yet.

"If we're still going to the cemetery, we'd better hurry. It'll be dark soon, and we wouldn't want y'all turning into pumpkins, now would we?" Gwen runs her finger across Morgan's hand and points at the chocolate puddle of sprinkles in front of me. "And you have to eat."

The cemetery gate is locked when we arrive, but I anticipated this, and had said as much on the way over, because the graveyard closes its doors at five o'clock sharp. Mordy parks two blocks away from our destination, to hide his car from being seen, and I lead them to an opening in the back. When we were kids, Gwen and I would routinely sneak in here at night and rearrange the floral pieces. Not something I'm proud of, if we're being completely honest, but they say vision is 20/20 in hindsight, so...

Thankfully someone has torn a fresh hole in the once-repaired fence, and we climb through it, carefully avoiding the protruding pieces of rusted metal. When we're safely on the other side, I ask Gwen and Morgan why they specifically wanted to come to this cemetery.

"Because I dream about it every night," Morgan replies. "I've been here for seventy-two days now, and every night those gates open for me with ease, and I spend the entire fuckin' time looking for something."

"What are you looking for?" Gwen asks.

Something must've happened between those two, and I'm surprised Gwen hasn't mentioned it to me. She usually loves to tell me every detail of her love life despite my objections that I don't need to know the color of her girlfriend's nipples, but something about the way she interacts with Morgan feels different, almost secretive. I'm not going to stick my nose where it doesn't belong, but Morgan is still possessed by whatever-the-fuck, and Gwen could be messing with fire. I watch the two of them match each other's pace and stroke each other's arms. It's a lovely sight.

"So," Mordy says, stopping in front of me, my nose slamming into his ribs. "I need to get something off my chest before we continue."

I rub my nose. "Okay," I say. The girls are far enough away that they're not in earshot anymore. "If this is about what happened at Little Henge —"

"It's not." He raises his glasses, placing them on top of his head. "For the past couple a weeks I've been pretty tore up, completely lost in my feelings. When I came to Avalon, I didn't come here to help anyone. I just wanted talk some sense into my uncle and get the fuck outta here, head back to California."

"I know," I say, looking at Mordy's grass-stained pants. "There's not a lot to do out here."

"No." He shakes his head. "The people are what make this place bearable. You make this place bearable. You all do. But being around you does something to me, fucks my brain all up."

My phone buzzes several times in my side bag. Someone must be actually calling me because it just keeps going, but I don't want to detract from what Mordy's saying or break his concentration, so I leave it alone to mess with later. He takes a step forward, engulfing me in his slender frame. His arms wrap around my shoulders and he leans into the hug.

"You are a magickal, dope dude, Lance Lotte." His lips touch my earlobe. "You're an old soul, and you are true to yourself and others. I can't just fall out of love with you overnight, because I'm not built like that—I don't think anyone is—but I want you to know that I've got your back. No matter what. You, me, your nut of a sister, my nut of a sister, we are all in this together, as family."

I take a fistful of his T-shirt into each hand, then rest my head on his chest and begin crying. I'm not sure if it's exhaustion, the hysteria from earlier or my allergies, but the deluge rushing down my face won't stop. Mordy stands very still for the next few minutes, letting me work through whatever the fuck it is I'm working through. When I'm finished, he unsnarls his long arms from my grasp and places his hands on my shoulders.

"And I respect the fuck outta Arthur," he finally says, looking into my eyes. "Weird, huh? Yeah, I know. But a man like that, who will wait around for another man to sort out his personal shit, especially in this goddamn town, that's a diamond in the rough right there." He pauses, then continues, "Now don't get me wrong, I would do the same for thing for you, but then again so would Gwen, and my sister, for that matter. We will do whatever we have to do in order to save Arthur. You are not alone."

I laugh and wipe my snotty nose with a sleeve. "Sounds like our holler magick is rubbin' off on you."

Mordy pats me on the back and replies, "You act as if I actually had a choice." The twinkle in his eye sends a ripple of a sob through my chest, and I do everything I can to catch it before it turns into another wave of melancholy.

Gwen is sitting by herself in a patch of dirt when I find her. Morgan is off somewhere else, examining the tombstones, trying to see if the graveyard from her dreams is, in fact, this same exact one. The big pile of plucked violets sitting at Gwen's bare feet indicate my sister is likely preparing for a protection spell of some kind—that, or a floral liqueur for later. Knowing her, I'd say there's a fifty-fifty chance of it being either. I sit on my haunches and join her.

"Morgan's really sick," Gwen says, tying a violet stem into a knot and hooking it through another flower. "Whatever it is that's in there, it's drainin' her like a swimming pool. Do you know that she sleeps like, sixteen hours a day? *Every* day? The shit her uncle's doing is keeping her alive, but at what cost?"

"What do you mean? Keepin' her alive?"

A twig snaps, calling our attention to the graves behind us. "I mean that he has to exorcise her every goddamn day. A ritual that takes hours sometimes to complete. She's barely allowed to live, Lance."

I'd known things were bad, of course I'd known they weren't good, horrible even, but I hadn't known the extent of it. Not truly. That Mordy didn't feel comfortable telling me about it...hurts. Maybe he doesn't trust me. Or maybe he thinks it's a family affair. But Morgan *is* our sister now, and we have to find a way to rid her of this possession. *There's no other option.*

"Do you know which way she went?" I ask. Gwen shrugs, and points to her left with a knotted string of flowers. "All right," I say. "I'll be back in a second. Don't go anywhere."

From the looks of things, the sun will be setting in the next fifteen minutes or so, and it will take that long to walk back to the car. Mordy isn't as strict about being inside at night as Morgan, but that's probably due to the fact that he isn't sharing his body with a goddamn demon. When I round the corner, a black form flashes before my eyes, and I have to ask myself if I actually saw it, or if it was a fleck of dust in my line of vision.

I rub my eyes. "Morgan?" I say. "Are you over here?"

I take two steps forward, and a huge, black, shaggy-haired dog jumps on me. The sound of claws ripping my hoodie ricochets off the large concrete pillars beside us. Its body is heavy, much heavier than mine, and the only thing I can do is shield my face with my relatively puny arms in the hope that someone will find me before I succumb to the beast's attack.

"Far below, where the one-eyed raven king crows, our goddess — the holy queen — peacefully sleeps, while the hounds of hell are free to roam and creep. But where you shall go, no one will ever know." Morgan's voice slices through our blend of growls and human cries. "Now get the fuck off of him, you big ugly shit!"

After one deep, terrible howl, the gigantic animal releases my arms from its grip and backs away slowly, a mixture of foam and my blood dripping from its yellow fangs, then suddenly transforms into a swarm of angry blowflies. Morgan rushes to my side, swatting at the flittering insects, her eyes awash with pain and confusion. The swarm hovers a few feet above our heads before flying off, a ghastly black mass heading in the same direction.

"I'm all right. I'm okay," I say, inspecting the gashes on my forearm. "What the hell was that?"

"A shuck." Morgan gets down on her knees and places her hands on both sides of my head, her irises completely swallowed by the pupils. All traces of her identity have been completely replaced by something else entirely.

The entity.

Morgana le Fay. I wrench my head out of her hands and put a few feet between us, my body moving faster than my mind.

Her eyes narrow and a shadow sweeps her face. "Tell us what the death queen said to you." Her voice is not her own, an amalgamation of oscillating sounds, no hint of Morgan anywhere. "Or else your crusade ends here," she hisses. "Paladin."

"Morgana le Fay." I use her name. Her true name. "Your fight is not with me. I'm—I'm trying to save Arthur," I stammer.

Her eyes soften for a second. "The death queen," she repeats, her voice more or less the same pitch. "What did she say?"

I say the first thing that comes to mind. "A life for a life."

"No! There has to be another way!" Morgana punches the ground several times, leaving the skin across her knuckles broken and peeling. "Wait." She raises a bloody finger and points it at my head. "What if we find the scabbard?"

"*What scabbard?*" she asks, her voice changing in pitch. "Oh, don't play dumb, girl." Her hands then explode into the air like fireworks, soil flying everywhere. "Search our memories. You know the legends, the stories. The holy sword's sheath. *Oh, right! Why didn't I think of that? Let's just go to the fucking store and ask for one. I wonder if Macy's has them.*"

I'm not sure what's happening, but I think Morgana and Morgan are actually arguing with each other.

"The tomb. Where is the tomb? *What tomb?* The one we see every night. *There's not going to be a king's tomb in this cemetery, you dumb bitch.* Call me that one more time and I'll take a blade to our throat."

"Whoa! Okay," I interject, finally getting up from the ground. "Hold up. No one is going to be slitting anyone's throat."

Morgana turns to me, her face flushed with frustration and anger. "You," she squawks. "You never do enough! Every time, it's you. It's your fault! You and that fair-haired girl! No one has ever been able to stop Emrys. No one. The last time you ended up..." Her voice trails off, never finishing the accusation.

"Look, lady, I know I'm a fuck-up," I reply. "You don't need to tell me. I already know that it's in my blood. But we won't lose, not this time around. I will do everything in my power to protect Arthur."

"I am so tired," Morgana says, dropping to the ground. "I just want to go to sleep. I'm tired of doing this."

"Of doing what?" I ask, heading straight for the crack in Morgana's outer shell. "Fighting Emrys?"

"Being reborn. I don't want to live anymore. I've lived enough lives. Aren't you tired?"

Me? If I have someone living else in this skinsuit, that's news to me.

When I don't answer, Morgana pulls herself up from the ground and starts flailing her arms in the air, screaming for me, for us, to do something, anything. The last time I'd witnessed a meltdown like this, we'd been at the lake house and Mordy'd had to swaddle her until the spell passed. She's dangerously close to a set of concrete stairs, so I sprint to her side and latch onto her arm before she can smack into the side of the building. Her body goes flaccid in my arms, and seconds later, I nearly collide with the top stair.

"Lancelot," she blubbers, spit spraying out of her mouth. "The scabbard. It's the only way. Your dying won't save Arthur. It never does and it never will. Two deaths won't make a life, you have to remember that."

We stumble up the stairs, her arm intertwined with mine. After we reach the top, I position Morgan's head in my lap and prop mine against the tomb, or mausoleum, or whatever the fuck it is. I am tired, I realize.

Coming home wasn't a mistake, but it wasn't supposed to be like this. My plan had been to lie low, work as much as Emmett would let me, then head back as soon as my dorm became available. No drama, no fights, nothing.

Magick, witchcraft, none of it has ever meant anything negative to me, not even the darker aspects of brujería. But killing a man to save a man…murdering my boss to save my boyfriend...the idea is ludicrous. *I don't know if I can do it.*

"Lance?" Morgan's eyes fly open and she springs forward like an overwound clock. "Lance?"

"Yes," I say. "I'm here. Are you okay?"

"The scabbard," she says suddenly. "I know where it is."

"What?" I smack my head on the pillar directly behind us. "Fuck! Where?" I ask, clutching the back of my skull. "Jesus Christ!"

Morgan clambers away from me. "In here!" she shouts. "The one-eyed raven, he's led me to it before. I don't know why I didn't see it before now."

I jump to my feet and rub the back of my head. "Do you know where it's kept?"

Morgan places her hand on the doorknob. "No, not exactly. I've never been in here, because he usually just leads me to the door, never actually follows me inside or anything like that."

We both walk into the mausoleum. The room is compact, unremarkable, and unlike the other tombs, there are no flowers or decorations anywhere, no pictures or etchings, just a plain bronze casket in the center of the small building, suffused with the now-dying sunlight. The stench of decay and rot hit me like a backpack full of books—I don't know if I'll be able to stand it. Morgan takes my hand anyway and guides me over to the metallic box. Our eyes meet briefly before we both place our hands on the lid, and I swallow, uncertain of what we're about to do, or possibly undo.

"You haven't told my brother that you're planning on dying, have you?"

"I don't plan on dying," I reply. "I just plan on helping Arthur live."

Morgan snorts. "And if the scabbard is missing, then what? What will you do? You heard Morgana. Both you and Arthur will die. What do you think that will do to my brother? To your sister?"

"I'm not going to die," I say finally. "You saw them. At the lake house. The children."

A grin cracks through her glower. "You should know that my visions aren't always correct. Foresight is an imperfect magick."

"Yeah," I reply. "But we don't really have a choice either way, do we? Because we both know that I'm gonna do whatever I have to in order to keep my best friend alive. That I would do the same for Gwen, Mordy and you."

After one last, long look at me and my resolve, Morgan's attention fixes on the rectangular box, and we both grip the sides of the bronze casket. I'm not sure how heavy the lid is, but it feels like it weighs six hundred pounds. Once we realize it's not going to budge without another set of hands, we let go and take a step back. Morgan is already so weak from Morgana's always-untimely appearance that I don't think it's going to happen for us. I'm ready to voice this concern, the fact that Morgan shouldn't lift six pounds, let alone six hundred pounds, when I hear Mordy and Gwen calling our names.

I race over to the door to let them know where we are. Morgan and I don't have time to fully explain everything that's just happened, or why we're standing in the mausoleum, because it is dark outside, and because the twins are out past their curfew. *Again. Myrddin is going to be pissed.*

"Mordy, you grab that side," I instruct. "Gwen, grab the end there. When I say 'heave ho', I want you to lift with everything you've got, because this lid is a bitch."

The first two heaves are pointless, and do nothing to loosen the top. Mordy looks exhausted after our second attempt, but I implore him to try once more, the desperation in my voice as thick as oil. When the lid moves ever-so-slightly, life returns to Morgan's eyes, and I readjust my grasp on the metal.

Inside the casket lies the corpse of a young man. When Gwen starts sobbing, I take this as a sign that either she knows him, or that the sight of a dead person is too much for her, and ask Morgan to take her outside. The two women exit the room while Mordy and I lift the listless body out of the box, the smell of death now filling the air. Mordy pulls his shirt up over his nose and pinches the area between his eyes.

"Holy shit, man. What the hell are you doing?" he finally asks. "Are you looking for something?"

When I plunge the snake dagger into the inside of the casket, Mordy leaps back a few feet, startled by my savagery.

"Damn, boy! Be careful!"

But I can't stop hacking until I find Excalibur's sheath. I won't stop. Because fuck, it's not like I *want* to die, or have any intention of dying. We'll find the scabbard, Morgan will explain its significance, and I guess I'll kill the Merlin, even though I really don't want to do it.

I remove the interior of the casket and come up empty-handed. There's nothing but stuffing and cloth inside the damn thing. Mordy peers into the box and whistles. I know I look like a maniac, tearing a dead person's forever home to bits, but it's not like I'm doing it without purpose or anything. The scabbard means life or death for Arthur, for me, and Morgana's madness has infected me, spreading to my heart first and my head last. Anxiety and restlessness have replaced any rationality that I might have had before coming to this fucking graveyard.

I fall to my knees and hold on to my sides, my head swaying back and forth. *We're going to die.*

"What the fuck is this?" Mordy asks. "Yo, help me turn this shit over."

Underneath the lid, Mordy has discovered a heavy object that's being held in place by several leather straps, something that feels like a sword, he explains. I saw through the straps with my death dagger, and the large weapon falls into the lid, then drops onto the floor, the sound of metal hitting concrete echoing throughout the tiny room.

"Holy shit," he exclaims. "Would you look at that? Another fuckin' sword."

I'm afraid to touch the sword because of what happened at Arthur's earlier, and instead scuttle away from it, putting several feet between us. Mordy picks up the weapon and inspects the scabbard. I'm not sure what we're supposed to do with two magickal swords, or what we're supposed to do with the scabbard.

"This is what you were lookin' for, isn't it?"

I nod once. "Yes. Morgana said Arthur would need it."

Mordy's forehead scrunches. "Morgana? You spoke to Morgana?"

I don't say anything, stuck in my feelings, trying to figure out why the fuck I'm sitting in a mausoleum next to a decomposing corpse and another magickal sword.

"Looks like Arthur's sword," he says. "Might be its twin." He holds out the sheath, inspecting the surface closely, then draws the sword from it, and I know he's right as soon as I see the tip of the blade.

"Excalibur has a twin sword," I say, getting to my feet. "The Galantine. According to legend, it's a sword that rivals Arthur's in every way."

Mordy turns to me. "Oh yeah?" He sheaths the blade and holds it out horizontally for me to take. "Go on."

I approach the blade with caution. "Yes." I pause, and continue. "It was given to Sir Lancelot by the Lady of the Lake." I take the leather case into my hands and unsheathe the sword, its power rushing into me like a heavy current. The tide of energy slams me into the wall, and I drop the blade.

I soon find that I can't breathe, and Mordy slowly fades from my line of vision. Everything dims to black, and I can't see. I swear to God, if I'm being summoned to the Underworld, I'm going to be pissed, because I haven't had time to even use the Xiuhcoatl. I can't return it just yet.

"I am surprised it's taken you this long to find Galantine," a soft, feminine voice calls from the darkness. "To find me."

"Mictēcacihuātl?" I ask, still completely enshrouded by darkness. "Where are we?"

"At the bottom of a lake," the voice responds politely and very matter-of-factly. "And I'm called Viviane, not Mictēcacihuātl."

"You're the one who spoke to Arthur." The sound of rushing water surrounds me, yet I can't see it or touch it. "You are the Lady of the Lake."

She laughs, the sound eerily similar to that of the inside of a conch shell. "I am. Why have you waited so long to come to me? I have been waiting here for years."

"Are you kidding me?" I reply. "How the hell could I have known? If Mordy and Morgan had never come here, I might have never known. You're literally at the bottom of a fuckin' lake."

"That's not true. Your eyes have seen all of the signs. You were born with a third eye, Lancelot."

I can't argue with that. Auras, spirits, numerology, the mystical *and* the mythical — I've always seen and believed in everything, not because I wanted to, or because I went seeking for it — phenomena always just made their way toward me. It had been one of the reasons why I had been asked to stop coming to church — telling a Southern Baptist preacher in front of his congregation that angels are speaking to *you* instead of *him* can be quite upsetting when he's trying to collect the tithe.

"All right, so say you're right. I'm here now. What do you want from me?"

"Nothing," she says. "I only wish to leave you with this bit of information…"

The dark space is suddenly as cold as the first day of winter. I shudder and rub my hands together. I wonder if we're in an underground cavern or something like that. "Okay," I say. "What is it?"

"As much as it pains me to say this, you must drive Galantine through the Merlin's heart."

I groan. "Yeah, murdering that man is already on my list."

"He cannot drink from the Grail. You must destroy it as well. Only white fire can do this."

"White fire?" I ask. "What the hell is that?"

"The white witch traveling with you, she is the one whose counsel you seek."

"White witch? Who? Do you mean Gwen?"

"Lancelot," she says. A dainty hand rests on my shoulder, and I strain my eyes to see the rest of her body. "You are our only hope. The necromancer has walked this earth for long enough. Destroy the cycle of rebirth, please. It is time for my husband to be stopped."

Husband? Olivia Crabtree.

"Wait," I shout, groping the darkness. "There's so much more I need to know! Don't send me back just yet! What do I need to do with this goddamn scabbard? Olivia! Viviane!"

When I finally regain my senses, I find myself sitting in the back of Mordy's SUV, my head propped against the warm window. Morgan and Gwen are seated beside me, each of my hands resting in one of theirs.

"Lance," Morgan says. "Can you hear me?" I stare at her blankly. "He's not saying anything. Should I pinch him? His eyes are wide open."

"Hey," I say, putting my hands up. "No need for violence. I can hear you all right."

Gwen is the next to speak. "Goddamn it. You're going to send me to an early grave. What happened back there?"

An image of Olivia pops into my mind. "The Lady of the Lake spoke to me."

"Are you serious? What did she say?" Gwen is a bundle of nerves. "Well?"

"That we need to destroy the Merlin," I say, my eyes landing on the hilt of the sword that now rests in between the passenger seat and center console. "And his godforsaken Holy Grail."

Chapter Fourteen

The Banshee

"Will you move in with me?" Arthur pops the question like he's been holding it in for a while now. "Er. I mean…"

"What?" I say. For the past two and a half months I've been staying with him, so I don't understand his request. "What do you mean? What do you call what I've been doin'?"

He squirms underneath my weight and shifts his arms, placing them behind his head. "I dunno. I'm not really sure what I'm trying to say here."

I push up from the truck bed and scan his face, searching for a motive, anything to indicate how he's feeling.

Arthur's been acting strange lately, not like before, when he had been concerned with Mordy, but overly affectionate and adhesive. Last week when I'd come home from the mausoleum with my arm covered in blood, wearing a tattered hoodie, he'd insisted that I be more careful, more attentive of my surroundings, even raising his voice at me. I had never seen him so passionate about anything before. We haven't spoken about me returning to Lexington yet—which will happen in two weeks—and I'm not sure if I should use this opportunity to discuss it.

"I guess what I mean is… I want you to actually live with me. Obviously not while you're in school, but like, when you come back. It would be our home. You don't have to if you don't wanna. It's just a thought. Actually, never mind, forget I said anything." Sometimes Arthur acts and sounds like an unsure teenager, an indecisive kid trapped in an overgrown body. I bend down and kiss him, to stop his lips from quivering.

"How long have you been sittin' on this?" I ask, brushing his lip with my finger.

"I don't really wanna tell you because you'll think I'm a freak," he says, keeping his eye on the side of the truck.

I have witnessed demonic possession numerous times now, spoken to an Aztec goddess and accepted some snake dagger from her, and opened a fucking casket in search of a magickal scabbard, and he thinks *I'm* in a place to judge *him*. "Just tell me."

He shakes his head and attempts to change the subject. "When did you say Gwen was supposed to get here?"

"Arthur." I drag my knees across the aluminum and straddle his torso. This catches his attention immediately, and he turns to me. "You've never been shy around me."

"That's not true," he says, his hands sliding up and down my thighs. "There are lots of things I keep to myself."

"At this point there's nothing you could say that would freak me out, so why don't you just tell me?"

"Since you got here," he admits, in a whisper. "I mean, fuck, you're about to leave me in two weeks, and then I won't see you until November. That's what...three months? Holy shit, that's a long time. I won't see you again until Thanksgiving!"

So there it is. "Is that why you've been acting weird? Hey, don't close your eyes. Look at me."

"Things were really awful for me last year," he replies. "I don't want to make you feel bad, because it wasn't your fault, but I was a fuckin' mess. You have no idea. Gwen had to talk me out of driving to Lexington more than once. And yes, I already know that I sound like a fucking psycho."

"If we're going to do this, you better not argue with me about paying rent. I mean it."

The streetlight directly overhead flickers a few times before turning on, and I fasten my mouth on his before he can protest or object to my conditions. I don't want to think about the possibility that I might be gone by the end of this week, that I might not live to see next Monday, that I will have to trade something precious in order to keep Arthur alive.

I snatch the hem of his shirt and press my body into his with an urgency I haven't felt since arriving here two months ago. Arthur doesn't know about the trade—nor do Mordy or Gwen, for that matter, because how the fuck am I supposed to tell them that I might have to trade *my life* for Arthur's? Mordy certainly wouldn't allow it, and neither would Gwen. The only person who knows is Morgan, and every time it gets brought up, I dance around her tune, carefully avoiding the refrain.

"Lance," Arthur says, retreating from my lips. "Can I be weird for a minute and ask you a question?" I adjust my head on his shoulder, and nod. "Do you believe in the concept of soulmates?"

"Yes," I reply. "I do."

"And if I told you that I think you're my soulmate, would that freak you out?"

I take his hand into mine, interlocking our fingers, and extend our elbows in an outward motion. "A little."

"Because sometimes I feel like I've known you my whole life, like I can't remember a time when I didn't feel this way about you." He pauses, and continues, "It's like when I first saw you, everything unfolded in slo-mo and the earth stood still, like I was hit with the world's biggest case of déjà vu. I sound fuckin' nuts, I know."

I bring his knuckles to my lips. "I feel the same way."

Because we *have* known each other our entire lives—present and past—we just didn't know it.

"I have something I need to talk to you about, but now's not the best time, I think."

"Okay," I say. "Well, I'm not going anywhere." *At least I hope I'm not.*

Earlier today, Gwen had asked Arthur if he wouldn't mind giving her a lift after she got off work. Her car had broken down on the side of the highway two days ago, and she refuses to ask our parents for help. We've been sitting out here in his truck for the past hour waiting for her shift to end.

Lately, things haven't been so hot for my sister. Lena hadn't given her a week to pack like had originally been planned, so Arthur had offered to let her crash at his place a few days ago, and she's been staying with us ever since. We haven't lived with each other for the past two years, and it's been really nice having her around, waking up to the sound of her making pancakes, and sitting outside, underneath the stars, talking till sunrise. Just the three of us hanging out, like old times.

"Hey, y'all." Gwen's head suddenly appears over ours and she drops a bag of fragrant cinnamon rolls on Arthur's chest. "Liv said to toss those, so I figured I'd bring 'em home. What you two doing out here?" Her eyebrow arches and she crosses her arms.

"Waiting for your broke ass," I reply. "What else?"

"Are we still on for tonight? Is it really necessary?" Gwen's voice is shaky and low. "Are you sure you think it's wise to break into your work? That's literally breaking and entering, Lance."

What Gwen doesn't get is that sometimes you have to break the law in order to help the ones you love, or at least that's what I've been telling myself for the past few hours. Mordy would agree, but then again, I think Mordy would be down for hooligan shit at all times. He's good like that.

"Yes, I know. But what if this helps us find Tammy?" I feel Arthur's body tense underneath mine. Ever since he found out Emmett might have had something to do with her disappearance, just mentioning my boss's name has put him on edge. "Arthur will pull up behind the store, and I'll be in and out of there in no time."

"Whoa. Absolutely not," Arthur protests. "You're crazy if you think I'm letting you go in there alone. Emmett could be a deranged lunatic for all we know. What are you gonna to do if he *is* an evil wizard? You said it yourself, you're not prepared to fight him yet. You can't just waltz up in there and stick a goddamn knife in his side."

I climb out of the truck and hop down onto the pavement. "Fine. We can all go in there together, but don't say I didn't warn you if—and when—we get busted for being in there. That's not on my ass."

* * * *

Midnight rolls around before we know it. Arthur parks his truck in an alley next to the store and the three of us do our best to walk in the shadows. I text the twins to let them know that we're going into Camelot's, and that I'll keep them posted if I find anything of importance. So far no one is patrolling this area of downtown, and I take it as a good sign.

"How are we going to break in there anyway?" Gwen whispers.

"I have a key to the back door," I say.

Gwen grabs my arm and pulls me aside. "A fucking key," she hisses. "Why didn't you say so before?"

I shrug. "Because I'm a dick, and because you never asked." I retrieve my arm from her vise-like grip. "Now stop talking and get out of my way. Arthur, please make sure you keep an eye on my sister. All we need is someone setting off the alarm. And don't look at me like that, you know damn well you're scared of the dark." Gwen sticks her tongue out at me. "All right, here we go."

The back of the store is dark, hidden by black forms and shapes that seem to move on their own. It would make sense if there were a fan or something overhead to generate an airflow, to fondle curtains or large sheets of construction paper, something, but there isn't anything other than heavy boxes of shit blocking nearly every path leading out of the room. I don't know why, but the storage room smells like a dumpster, stuffy and acrid, full of dry air, much like a tomb. Gwen is the first to say something about it.

"What the fuck is that?" she snarls. "Does it normally smell like this?" She cups her mouth with her hand.

"Not normally, I don't guess. Can you make things lighter in here?" I ask. "I'm afraid if we turn the lights on, it might be too obvious. And someone might see us."

"Holy shit! It smells like vinegar and rotten eggs back here," Arthur adds. "Jesus, it's strong enough to knock you out."

Gwen reaches into her purse and pulls out her cell phone. "What's wrong with using the flashlight on our phones?" When I see her eyes widen, I know that her phone is dead, or nearly dead. Lately, I have had to leave my phone plugged into the wall whenever I'm at work because the battery drains almost immediately when I walk through the door. "Oh, shit," she says. "This is a new discovery, yes?"

I nod. "It is. Ever since Morgan shattered that glass everywhere, the energy in this place has been on the fritz. One day the phone will stay on one hundred percent all day, and the next, it will die as soon as you walk in here. I thought maybe my phone was just fucked, but then Mordy told me his phone drains anytime he walks down this block. I don't think it's mere coincidence. I think it's this place that's doing it, because it only ever happens when I'm here." Arthur checks his phone, and it's dead, too. "See?"

I can tell Gwen is disturbed by the whole situation, and the sooner we get out of here the better. The store is so dark that I can't see anything, and I keep falling over boxes, tripping over racks of plastic-wrapped fabric. Emmett must have received a new shipment of products, because this room was empty the last time I was in here, not even two days ago.

"Do you know where we're going?" Gwen asks. "Because I'm starting to freak out a little."

When she finally casts her enchantments, a tiny white orb appears in the middle of the room, so small that I almost miss it. Gwen goes to the light and cradles it very carefully in two hands.

"Hello there," she purrs, her voice low. "I won't hurt you, and I'm sorry to have bothered you, but we need help getting through these halls." The orb's color changes erratically, first yellow, then green and finally red. It's like watching a faulty streetlight in a storm. I take a step forward and it shoots out of Gwen's hands, heading straight for Arthur.

"Oh shit, Queenie!" he yells. "What does it want with me?"

A befuddled Christmas firefly, the orb zooms around Arthur, cycling through colors, until it suddenly drops to the ground. We all stare at the little ball of light in silence. The faint sound of bells fills the room, and I stare at the creature in awe. *Just what the fuck did Gwen conjure up?*

"Hob's lantern," Gwen says, as if answering the unspoken question. "Arthur, it's chosen you. It clearly doesn't want to fool with me."

I can't actually tell if Gwen's feelings are hurt, or if she's getting irritated by the darkness and smell, but we really don't have time to address this, whatever it is.

"All right then," I say. "Pick it up. We don't have all day." Arthur shoots me a concerned look. "Okay, I don't think it will hurt you. It's a goddamn ball of light."

Arthur leads us out of the storage room and into the hallway. The hob's lantern is barely bright enough for us to see, but I've worked here for over two months, so I'm familiar with the setup, and it will just have to suffice for the time being.

To our left are two rooms, a unisex bathroom and a utility closet, and to our right are two more rooms, a poor excuse for a break room and Emmett's messy-ass office. When we come to the front of the store, the place where I spend most of my time when I'm here, headlights appear in the distance, and we all duck down in a panic, knocking into one another like bowling pins.

We're supposed to kill an all-powerful, thousand-year-old necromancer, and the mere sight of a car provokes instant hysteria. Yeah, okay. Sure.

After the vehicle is no longer in view, we hurl ourselves to our feet, determined to get the hell out of here ASAP. Gwen takes my arm and Arthur holds the orb outward like it's the most valuable diamond in the world or something.

When we search the front of the store, we find nothing remotely incriminating. I see that Caspian has taken the liberty of crossing out my name with a Sharpie on the store calendar, replacing it with his own. *Stupid ass.*

"I have an idea," I say. "Ain't nothin' up here. Why don't we look in the back? Arthur can stand in the hallway. I'll go into Emmett's office, and you can check out the break room."

Gwen bristles. "Are you kidding me? You want me to go into one of those rooms by myself? Have you lost your fuckin' mind?"

"Arthur is going to be right there, dude. If you need him to stand closer to your doorway, fine. I just think those will be the best rooms to search if Emmett is hiding something. Make sure you open all of the lockers. Sometimes Caspian takes an hour lunch break, and there's no telling what he's doing back there."

"Is Caspian the short, goofy guy who has purple hair and a jailhouse neck tattoo?"

"Yes," I tell Gwen. "The other guy got fired a few weeks ago. It's just been me and Caspian steering the ship for a while now. I thought I already told you that."

All three of us amble toward the back of the store, afraid of what we might find — or what might find us. My eyes adjust well enough to the darkness, and I head straight for the office. Gwen chases after Arthur, muttering words of discontent, and I hear her bang a leg on the side of the wall. If we get out of here alive tonight, I'll be shocked.

Disorder.

Emmett's office is messier than usual. With crates overturned and papers cluttering the floor, it's difficult maintaining my balance. The trash can is on its side, the contents overflowing onto the floor. Things have never been orderly in here, but this is a maelstrom of madness. *Just what the hell happened in here?*

I hear a string of curses coming from Gwen in the next room, and my guess is that the break room is just as messy, if not more so, knowing that poser Caspian. I walk over to the large mahogany desk and do my best to comb through the documents without disturbing them too much, because there's no telling if Emmett is one of those freaks who has a photographic memory.

Receipts, bank statements, nothing of any real use. I leave the desk and turn around, ready to exit the dingy room, when something catches my eye—a piece of glinting metal. The light in the room is so scant that I have to kick a massive pile of wadded-up newspaper ads out of my way and bend down to get a better look at whatever is seeking my attention.

A piece of purple plastic attached to a metal wire. A removable retainer. Why would Emmett have a retainer in his office? Maybe it belongs in the lost and found, but I don't think so. I place it in my pocket and leave the office.

Arthur is standing in the hallway, his neck craned in my direction. When we make eye contact, he rushes to my side, unable to conceal his feelings.

"Jesus," he says. "Did you find anything?"

I chew on the inside of my cheek. "I may have, but I'm not sure. What about Gwen? Where is she?"

At that, Gwen emerges from the break room, carrying something in her arms. When she comes closer I see that she's stumbling. I bolt to her side, afraid that she might have hurt herself, or that something might have hurt her. Her face is covered in a mixture of snot and tears, and her body is shaking.

"Holy shit, Gwen!" Arthur exclaims. "Are you all right?"

She presents us with a pair of black and white polka-dot flip-flops. Arthur takes one in his hand and inspects it. I have no idea what's going on. *Am I missing something?*

"So...you found a pair of sandals?" I ask, toying with the retainer in my pocket. "Do you know whose they are?"

Gwen sniffles. "These...shoes...belong...to...Tammy."

I'm not sure what I'd expected to find in here, or what we would do if we *did* find something of hers. But now that I'm confronted with the real possibility that Emmett killed my sister's friend, I have no other choice but to follow the path Mictēcacihuātl suggested.

Emrys Caerwyn must be stopped, and only I can do it.

"I found something else," I say. Arthur's eyes widen as the orb hovers above my hand. "Is this Tammy's?" It's a long shot, but they might know, so I ask anyway.

A brief moment passes, and Arthur replies, gravely, "Yes, that's hers. Or at least, I know she wears a retainer. But I thought it was black."

"Black? How would you know that?" I ask, shoving the bumpy piece of plastic into my pocket. "Just how old is she?"

Arthur looks to Gwen, whose arms are folded. "Don't look at me," she says. "Answer his question."

"I know," he replies finally, "because we used to fool around." His explanation comes out in a mumble, and if I weren't standing close to him, I wouldn't have understood a word of it. Now's not the time to get caught up in my feelings, not when Tammy's life is at stake, but I would be lying if I said it didn't bother me. If I asked Arthur for a list of everyone he's messed around with, I'd have to order a forest's worth of paper. How I'm supposed to trust someone like *that* with my heart, I have no fucking idea.

"All right." I grab the shoes from Gwen's hands. "I think we've got enough evidence."

"Are we going to the police?" Arthur asks, trying to keep up with my stride. Gwen is moving at a much slower pace, her tread hindered by sadness. I'm annoyed with Arthur at the moment, and I just want to get out of the building before anything else can upset me, before I say something dumb. Trying to deconstruct my stupid jealousy has been difficult enough, and now I have to deal with this shit. Things are never going to be easy for us.

Arthur reaches for my wrist. "Tammy is a good friend of mine." I sigh because I don't want to have this conversation, not now. "And we were together briefly for one summer before I moved here. Lance, I was thirteen. We reconnected last year. I'm sorry, I should have told you."

"We can talk about it later when we have the time," I reply. "I just want to get out of here. Let's not lose focus of our goal right now."

"Right now all I see is you. I hope you know this."

Arthur is an earth sign, patient and humble, always willing to assess a situation before it gets out of hand. I don't turn around, but I know he's standing right next to me because I feel his energy radiating from his chest, his center.

"I know," I say. I don't actually want to discuss this with him — things are too heavy at the moment — but I appreciate his willingness and readiness to communicate. "But let's not do this right now."

Gwen finally joins us, and chooses to remain silent, which is probably for the best because I know she's processing some things. Arthur lights a path through the maze of boxes, and lets Gwen and me go in front of him.

Halfway through the storage room, we hear the sound of a door slamming and voices shouting. Gwen's hot pink talons dig into my forearm and she nearly lands on top of me, sending both of us crashing onto the floor. Gwen is three inches shy of being as tall as Arthur, and I'm not a big man, so it doesn't take much force to upset my gait, to send me flying through the air like a Chinese lantern.

"Hey," Arthur whispers. "Where are you guys?"

I'm not sure when or why it happened, but the orb vanished at some point, leaving us stranded in the darkness.

"Over here," I reply. "Will you get up? You're literally crushing my foot."

Another high-pitched shriek cuts through our hushed murmurs. It sounds like it's coming from next door, from Baubles & Books.

Gwen's grip tightens. "That's Olivia. Lance, we have to do something!"

"Calm down," I reply. "What can we do right now? We don't have the swords, the dagger, nothin'. And our phones are fucked. Just be quiet so that we can hear what's going on."

We stand as still as ice, huddled together and barely breathing.

There are two overlapping voices now. A man's voice and a woman's voice. Gwen thinks Olivia is in imminent danger, and if the man shouting at her is Emrys Caerwyn, that might be true.

"I won't do it!" Olivia shouts. "Not again, damn you. Our union was broken by the law. I have allowed you in my store as a service, a gesture of goodwill, but now I would like for you to leave."

"Oh no," Gwen whimpers. "He's not going to like that."

Heavy objects plummet to the floor and jostle the wall like we're under siege. Half of Baubles & Books is covered in bookshelves and small dining tables. There's no telling what's being torn asunder over there.

The man begins shouting at Olivia in a language that none of us understand. Gwen casually mentions that

Olivia is fluent in both Welsh and Gaelic. I stare at her in disbelief even though she can't see me.

"Olivia speaks Welsh and Gaelic? Don't you think that in Bumfuck, Kentucky, it's a little weird to speak Welsh? Most folks can't speak English."

Gwen replies, "What? I thought it was because she's Wiccan. I just thought she was super into her heritage or whatever."

If the Lady of the Lake is indeed Olivia, it would make sense that she has some arcane understanding of these languages...but that's not tea I'm willing to spill during our current circumstance. Morgan is the only one who knows the full extent of things, simply because I don't know how the rest of the group is going to take any of this shit. Actually, I do know, and I'm just afraid how they'll react.

"You think a divorce absolves you from everything you've done in the past? That's not how the universe works, my dear. You of all people know this."

"Leave now," she insists. "I do not fear you or your maledictions. If you try *anything*, I will destroy the Grail."

For the next few minutes we sit in silence, horrified by the events unfolding next door. Gwen is hanging on to my arm and hyperventilating now, which means we need to get the hell out of here immediately, because we can't stick around and wait for her to pass out from a panic attack. So I tap on her shoulder and place a finger on my lips, then motion upward using my hand, hoping that Gwen's eyes have adjusted to the darkness like mine have. Soon after, the three of us slowly maneuver ourselves around the cardboard chaos and somehow find the back door hiding in the murk.

As soon as my hand leaves the door handle, a loud wailing from within Baubles sends all three of us to our knees. Arthur jumps to his feet and I desperately reach for his shirt in hopes of stopping him.

"No," I say, firmly. "Don't, Arthur."

Something inside of me lurches at the keening. I don't know how, but I've heard that scream before. Known by many names—*Bean-nighe*, *La Llorana*, the *Caillech*, the White Lady, *Doña Marina*, the Banshee— the songs she often sings are different, but her message is always the same...impending death.

Chapter Fifteen

The Round Table

Emmett and Caspian arrive at the shop within minutes of each other. I got here an hour and forty-five minutes ago because I couldn't sleep last night — not after hearing Olivia's screams — and had gotten a ride from Arthur on his way to work this morning.

Gwen and I had hung out before the doors opened at Baubles, splitting an overly ripe banana and sharing a bag of granola. Even though it feels like the pits of hell out there, we'd sat outside in the heat because we had both been too scared to enter Camelot's. Luckily for Gwen, she doesn't work here, but then again, I'm not entirely sure how she's going to swing her shift either, seeing as how she's been a total mess since everything happened.

After we'd gotten home from the store, we hadn't talked, even choosing to sit in silence during the car ride home, then going straight to bed afterward. Not a peep. Gwen and I had slept on the futon in the living room, while Arthur had slept in his bed. We hadn't talked about it this morning, either.

Tammy isn't a friend of mine, and our relationship has been contentious due to my immaturity and tendency to get defensive over things, so I couldn't possibly understand what either of them are going through. There's so much that our group needs to talk about. It's just that finding the right moment to discuss this shit has been so damn hard. If I'm not falling victim to glamouring and turning into a human garbage truck, then I'm fucking with cadavers and finding magickal weapons in graveyards.

I'm not sure what I'd expected when I got on that Greyhound bus, but it sure as hell hadn't been this.

When Caspian enters the break room, he's wearing a smile and a new band T-shirt. *Must have been a sale at the douchebag factory.* He doesn't acknowledge me, instead skating past like he's on some kind of mission. The more I look at him, the more I dislike him. He isn't physically ugly, quite the opposite actually—stocky and broad-shouldered, with faded blue hair and a flawless complexion—but he has the social skills of a raccoon. I won't miss him when I go back to Lexington, that's for sure.

"Emmett needs to talk to you." The statement startles me, and even though it's just the two of us, I look around to make sure he's talking to me.

"Oh. Okay. Thanks for telling me," I reply. "By the way, you have ketchup on your face." I hear him scoff as I exit the room.

Emmett is standing by the window when I enter the front of the store.

"Mornin', Emmett. Caspian said you wanted to see me?"

"Lance," he says. "Were you here last night?"

My heart seizes inside my chest. "Uh, yes. I forgot my charger," I lie. "And I stopped by to see if it was here."

"And?" He doesn't turn around to face me. "Was it?" I can tell by the way he's holding his hands behind his back that Emmett did not come into work to play.

"No, sir," I say. "It wasn't. I don't know where I put it."

"I see," he replies. "Are you aware that you left the back door unlocked last night?"

Shit. "Oh my God, I had no idea." Emmett must have returned to the store after his falling out with Olivia. "Was anything missing this morning?"

A long, airless pause. "Yes. A couple of things," he replies coolly. "But it doesn't matter. I have what I need." I'm not sure what he's alluding to, but I'm fairly certain it involves my boyfriend's ex-girlfriend. I ball my hands into fists and shove them into my pockets — a blow-up at Emmett would not do, not now, when it's just him, his henchman in the back, and me. "I'm going away for a while," he says. "Caspian will be left in charge, but I guess that doesn't really concern you, now does it? Because I believe you're going back to school very soon, yes?"

"I am," I say, unsure as to where the conversation is headed. We haven't had time to discuss any of this because he usually sends me home before I have the chance to bring it up. "I go back in two weeks, actually. Where are you goin'?"

"Wales. Carmarthen, Wales. It's where I grew up."

According to every legend I've ever heard or read, he's right — Carmarthen is where the Merlin was born. A product of sexual depravity and devilry, Emrys Caerwyn was brought into this world with the cards stacked against him. His father had been a sea demon, known to the world at that time as Afanc, and his mother, Adhan, had been an unsuspecting nun. Why he's telling me this, I don't know. Maybe it's to scare me, or maybe it's to warn me. I doubt it, though. For the past few weeks I've been walking on eggshells when I'm around him, trying to roll with the punches, always accepting reduced hours and being sent home early. But what I don't understand is that if he knows I'm a reincarnation of King Arthur's right-hand man, Sir Lancelot, Knight of the Round Table, why hasn't he turned me into sausage, or made me disappear like Tammy?

"My suggestion to you..." Emmett finally turns around, with a sort of fire in his eyes, and he smiles at me, a dreadful smile. A smile that feels like someone's just stomped on both of my feet. "Lance A. Lotte, is to take the rest of the day off, spend it with your family and cherish the next two weeks in peace." He pauses and scratches the gray stubble on his chin. "Oh, one more thing I've been meaning to ask... Is the boy who drives you here called Arthur?"

I gulp. "Yes, his name is Arthur." I don't dare tell him what Arthur's last name is, even though he probably already knows. He probably already knows everything. All of our plans, all of our secrets, all of our faults.

"Hmm," he murmurs, in a way that makes my joints ache. "And he lives out by that used tire place, right?" He taps his cheek twice with an index finger. "You know, those houses are in poor shape. Why, a flood, or a simple fire, could wipe out that whole trailer park. He'd better be careful out there. There's no telling what the end of summer might bring." The last ten words of

225

his warning twist inside me like the blades of a lawnmower, relentless and sharp, meant to shave and destroy. If he intended to cut me down to size, he's succeeded.

I don't respond to his threat, and instead offer my resignation on the spot, ultimately agreeing with him that I should spend the rest of my vacation relaxing and resting. And for a brief moment, Emmett Crabtree returns, a bushy, gray-eyebrowed elderly man who walks with a cane and has a terrible time using any technology built after 1995.

It's difficult to believe that this scraggy old man has abducted children and women.

"Give your mother a kiss on the cheek for me. I always did enjoy the sangria she brought to the Fourth of July block party."

And now he's bringing my mom into this mess? Oh hell no.

* * * *

Gwen and I meet up after her shift. Mordy and Morgan have called a meeting, and would like to assemble at their uncle's house tonight. Arthur agrees to this without complaint and offers to drive us over there after he gets off work. My body is sore all over, and all I want to do is sleep, maybe take a bath, drink an ice-cold beer, but I don't think that's in tonight's reading.

Tío Myrddin walks out to greet us. His long white robe is the first thing I observe, followed by a small white cap on his head and several necklaces made of seashells and pocket-size bones around his thick neck—probably more chicken bones. He hugs me immediately, and places his arm around my neck, escorting me up the porch steps.

Gwen and Arthur trail after us, speaking softly to each other out of earshot, carefully carrying Excalibur and Galantine, because Morgan had asked us to bring the weapons. The two of them had spoken briefly about Tammy during the ride up here, consoling each other, and I'd almost felt like a third wheel, intruding on their conversation in the truck. I may not know her, but I want to save her and do everything I can to protect her.

The first room Myrddin leads us through — the living room — is covered in what looks like hundreds of black and white candles, all ferociously burning, every flame pointing south.

In the center of the room, painted on the creaky wooden floor, is a symbol drawn in white chalk. I'm not a scholar or a priest, so I don't know exactly what it means, but from the way Morgan's uncle is dressed, I assume it has to do with protection and the Orichás.

Every room we walk through is decorated similarly, with black and white candles, the only difference being the symbols in the middle of the floors. A different symbol for each room.

"Where are Mordy and Morgan?" I ask as we pass through the kitchen, the only room seemingly not covered in melted wax and chalk. A combination of smells from fried corn tortillas, garlic and freshly baked bread invades my nostrils, and when I scan the room I spot a gigantic steel pot cooking on the gas stove, steam rising from the metal. The sight of brown, knotted bread on the kitchen table makes my mouth water.

Coming here on an empty stomach wasn't the brightest idea, I chide myself.

"They're waiting for you outside." Myrddin opens a screen door leading out to the back porch, and we walk through the laundry room in single file. "Watch your step! That last stair is barely hanging on."

Outside, sitting across from each other, are Morgan and Mordy. Both are dressed in black T-shirts and jeans. It's the first time I've seen them wear anything other than the color white. I rush to Morgan, practically bowling her over with excitement. My arms slide around her waist and I hug her tightly.

"Wait, is it already over? Did you make it?"

Morgan laughs, patting the top of my head. "Yes, friend. Iyaworaje has ended."

My gaze shoots across the fire and lands on her brother, who is sitting with his legs crossed, looking sedated, exhausted. I'd had no idea their year in white was about to end.

Damn, I wish I had known. Because I'd made the both of them flannel sachets of sage, anise and lavender the other day, to celebrate this moment, and I hadn't thought to bring them. They're sitting on Arthur's dresser. I'd put a lot of effort into sewing them by hand, pricking my finger repeatedly, like I was trying to go to sleep for the next hundred years.

"*Tío* Myrddin," Morgan says. "This is Gwen, Lance's sister, and Arthur, Lance's roommate."

Morgan hadn't outed us to her uncle. I squeeze her shoulder in approval, and she winks at me.

Now, crouched down beside his nephew, *Tío* Myrddin inspects Gwen and Arthur through the smoky pile of sticks, not with scrutiny or malevolence, but out of curiosity and wonder. Perhaps he is just as interested in them as they are in him.

Arthur is wearing a dirty white T-shirt, a pair of blue jeans, muddy work boots and a backward ball cap. None of us had thought to change into actual decent clothing. Standing beside him, Gwen is dressed in a pair of pink Daisy Dukes and a green tank top that reads in glittery lettering *Real Men Are Feminists*. She must be nervous, because she's tonguing the stud in her left cheek with a sort of furious determination, and I'm not sure why I didn't realize it before, but she isn't wearing any shoes.

I can see why the face Myrddin's wearing might be a little heavy.

"Mordy has told me a lot about y'all. Your meemaw is a hell of a woman, Arthur."

Arthur laughs. "Thank you, sir. I know."

"Used to run around with her when we were kids." He chuckles. "Has the purest of hearts, that one." By Arthur's beaming, I can tell that he agrees with *Tío* Myrddin's assessment of his grandmother. "Have yourself a seat. Gwen, you too. I think it's fair to say that we have all become family in some way or another, whether we willed it or not. Mordy, your marshmallow's gonna be too black to eat, boy."

No one argues with *Tío* Myrddin, because he's right, and we all know it. Even the fire knows it, its flames dancing along to our responses, shrinking and growing with our emotions, our laughter.

Morgan leaves the fire, enters the laundry room through the back porch, then returns moments later with a tremendous amount of bagged leaves. High above the bonfire, the moon hovers directly overhead, offering lustrous streams of silver light. When Morgan tosses a bag to each of us, I smell the clean, crisp fragrance through the plastic immediately. *Oregano.*

"Damn," Arthur says. "That's strong as hell. What is this?"

"It better be," Morgan replies with a shake of her head. "For all the shit I went through to get it. *Tío* Myrddin had me sneaking around on all fours, looking for this shit in the cemetery. You ever been chased at night with a shovel? I'm surprised that dude didn't call the cops."

"Shew, you ain't kiddin'," *Tío* Myrddin agrees. "He was madder'n a porch full of rattlesnakes and rocking chairs."

Everyone starts laughing after that—except for Mordy. Other than an initial nod, he's not communicated with anyone yet—other than his uncle, that is. *I wonder if he's okay.*

When Mordy catches me staring at him I don't look away, smiling instead, but he turns away from me and swiftly grabs a fistful of oregano. I don't get it. Something's pissed him off. He doesn't normally act like this. In fact, I've never seen him angry.

Is it me?

"Mordred," Morgan whines. "Calm down." At that, Mordy jumps up from his seat, alarming all of us, and starts throwing leaves into the fire. The oregano fizzes and produces a shrill, human-like whistle while turning to ash. "Goddamn it," Morgan says. "I said calm down."

"Calm down my ass!" he shouts, and shifts to face me. "Don't you have something to tell the group, Lance?"

I look to Morgan. Her face is sympathetic, but all she can do is shrug. Somehow Mordy knows. But just how much, I'm not sure.

"What is he talkin' about?" Gwen asks. "And why is he so mad?"

Secrets. The trade. A compromise. Death.

"Yeah," Mordy says, launching the bag into the fire. "What could have possibly crawled up my ass?"

"Do you have any idea how difficult all of this has been on me?" I shout. "Why would I keep this to myself? Why would someone keep the fact that they're going to die to themselves? To spare everyone the pain and suffering they're dealing with!" Gwen reaches for my arm, but I shrug it off, and stand. "I never had any other option. All roads in my life have led to this moment. You know it as well as I do, Mordred. The cycle will be broken, and I am the only one who can do it."

"Death?" Arthur says. "What are you talking about? Who's dyin'?"

Mordy points at Arthur. "Lance made some kind of deal where you'll get to live if he kills the Merlin, but in order to do that, he has to essentially sacrifice himself for you. It's fucking stupid!"

Even though I've now got a hornet's nest buzzing within my ribs, I'm oddly glad all of this shit has surfaced, because honestly, I didn't know how I was going to bring it up.

Arthur doesn't offer anything in response, instead keeping his eyes focused on the fire.

Gwen explodes. "What the fuck is he talking about, Lance? What do you mean a trade?"

"A life for a life," Mordy replies, our eyes now locked. "Isn't that right, Lance?"

Gwen inhales. "No offense, Mordy, but I need to hear this from my brother. So could you please just let him explain himself, because what I'm hearing can't be right." Her voice cracks. "Right, Lance?"

"I don't know what y'all want me to say. When Morgana attacked me the first time, she mentioned a trade, and then when Mordy and I went up to Little Henge, Mictēcacihuātl said the same thing. All I know is that I'm the only one who can do this. I don't know why. I didn't ask for any of it. If I never came back to this fuckin' town, none of it would have happened." I don't know when I started crying, but now that I am, I'm not sure that I'll be able to stop.

Everyone is attacking me, and I don't know, maybe I deserve it, maybe it *is* my fault, because I kept all of this hidden from them, but I had not come emotionally prepared for such an intervention. No one tries to stop me, either, when I walk around the side of the house, headed in the direction of the front porch.

I lay my head on the splintered wood and close my eyes, unable to cork the salty tears. The wooden floorboards beneath my arms and legs are still warm from the summer heat.

Learning how to love another human being is the hardest challenge I've ever had to overcome in my life. Bouncing from house to house and county to county, as a small child I'd struggled with trusting others and accepting kindness, always thinking folks had ulterior motives, something they could use against me if I opened my heart to them. Lying had always come easier than loving.

When I'd first joined the Lotte family, Fred and Anna had been so patient, welcoming me into their home and family with an understanding that I was different, that my needs would be greater than their own daughter's, that they would have to devote more time to me than her.

During the first week, I'd stayed in bed, burrowed under my quilt like some frightened mole, afraid to interact with any of them. But then Gwen had rebelled against her parents' advice, sneaking into my room one night with an unopened box of Popsicles, one of those twenty-four packs, and we'd eaten every single one, not uttering one word while doing this. Afterward she'd crawled into my blanket fort, and we'd fallen asleep on the floor.

That was my introduction to Gwen.

That had been our setup for the next few years. I hadn't slept alone until I was a junior in high school.

The thought of losing any of them—Gwen, Mordy, Morgan, Arthur—the feeling is acidic, chaotic and eats away at any and all logic. Saving Arthur, saving any of them... I will do anything and everything I can to protect them. Because I realize now that it's not just Arthur, it's everyone—*Tío* Myrddin, Fred and Anna, even Arthur's morally bankrupt father. Every living thing in Avalon.

We have to do this for every resident, because when you love something, you love the good and the bad, and there's nothing anyone can do to change that. *I love Avalon, and I love Kentucky.*

To my left I hear the sound of movement and promptly pop up, scrambling for composure. The collar of my shirt is soaked, and when I wipe my face black marks that were once my mascara streak my hand. Arthur steps into my line of vision, holding two water bottles, one resting in the crook of each elbow.

"Hey," he says. "Thought you might need some water. It's hot as hell out here."

"Oh, hey. Yeah, it really is." I accept the water and bring my knees to my chest. "Thanks," I say. Arthur takes a seat next to me. "Sorry about all that."

"About what?" he asks. "Oh, you mean that whole sacrifice thing? Yeah, I gotta admit…things got a little out of hand back there. Are you okay?"

I remove the plastic cap and take a long swig of water, drinking more than half of the bottle's contents. For the past few weeks I've felt drained, unable to take care of myself. I haven't eaten anything since lunch today, and it's past nine o'clock. I feel like passing out.

"I'm alive," I squeak. "Did you come out here to yell at me too?"

Arthur reclines his body, using his elbows to prop himself up on the floor. "Nah," he replies. "If the roles were reversed, I'd do the same thing. Wouldn't think twice about it. For you or Gwen. Besides, I can't stand to see you cry. I hate it more than anything in the world."

"I didn't keep it from y'all because I was intentionally trying to be deceptive. I just didn't know how to tell you. There's no way you would have believed me if you hadn't found that sword. You would have been like 'Oh, that Lance, he's snapped. I knew he was a little off, but now he's past the point of no return'. I mean, just think about it."

"You regret comin' back, don't you?" His voice is a well, deep and full of sorrow. "You implied it back there."

I take a deep breath. "I just didn't expect to come back to this, you know? The worst thing that I thought could happen was comin' back to you bein' in a relationship, not this — not killing a druid that's been around for eons. Certainly not multiple visits from ghosts, ghouls and goddesses. It sucks, man. All of it."

Arthur remains solemn for the next several minutes. "We could leave here," he says. "I have a few thousand dollars in the bank. You, me, Gwen, we could leave tonight. You don't have to fight Emmett. I know rent is high in Lexington, but we could live somewhere shitty for a while until we get on our feet."

I drop my water bottle on the porch and slink toward him. He doesn't budge from the porch, but his eyes follow my movement with careful precision.

"I regret a lot of things," I say. "Mostly I regret keeping these feelings to myself for so long." My hands glide across his paint-stained shirt, and I pull myself up against his body, then rest my ear against his chest. "I just want to be able to do normal shit with you. For a while there, it actually felt like we were dating, but now it feels like we're racing against time."

"Hey," he says, twirling my ponytail in his finger, his breath hot against my overgrown undercut. "You've made me so happy these past couple of months. I'm not ready to just give up, and you shouldn't either. I'm not going to let anything happen to either of us." I slump farther into his stomach, head-first, desperately wanting to believe him. "I don't get it. You always put people before you. It's like you don't love yourself or something, like you think other people are important, and that you're not." I draw away from him, afraid he'll see my tears again, but his gentle hands stop me. "You know, you don't have to love yourself in order to let other people love you. It doesn't work that way. I know you struggle with that stuff."

Now, looking at Arthur's backward cap and his dirty work clothes, I absorb his words, his energy, his being, and think to myself how lucky I am to be right here, in this moment, with this man.

"I love you."

"Say that again," he replies, his eyes sparkling in the moonlight. "I never get tired of hearing you say that."

"I love you," I say, before my lips attack his. "I love you."

Tío Myrddin and Gwen are sitting side by side when Arthur and I return. Mordy tries to stand up immediately, but Morgan yanks on his hand, jerking him back to the ground.

"Ah!" *Tío* Myrddin exclaims as he acknowledges us, his palms juggling a stack of brown bowls.

Arthur and I are holding hands, and when I try to drop his, he squeezes mine tighter. If the sight bothers *Tío* Myrddin, he's doing a helluva job hiding it.

"You two are just in time," he says. "We are getting ready to have some black beans and rice. Morgan's got the knife, if you want some bread. She made it. Her first attempt!"

Morgan turns a soft red in the firelight. "It better taste good. Kneading that dough was a bitch!"

I accept a dish from *Tío* Myrddin and walk over to where Mordy's sitting. The aroma of lime hits me instantly, and I realize just how famished I am. He reaches into the large metal bowl sitting in front of him and spoons an enormous amount of beans into my bowl, then looks up at me.

I hurt him most of all by keeping all of these things a secret. We don't break eye contact for several seconds, and probably wouldn't have, if Arthur's warm hand on my shoulder hadn't urged me to move so that he could get some food too. Gwen doesn't say anything to me as

I find a seat next to her. She keeps her head glued to the large piece of bread in her hands.

I press on her shoulder with my free hand. "Do you hate me?" Gwen shakes her head, but doesn't speak. "Okay, because I love you, and I'm sorry that I'm your older brother who seems to be the world's biggest fuck-up." She abruptly places the bread on a plate in her lap and crushes me with her arms, nearly spilling the rice from my bowl all over my legs. "Jesus, Gwen!"

"We've already discussed it." She snuffles, hot tears streaming down her cheeks. "You're not going this alone. And if you don't like it, tough shit."

* * * *

After dinner, Morgan hands me a bag of oregano.

"We're burning oregano tonight, to reverse or end any hexes placed on any of us within this circle," she says. "*Tío* Myrddin has had several chickens turn up dead recently. All in bloody, gruesome ways. Lance, I'll spare you the details. But we believe someone is targeting this land."

"And because I've been having vivid dreams lately," Mordy chimes in. My heart is relieved to hear him speak. "Dreams about you, Lance." I swallow. "Queen Mab over here came to me last night and showed me all of this fucked-up stuff, told me you already knew about it. I'm sorry for blowin' up at you."

Morgan nods. "I have mini-pouches full of oaken ash to give you all as well. In preparation for the days to come."

"Oaken ash?" Arthur asks. "Do you mean like ashes from an oak tree?"

"Yes," *Tío* Myrddin replies. "It is believed that Emrys Caerwyn was conceived in an oak grove, and because of this, druids have worshiped and revered oak trees for centuries. Now, I'm not one for cuttin' down trees and burnin' 'em, but I believe this ash will help us draw power from the Merlin." Morgan hands us little canvas bags with drawstrings. "My suggestion to you is to keep them on you at all times, even when you're at work, Lance."

"Oh," I say meekly. "Emmett basically fired me today."

"Well," he replies. "That solves that problem, I reckon. Morgan, do you have the swords?"

Mordy had asked Arthur while he was at work to bring Galantine, Excalibur and the Xiuhcoatl to the fire. I guess when I had been off throwing myself a pity party, one of them must have gone to Arthur's truck to retrieve the weapons.

"Good," *Tío* Myrddin says. "So what we're going to do tonight is cleanse and bless the blades. This will happen by igniting the blade and then dousing it in holy water. But there's an important component of this ritual that I need to get out of the way right now...and that's the belief portion." He turns his eyes on Arthur. "Everyone here is a witch, aside from you, Arthur Pendragon, and that could be a problem. Do you understand why?"

"You're right—I'm not a witch," Arthur agrees. "But I've been around them for the past few years, and that's never stopped anyone from performing a ceremony when I'm present."

"Right, but this is different, because it is elemental in nature. We are calling everyone and everything inhabiting this land, all of the tree spirits, ghosts from slave plantations now long gone, and quite possibly demons, if they live here. We require total land devotion." His eyes shift to Morgan. "Now, I need you to state before everybody here that you believe in magick, that you will continue to believe in it and that you will use it if called on to do so."

Arthur sits real still for the next few moments, taking in everything *Tío* Myrddin's just said.

He clears his throat. "Uncle Myrddin, I believe in God, and good and evil—hell, not so much, but spirits and ghosts, sure. I guess belief in those things is similar to your belief in magick. And no, I'm not a witch, as you stated before, but I do believe in everything I've seen and heard these past couple of months, and they have all been directly related to witchcraft. If you're asking me to believe in the power of this circle, there's no need, because I've believed in it since I met your niece and nephew."

Tío Myrddin brings a hand to his side and says firmly, "Hand the man his sword, Morgan."

Chapter Sixteen

Merlin, the Oathbreaker

"Do you have any idea how hard it was for me to ask Pastor Wilson to bless this goddamn sword? And don't give me that look. It *was* hard as hell. You try walkin' into some Southern Baptist preacher's house and gettin' him to bless a magical weapon."

Gwen jeers, "Oh, whatever!" I look up from the book sitting in front of me on the table, baffled by her sudden wrath. "It was only hard because you fucked his daughter." I sigh and return to the book. *This conversation is not worth my time, and I need to focus on spellwork, on transmutation.* "And don't even try to save face because Lance is here. I know all about it. The whole damn school knows about it."

Arthur chokes on the apple juice that he's just chugged straight from the bottle. "I'll have you know that I never had sex with that woman! And if anyone's to blame here, it's her. I was sixteen, and she was a sophomore in college!"

I rub my temples. Gwen and Arthur have been going at it like an old married couple for the past week. Living with Arthur was supposed to be temporary, only until Gwen sorted out her finances, but I'm not sure he can take her jabs much longer. Last week they'd gotten into it because Gwen had left for work without plunging the toilet, and Arthur had had to deal with the aftermath when he'd gotten home from work.

Ideal roommates they are not.

"What did he say to you about the sword?" I intervene. "Did he ask you a bunch of questions?"

Arthur opens the fridge and places the juice back on the shelf, then pulls out a couple of sticks of string cheese.

"Actually," he replies, peeling apart the plastic packaging, "when I told him I was gonna fight demons with it, he immediately took me out back to this creepy cellar, where he keeps all of these portraits of Jesus and Mary and shit. I don't know what he's going through, but he had all of these metal canisters of holy water down there, said that an angel came to him in a vision a few months ago and told him he needed to start stockpiling it. Man, it was weird."

"But it's done now?" I say, getting up from the table. Arthur shoves an entire cheese stick in his mouth and gives me a thumbs-up. "Good. That means we've cleansed and dowsed every weapon. Morgan has all of the dolls we made. Gwen, you got all of the talismans finished, right?" She nods once. "All right. Now all we have to do is wait for Mordy to text with the go-ahead." I glance at Arthur, who is now eating peanut butter out of a jar with a spoon. "I know how strange all of this must be for you, Arthur. I'm sorry you got dragged into it."

"Dragged into it?" he asks, metal spoon mid-air. "If that old man is truly a thousand-year-old wizard, and we are all related to characters from some fairy tale, I'm not sure I even had a chance. I don't think any of us did. Seems to me like we were all meant to come together to fix some cosmic mishap."

Honestly, I'd expected everything to be more difficult for Arthur, to be more of a spiritual challenge. But last week at the initiation fires, he'd accepted everything *Tío* Myrddin had said and offered. There had been no hesitancy or reluctance to believe, no need to suspend disbelief. Arthur had received every amulet, charm and blessing with gratitude, and had even asked *Tío* Myrddin question after question regarding Santería like he was a toddler who had just discovered the word *why*. I haven't asked him if he believes what Morgan told him that night, that he is a reincarnation of King Arthur, his literal namesake, because I'm not sure that matters anymore. As long as he believes in what we're doing, it should be enough. At least, that's the collective hope.

Around eight o'clock, I receive a text from Mordy stating that he and his sister are ready to go, that we should plan to meet at Emmett's house a little before midnight.

The witching hour. The moment when witches and spirits are at their most powerful — which means Emrys will also be at his most powerful, unfortunately.

Gwen and I make a huge spaghetti dinner for the three of us, and we cram in together on the futon, watching old reruns of *The Munsters*. None of us are actually hungry, but we make a concerted effort to shove the noodles and garlic bread down our throats. All I can taste is sorrow and despair in every bite, the individual sands in an hourglass.

Arthur goes back to his bedroom and closes the door. I don't follow him because I think he needs time to himself. What we're about to do is insane, unheard of, incredible. I don't blame him for needing some time alone, time to meditate and reflect.

Gwen and I step outside the trailer, then make a huge pentacle in the middle of Arthur's gravel driveway out of sticks and daisies that we've collected, and position our bare feet inside the heart of it. Gwen takes both of my hands into hers and we send silent prayers into the universe — hers to Diana, the Moon Goddess, and mine to Mictēcacihuātl, who I hope is still listening.

Standing here with my sister like this, under the marvelous protection of the lunar queen, I've decided that black and white witchcraft don't have to be at odds with each other. Not anymore. There's no rulebook, no regulatory body, no statute that states we must be at war with each other.

No one path is right.

Besides, brujería exists without hierarchy or rules, and if I need to shape it into something to better fit my life, my belief system and my family, I can do it, because that's how magick works. That's how all magick works — regardless of what it's called.

The sound of Arthur opening the screen door draws our attention toward him, concluding our ritual. Dressed in a tie and three-piece suit, he leans against the frame of the door. Now's not the time for romancing, but if I make it through the night, I'm going to ask him to wear that outfit to every appropriate outing, because *goddamn*.

"What are you wearing?" Gwen asks, stepping out of the symbol. "You look like you're going to a funeral."

"Well, this is what I wore when my Uncle Jasper passed away last year. Mordy suggested it. Well, not this exactly, but he said I should wear something that holds sentimental value, and I loved Jasper."

Of course I would get turned on by something Arthur wore to a funeral. Only me.

I follow Gwen up the stairs into the house, and prepare myself for the upcoming confrontation. There's so much I want to say to both of them—about how much I love them, how I want to grow old with the both of them, how special they are to me. But I know this will sound like giving up to them, so I don't, and try my best to soothe the sickness that's slowly creeping into my soul.

After Gwen's finished weaving sprigs of lavender throughout her hair, I take her place in the bathroom and remove the ponytail holder from my bun, letting my hair tumble to my shoulders. I haven't cut it since I arrived in Avalon. There had been a time in my life where long hair had made me feel dysphoric—like less of a man—but now I can't imagine having short hair. Seeing Arthur with short hair had been a shock, and I'm sure if I got mine chopped off, I'd have a similar reaction.

I reach into the makeup bag sitting on the sink and root around for the face paint I purchased a few days ago. When I find it, I unscrew the top lid and plow my fingers through the white waxy substance, then smear a big glob across my forehead. It's the cheap stuff, Halloween makeup actually, and I can only hope that it doesn't liquefy when I step outside and start to sweat—even more so than I already am.

The black tube of lipstick is the next thing I apply to my face. Large circles around my eyes, a spade on my nose, and vertical lines across my mouth. Then on my neck, hands and bare feet I lather an herbal infusion made from St. John's Wort and olive oil—for added protection, *not* because I like the smell.

At first glance it might appear that we're going overboard with this protection shit— lavender to ward off the evil eye, oregano to break curses, St. John's Wort for providence, star anise to increase Morgan's psychic abilities—but witches have *always* borrowed power from the earth to expand their magickal abilities. And if we're going to defeat a druidic priest who is commanding nature to do his bidding, we'll need all the help we can get.

I fasten the necklaces I received from both Arthur and Mordy around my neck, carefully avoiding the sharp bones, then slip a pair of black socks over my oily feet and open the bathroom door.

Gwen and Arthur are sitting at the kitchen table, sharing a pot of tea. *Wormseed.* The fragrance hits me immediately. An herb popular in Mexico, wormseed is known for its many health benefits, but I know they are drinking it to cleanse themselves spiritually. On its own, the tea is pungent and bitter—I don't see how they have mugs full of the stuff.

When I pull out a chair and join them, I can feel Arthur's intense gaze boring into the side of my head. I wheel my face around to counter his ogling, and observe him carefully examining my face and hair.

"Got a staring problem?" I ask, accepting a cup of tea from Gwen. "Mr. Pendragon?"

"You just never wear your hair down anymore." He reaches out and places a strand behind my ear. "I like it, is all."

Gwen makes a gagging sound. "Get a room."

"We have a room. A whole house, actually."

Gwen's tongue protrudes from her freshly painted lips and she rolls her eyes at Arthur. "Whatever. I'm moving back in with my folks on Wednesday, so y'all can get back to fuckin' like bunnies if you want."

Arthur's relief is visible. "Well," he says, "I, for one, will hate to see you go."

"Oh, shut the fuck up!" Gwen whoops, then picks up a hand towel that's drying on the back of a chair and chucks it at Arthur's head, setting off a cacophony of laughter around the table.

Coming back here was not a mistake. I would face injury and death for these two people a thousand times over.

* * * *

Moonlight and meditation are the only reasons we're able to make it up the steep hill — the hill leading to Emmett's monstrous estate — without headlights.

When Arthur's truck finally comes to a rumbling halt, I notice Mordy reclining on the hood of his Escalade. Moments later, Morgan's head pops up from behind the vehicle like corn in a microwave. Her near-perfect pair of oval, black buns is the first thing to enter my field of vision.

Mordy jumps down from his SUV. "I don't know why we said no headlights. You can hear that engine a mile away!"

Arthur opens his door and hops out. "Ha," he says, scratching his head. "We can't *all* be hipsters with nice rides, now can we? I mean, *someone* has to make y'all look cool, right?"

They bump fists, talk briefly, and Mordy turns his attention toward Gwen and me. We haven't moved from the truck, still in shock because of what we're about to do, and I roll down the window. When Mordy places his hands above his head on the warm metal and leans into the frame, I realize that he's dressed in all black—a pair of sweatpants and a hoodie, clothes too hot for the season, really—then it hits me—his enlarged pupils, tiny eclipses staring back at me. I reach up and tilt his jaw left and right.

"Are you high?" I ask firmly. "Goddamn it, Mordy." At least three-quarters of each eye is inhabited by an astronomic black circle. I don't know how the fuck he can see.

"Chill, Mister Rogers," he replies. "I'm sober. It's belladonna. *Tío* Myrddin and Morgan made a batch of the stuff a few nights ago. It's supposed to help you detect psychic attacks. Morgan let Morgana help make the stuff, so it's really potent."

I let go of his chin. "Morgan looks like this, also?"

"Yes," he says, his face a few inches from mine. "And you should, too. You'll need to be aware of everything once we step foot inside that house. There's no telling what kind of shit he's conjuring up in there. And you are *not* to face him alone. Do you hear me?" He flicks his silver tooth with his tongue.

A well-dressed wraith, Arthur, materializes beside Mordy, carrying Galantine, Excalibur and Xiuhcoatl in his hands. "Do you hear *all of us*?" Arthur says, handing me the death dagger. "You're not going in there with banners raised, man. It ain't happenin'."

I groan. Ever since they found out about the trade, it's all either of them have been able to talk about. Gwen hasn't brought it up, probably because she's afraid of losing me, or because she doesn't want to acknowledge the possibility that I could die tonight. Mordy has apologized to me through texts, and I've readily accepted his apology, but it's a topic he won't drop.

Gwen takes my hand into hers and gives it a little squeeze. "We got this," she whispers. I examine the lines of her face, the high cheekbones and golden studs now in the centers of her cheeks. Her beauty never ceases to amaze me. Fair-skinned and blue-eyed, wearing a crown made of laurel and a loose, handmade dress made from white cheesecloth, she is easily a queen from faerie tales long ago.

Morgan is already strategizing a mental game plan by the time we exit the truck and join her. Halfway bent over, she extends her hands, and her careful fingers graze the tops of an overgrown, neglected lawn congested with fluffy dandelions that almost immediately lose their shape when any amount of air rouses them.

"Yo," I say. "You ready for this?"

Morgan stands up and wipes the white fuzz on her black pants. "The first thing we gotta do is heal these trees. Look at the trunks. He's straight stealing energy from them. God, at this rate, the wilt is gonna kill them."

"What wilt?" I ask. "Where?"

"Holy shit, look at the size of that hole!" Gwen comments. "Poor babies!"

Gwen and I walk over to examine one of the towering oaks, tall grass brushing against our knees as we move toward the tree. Gaping black craters, as big as my side bag, consume the outer and inner bark, a ravenous disease devouring anything and everything in its sight. Morgan had referred to it as 'the wilt', but it's something more insidious, something far more nefarious than a simple fungal disease.

"I don't get it," Gwen says, placing her hand in one of the holes. "Why would he kill these trees? Druids worship oak trees. The term druid literally comes from the Gaelic word for tree."

"Right? It makes no sense," Morgan says. "But whatever the reason, we gotta stop it. Can you help me tie these charms around the branches? Not too tight. Don't wanna hurt these wooden babies."

One by one, Gwen, Morgan and I tie paper talismans around the skinny limbs, doing our best to handle each green leaf with great care. Every individual charm contains a hand-painted healing symbol, drawing power from ancient shamanic magick — spiraling suns, the Eye of Horus and the Hand of the Goddess. Together Morgan and Gwen had come up with the symbols, then Gwen had been tasked with painting them. I'm just glad I hadn't been asked to paint anything, not after Mordy forced me to paint that rune and it turned out looking like shit. Who knows what kinds of stuff my crooked-ass symbols might have evoked?

Once the trees are covered in paper like a ticker-tape cannon just exploded all over the place, the five of us form a line and trudge through the embedded tract of land. The dagger in my side bag feels heavier than usual, and I wonder if it's because we're about to enter a den of death.

"Oh my God!" Gwen bleats, grabbing my wrist, and forcing me to lose my balance. "Lance, it's Olivia's car! She's in there with him!"

Before her panic has time to spread throughout our small group, I spin her around to face me, placing my hands on her shoulders.

"Hey," I say. "We can't go in there thinking the worst has happened. We have to hold on to the belief that we can still save Tammy and Olivia. There's no point in thinking otherwise."

"But what if she's dead? What if they're both dead? Oh God, Lance, are we actually going to do this?"

"Yes," I reply. "We are. And we're going to walk away from this house when it's all done and never look back. Do you hear me? We are going to end it once and for all."

Arthur slings his arm around the both of us, and we head up the stairs.

The closer we get to the door, the more derelict the front of the house appears — cracked windows boarded up with cardboard, nails projecting from missing floorboards on the porch, turned-over metal pots full of weeds and dirt. The neglect is astonishing, given how gargantuan his home is.

"All right, guys," I say, letting go of Gwen's hand. "It's now or never. We have no idea what the fuck we're about to go into, so let's try to stick together. Don't fight anything by yourself, and don't separate yourself from the group."

I don't have a particularly inspirational speech rehearsed, and we don't have an actual plan, just an expectation that everyone will make it out alive — everyone except for Emrys, that is.

At this point, there's nothing else anyone could do. We've doused ourselves in protective salves, sent prayers to nearly every god, angel and saint listening, and have tried to decrease his power to the best of our abilities.

Whatever happens next is fate.

Mordy is the first to enter the house, followed by Morgan, then Gwen.

"Hey." Arthur pulls on the sleeve of my hoodie, and I turn around. "Wait."

"What is it?" I ask, then look over my shoulder at Gwen and Morgan, who are now holding hands.

"Please don't do anything stupid tonight—like getting yourself killed. We're going in there together, as a team."

I blow air through clenched teeth. *We've been over this a hundred times now.*

I already promised everyone that we would fight the Merlin together, that we would tackle this problem as a group.

"I won't," I reply. "Don't you trust me?"

"Yes, of course. I just know how stubborn you are, how once you set your mind to somethin', you won't budge. Look, I know that King Arthur dies in the end."

His words shock me, stealing my breath away. I guess I just hadn't expected Arthur to buy into the reincarnation bit. He must've done research—without me—and discovered all of the bad shit. The incest, the betrayal, the bloody end.

"But I'm too fuckin' young to die. And so are you. I figure that somethin' must've gone wrong in the past all of those times that Arthur died. If we can just avoid the same mistakes, we can free Tammy and Olivia and escape with our lives. Live happily ever after."

"I really don't want to die."

Arthur uses his free hand to pull me close and hug my neck. "I know. So let's not."

The two of us walk into the house and find Mordy examining the front room.

Surrounding us on all four sides are water-damaged walls complete with peeling floral wallpaper and dark gray stains that look like hands reaching down from the rusted air vents above. A few feet below the ceiling are several large, mounted, taxidermied animal heads — some of the animals I couldn't identify even if I tried.

The floor beneath our footfalls crunches with each step we take, and I bend down to get a better look.

There are thousands of roaches and maggots writhing underneath an inch or so of fresh soil.

Everything smells of mildew and mold. I'm surprised no one's mentioned the fetid odor — more specifically my crybaby of a sister.

Now, I don't know if this is a case of the house trying to protect itself like Little Henge did or if it's just the natural state of things — a house forgotten over time — but I'm not afraid or intimidated one bit. The overall ambiance is grim and ghastly, much like the mausoleum where Mordy and I found Galantine, but this is somehow oddly comforting to me.

In the next room over, we discover a dilapidated stairwell that at one point offered safe passage through four floors of the house. Now missing pieces of wood and railing, somebody would likely break their neck if they attempted the climb.

"Holy shit, Lance!" Mordy exclaims. "Check this out."

Gwen and Morgan appear side by side, their presence a relief.

"Where were you guys?" I hiss. "We're supposed to stick together."

Gwen places a finger on her lips and motions upward with her index finger. Morgan doesn't speak, perhaps too spooked by whatever they just found.

Mordy calls my name again. I tell Gwen and Morgan that I'll leave with them in a minute, that they shouldn't go anywhere without us, and go join him.

Again the walls are plastered with weird dead things where I find Mordy.

Hanging from hooks are picture frames of various sizes encasing butterflies, moths, arachnids, millipedes and thousand-leggers. There must be over two hundred wooden bindings scattered across the walls.

"He's obsessed with death, dude."

"Yes," I say. "But like, in a bad way."

Mordy wags his head. "I agree," he says, his voice low. "He likes killin' things, and he doesn't do it out of necessity. I get the feeling that he does it for pleasure, that he likes torturin' things. Emrys is a fuckin' sicko, Lance."

"We have to stop him. For the sake of everyone in Avalon, not just us. This goes far beyond anything I could have imagined."

Mordy groans. "I wish my uncle was able to help us."

"Why didn't he come?"

I've been wondering about his involvement for a while now. His name is Myrddin, a Welsh variation of Merlin, after all. I know that we all have weird names — names associated with dead kings, queens and knights — but his name is different. His parents were from Cuba, not Wales.

"*Tío* Myrddin," Mordy says, "has already fought Emrys once. Long story short, they were younger, and the Merlin cast a spell on my uncle, a spell that forbids him from stepping within so many hundred feet of Emrys."

"A fuckin' magickal EPO."

Mordy nods. "Yes, precisely. So it's left up to us. We have to do what we can to take that fucker down. That's it. There's no other alternative."

I suddenly feel the dagger in my bag shift by itself as if in agreement with Mordy, and I reach down to grab it. The actual blade is as hot as a curling iron, and I have to carefully withdraw the hilt, avoiding my skin and the bag, because it truly feels as if it would singe the hair on my arm if I touched it.

"Xiuhcoatl, can you help us find the necromancer?"

The blade, once black, is surging with power, completely engulfing itself and my arm in a bright white light.

"Lance?" Arthur calls from across the room. "What's going on? What is that?"

All five of us come together in silence and marvel at the glowing blade.

"I'm not sure, but I asked it if it could take us to the Merlin, and this is what it started doing. Let's see if Excalibur reacts similarly."

Arthur removes the enormous weapon from his shoulder, and slowly rotates his arm, seemingly relieved by the steel's absence, then points the tip of the large sword at the floor. The blade begins to do the same.

"Galantine," I say. "Who has her?"

Gwen steps forward, letting go of Morgan's hand in the process. "I-I do."

Once she unsheathes the razor's edge and places it against Excalibur, all three weapons blaze in synchronicity. Arthur, Gwen and I regard one another in awe.

"And that's it," Morgan says, speaking for the first time since entering the house. "Where others have failed, you have succeeded." Our gaze turns on her. "There's no malice, no envy, no betrayal in your hearts, no room for anything but love. You three are as you should have been from the very beginning."

I don't know about the others, but each word hits me in the stomach like a punch.

Arthur taps my shoulder, and I wheel my head around, fighting back tears.

"See." A smirk appears on his face. "We got this."

I hope so. God, I hope so.

A lantern of sorts, our band of weaponry cuts through the nebulous veil encircling our group, and reveals chaos within the physical gloom—wooden tables hacked to pieces, cushions with stuffing ripped out, strewn about the floor, burns in the carpet, lawn-size bags full of bloody pelts, assorted feathers and bones with tendons still attached. Thankfully Mordy was the one who untied the first bag, saving us—but most of all Gwen—from losing our shit over the animal remains.

After minutes of sifting through the disarray, Morgan suggests we use magick to find the necromancer's victims, just in case they are located in different rooms. At first the idea frightens me, because I'm not sure if this will enhance his powers or cause problems for us, but I finally agree to her recommendation, mere seconds before Gwen starts squealing in the next room.

"What is it?" I hear Arthur ask. "Gwen, you have to calm down. I can't understand a word of what you're saying!"

The kitchen is an even bigger nightmare—with actual moss growing along the walls and a refrigerator that has been turned onto its side—and I find it difficult to believe that it has been used within the last century.

A fire must have broken out at some point, too, because half of the cabinets are charred and cracked from smoke damage. Chipped black and white tiles clack beneath our shoes as we make our way toward Gwen. There's no way Emmett and Olivia have shared an actual life of love or peace here, not together.

When we find Gwen, she's gesturing feverishly with Galantine, pointing it at some handbag — her hysteria visible, a culmination of how we're all feeling, I'm sure. The strap of the large white purse is painted with blood and has been snapped in two.

"Liv's! That's Liv's purse, Lance! What the fuck?"

There's no use in telling my sister to calm down, or to collect her thoughts so that we can discuss this matter as rational people. Olivia's bag is covered in blood, and she's probably being held captive by some lunatic. I'd say Gwen's reaction is as rational as they come.

"Morgan," I say, when she and Mordy appear by my side. "Can you find the Merlin? We don't have time to fuck with this house, and those stairs out there are useless."

Now that Olivia and Tammy have been taken hostage, we have no other choice but to use magick to find them — and the strongest witch here is Morgan. If we're going to find them before they die — *oh, please don't be dead* — we'll have to use everything we've got.

Black and white witchcraft. Life and death magick. All of it. Every ounce.

Morgan places her hands behind her neck and fidgets with something for a few seconds, then her arm shoots out suddenly, and hanging from her ring and middle fingers is a tiny skull attached to a leather string.

"I'm not sure how familiar you are with pendulum magick," she says softly. "But it has never failed me."

"Yeah," Mordy adds. "She was practically unstoppable at hide-and-seek when we were kids."

None of this can be good for Gwen.

A plant that wilts at the mere mention of cold weather, she is a relatively delicate flower, whose petals come off at even the slightest of breezes. Besides, her talent is healing others, not inflicting damage or harm on them.

I remove Galantine from her iron grip and tuck the scabbard under my armpit. "Gwen, you have to listen to me," I say. "We won't be able to do anything if we don't look for her, and we can't look for her with you like *this*. You have every right to be terrified and overwhelmed, but we need you with us in case Tammy or Olivia needs to be healed. We both know I can't take care of a plant, let alone nurse someone back to health. You're the only white witch here."

Her blue eyes bounce from Arthur to Mordy to Morgan and land on me. She knows I'm right—that I won't be able to do shit with someone who's got a broken arm or even an earache.

"We don't leave here until we find both of them," she says. "Do you hear me? Emrys Caerwyn is a monster. A creature of the night."

"You heard her, guys. Morgan, lead the way."

Pendulum magick is fairly simple, in that it requires only two things to complete a spell—an object on a string and a relatively steady hand. Morgan seemingly has both.

When she stills the skull with force, we all gasp and hold our breath, waiting to see if the tiny animal head will respond to her request for assistance.

"Is there anyone here in the house who wishes to speak with me? To any one of us?" she asks and waits for an answer. When nothing—or no one—responds, she asks again, "Is there anyone in this room who wishes to speak to me? Dead or alive?"

Seconds later, the pendulum swings back and forth like it's caught in a windstorm. Morgan takes a step away from the group and asks the same question again. This time the pendulum nearly ejects itself out of her grasp, and she has to jog to keep up with it. The four of us trail after Morgan, and struggle with matching her pace, the speed of it remarkable given the obstacles in our way.

The other two rooms we investigate are just as disorganized as the first few. With enormous china cabinets overturned and broken dishware everywhere, it's a wonder none of us have injured ourselves just by roaming the house with such scattered lighting. I hope Gwen is taking extra care, because she's wearing a pair of braided sandals. We should probably do better at sticking together from here on out.

When we come to the doorway that descends into complete darkness, I know with certainty that our journey is about to come to an end. Whatever trials we've faced, whatever ailments, they have prepared us for this moment. There's nothing any of us could have done. The fates spoke it, and so it shall be.

I grab Morgan by the arm before she can take a blind step into the unknown. "Wait," I say.

To my surprise she listens, and regards me for a split second. I can't help but laugh.

"How long have you been calling the shots down here?" I ask. "Did Morgan freely step aside, or did you bully her into this?"

Morgana places a finger on my nose and taps it three times. "You," she replies, "have always been a troublemaker. Always getting into trouble over that man." She motions to Arthur. "If you think this is bad, then you have forgotten the time Kilgharrah gave birth. When Arthur had to pierce the egg with Excalibur because the dragon had not emerged when it should have, and the damn eggshell was stronger than diamonds. She singed every golden hair on that body. Nasty business, that."

I'm amazed by how friendly she is toward me—toward Arthur—and wonder if this is Morgan's influence, or if Morgana has always been at war with her feelings toward him. Toward her brother.

Arthur arrives just in time to hear the bit about Kilgharrah. "Jesus Christ, I sure hope I don't have to fight a dragon."

"Dude, now's not the time to be jokin' about that stuff," I chide. "We are going into this shit with minimal details. There's no telling what the hell is lurking down there. In the fuckin' basement of all places."

"Who's joking?" Arthur forms an X with Excalibur and Galantine in front of his chest. "I just want to find Tammy and Gwen's boss, and get the hell outta here."

After Mordy and Gwen catch up to the rest of us, we exchange hugs with one another, and promise that we won't place ourselves in danger—alone—unless it is absolutely necessary. That it's perfectly fine to run if the opportunity presents itself during hypothetical—and almost certain—carnage.

"Our first and foremost priority is self-preservation. Don't let the Merlin separate us. We stick together. Gwen?" I turn to my sister and she steps in front of

Mordy. I take her hand. "Arthur will hang on to Galantine and Excalibur," I say. "What I want you to do is to stay out of the fighting, focus all of your power on healing us and whatever else might be in this house, okay? All right, everyone. Let's be swift about it."

It's not much of a pep talk, but it will have to do. We're racing against the clock.

The basement air is stale and musty. I can feel the moisture filling my lungs as soon as my foot hits the third step. Arthur is leading the way with Excalibur and Galantine because they're still lit up like glow sticks at a Pride parade. We can barely see, and the stairwell is creaky, so unless the Merlin has suffered significant hearing loss in the last two weeks, the bright lights and noise will alert him to our presence.

Arthur is halfway down the rickety stairs when he stops and holds out the swords. "What the fuck is that?" he asks. "Oh sweet Jesus!"

At the foot of the stairs is a figure, a mass of rumpled white fabric and golden-brown hair.

By the way Gwen pushes past Arthur and me, I can only assume that we've found Olivia.

"Oh my God," Gwen cries. "What did he do to you? Can you speak?"

Olivia's face is shrouded in bruises and blood. Her eyes are swollen shut from inflammation, and when she tries to speak, Gwen has to place her ear right next to Olivia's mouth.

"Do you think you could walk?" she asks Olivia, untying the rope knotted around her wrists and feet. "Lance, she's not gonna make it if we don't get her out of this house. I'm not sure what he did to her, but she said something about draining power. Though she may have said something else. I'm kinda guessin' here."

"You stay here with her." I reach into my bag and pull out several cloth bags full of oaken ash. "Sprinkle this around you, and wait for us to return with Tammy. Don't do anything stupid, Gwen. Stay here."

Even if Gwen had wanted to move Olivia, she couldn't have. Olivia might not be as tall as Gwen, but she's heavier, and Gwen isn't exactly the body-building type. Even dragging her up a flight of stairs is out of the question.

A man did unspeakable things to this woman, and he needs to pay for them—we're here to see that he does.

Morgana doesn't wait for the rest of us to catch up before she proceeds forward—an unyielding, determined juggernaut of fury on two legs.

The basement is largely unfinished, a mostly concrete enclosure with three rooms—one to our left, one to our right, and one at the very end, the only room with a door. The humidity gets worse as we move deeper into the damp structure, making it harder to breathe. There's a thick layer of dew clinging to everything in sight. There are rolled-up pieces of carpet everywhere, harboring germs, bacteria and God knows what else, as well as multiple heaps of firewood covered in brown fungus. In the middle of the hallway is a water drain, with several streams of dried paint flowing into it.

Mordy and I walk side by side while Arthur illuminates the path ahead. We carefully avoid the stacks of cinder blocks in the way, and try to keep from stepping on the back of his heels, but I'm so anxious I feel like I could pass out at any moment.

"So," Arthur says. "Is it just me, or does everyone think it smells like the inside of a belly button down here? Because fuck!"

"That's the stench of decay you smell," Morgana replies. "The Merlin is at the end of his rope. When I first arrived, I could tell that his powers were fluctuating, waxing and waning with each new moon. But now that he's abducting women, I am certain — without the shadow of a doubt — that he is planning his next reincarnation. His next cycle."

The cycle I must break.

"Is it the Merlin that smells like this, or is it the house?" Arthur asks, a foot behind Morgana. "Does he actually live here?"

Pipes knock overhead and we turn our faces upward. Water drips from the exposed metal tubing and gets in my eye. I rub my eye eagerly, determined to rid myself of anything having to do with this goddamn house.

Mordy scoffs. "Live here? That fucker probably lives in a coffin underground somewhere."

"Mordred," Morgana says, turning to face her brother. "I would like for you to put belladonna in both Arthur's and Lance's eyes. It doesn't sting for very long, just a minute or so, but the drops will be necessary for you two to see the Merlin's true form. There's no other way."

When my sight returns to normal and the burning sensation subsides, I turn to my friends, seeing them through a pair of fresh eyes for the first time, their auras as plain as the door in front of us.

Arthur's aura is white as usual, pure and selfless, a proper color for a king. Mordy's is different, a bright blue, fit for a faithful sidekick, a companion who will follow you *and* lead you toward the path of righteousness. Golden and tenacious, Morgana's aura is perfectly aligned with her goal — our goal — the goal to end a cycle of suffering.

"What is it?" I ask. "Why are you all looking at me like that?"

"Because you're covered in this silver stuff," Arthur says. "What color am I?"

"White," we all say at the same time.

"White?" Arthur shakes his head. "Well, hell, that's boring, ain't it? Vanilla in every sense of the term."

"Be sure to keep the ash close to your heart. It won't offer complete protection, but it will help some. Arthur, have you used a sword before?"

"I was on the fencing team for four years," he replies. "And took us to nationals every year."

Morgana bobs her head. "I'm not surprised. You are him. In every sense of the term. When we go through that door, you will likely see something very disturbing. You have a pure heart, and if you act on whatever it is you see in there, you will endanger us all. I need you to be logical. Do not think with your heart, but with your head. We cannot save Tammy if we all die, do you understand me?"

Arthur looks at me, then at Mordy. "I hear ya. One for all and all that stuff, right?"

"Right." Mordy holds out his fist, and we all take turns bumping it. "All for one."

The door flies open before Morgana has time to turn the doorknob, and a gust of wind tears through the basement, sucking our bodies into the room and slamming the door shut behind us.

After I get to my feet and help Arthur get to his, I spot a wooden structure in the middle of the room — a cage made of twigs and sticks in the shape of an X. As my eyes adjust to this room, which is completely and totally devoid of light, I can see now the contours of a body. Morgana's suggestion that I use the belladonna eye drops was advantageous after all. My breath catches in my chest and I stumble forward in the darkness, until a strong hand prevents me from going any farther.

"No," Mordy says. "You have one job. Until you see the Merlin, you stay with the rest of us. And even then, you don't engage him alone. He could be lurking in any one of these shadows."

"What the hell is that?" Arthur asks, using Excalibur to light the area in front of us.

Oh no. He must have spotted Tammy. "Wait, Arthur — don't!"

The sentence leaves my lips a mere millisecond before the Merlin materializes beside the wooden X structure. An old man whose yellowed skin is covered in scabs and boils, and whose long, white hair is stringy like ramen that's been cooked too long, the Merlin raises a staff and brings it down across Arthur's neck as he approaches the caged girl who is hanging upside down.

Arthur's blade obstructs the staff before it can land, but the force of the blow is so strong that it brings him to his knees. A low cackling escapes from the Merlin's mouth as this happens, and Arthur lunges at him again, this time agitating the great sorcerer so much that the Merlin throws back his cloak, revealing a chest that's missing half of its skin. The Merlin's heart beats wildly within a partially exposed rib cage, and we take a moment to absorb this visual information.

What the fuck.

Then an invisible hand lifts Arthur into the air and drops him on the concrete floor, and the sound of bones popping and cracking fills the air. Before I can rush to his side, both Mordy and Morgana wag their heads at me. Now, I'm not one hundred percent certain what the appropriate course of action is here—given that my boyfriend might have just broken every bone in his fucking body—but I'm pretty sure it doesn't involve sitting around doing nothing.

"No," Morgana says. "We must pray."

"Pray?" I ask. "Are you out of your mind? Arthur might be dying over there, and you want to meditate during the middle of a battle?"

"I was not addressing you, Lance." Morgana's voice is firm, domineering. "I was speaking to Lancelot."

Chapter Seventeen

Camlann Revisited

My body is not my own.

Or at least I don't think it is.

When I look down at my hands, they are much larger than normal—not swollen or inflamed, but my palms take up more space, and my fingers are longer.

And my eyes are now level with Arthur's—who, thankfully, has managed to get to his feet after being slammed down like he's in the WWE—which means I *somehow* grew over a foot and a half.

Arthur.

When I look at him, it feels like I haven't seen him in a hundred years—*maybe I haven't*—because I have to physically restrain myself from dashing to his side, stifling the mountainous desire to entangle him in a frenzy of limbs. Limbs that are now twice their usual size.

I stroke my chin and run my fingers across a bushy beard. *What the hell?*

"*Lance*," a voice suddenly intrudes on my thoughts, and I have to do a double take, re-counting everyone in the room to make sure another person didn't find their way into the basement, to make sure I'm not hallucinating.

"Yes," I reply cautiously. *"How did you get inside my brain?"*

"First, allow me to begin by thanking you for making it this far, for keeping him alive."

My eyes land on Arthur, and his brown eyes glimmer in the sword light as he tries to make sense of the chaos unfolding around us. I take a step forward, and resist the urge to join him, but it's not *my* urge, it's this body's — this body that is somehow simultaneously foreign and familiar to me. A second skin.

"You've gotten farther than any of us could have imagined. I'm impressed."

I flinch when the realization hits me. "Lancelot," I say, aloud. "Morgana summoned you, didn't she?"

"No," the voice says, *"I've been here all along. You and I, we are one and the same. But it will take the two of us to rescue Arthur. Are you willing to do what you must in order to save him?"*

I laugh. *"Do you really even have to ask? I think we both know the answer to that question."*

"Good. Then we are on the same page. Now about that compromise."

"Go on," I say, curiosity eating away at me.

"The first time Emrys betrayed all of us, I chose cowardice, turned my back on Morgana and her son, took Gwenhyvfar far away from Camelot and didn't look back. Arthur was never crowned king because he was poisoned shortly after Morgana was burned at the stake, along with her son. The unspoken compromise was Gwenhwyvar's life for Morgana's."

I look at Morgana and Mordred, who are now standing together, their hands interlocked, performing a spell of some sort. Everything seems to be moving at a slower pace, like we're moving through water.

I don't like this. I'm not in control of this body.

"No," the voice replies. *"You're not."*

"What are you planning on doing?" I ask. *"Tell me!"*

"Whatever is necessary. You can either help or sit back and watch. The choice is yours."

"But I made a promise to Arthur. To Mordred. To Gwen."

"What's more important, saving the man you love or keeping your word? You are a man. Act like one."

I don't want Lancelot hearing my thoughts — instead keeping them separate from his — and don't respond to his question. I'm not sure what I'd expected Lancelot to be like, but I'd thought the knight from the songs would have had more integrity, that the bards would have gotten his story wrong, at least a little.

"Fine, be that way. But we will do what we must. Don't get in my way."

When our shared body begins to move, I notice that I can't hear anything.

"Is this your doing?" I ask, sharply. *"I can't do anything. What have you done?"*

"I told you that I wouldn't let you get in the way. Now be quiet, and let me save Arthur."

"What about the others? I thought you cared about Morgana and Mordred."

"I never said anything about caring for them, only that I betrayed them. This is about duty, not love."

Lancelot walks toward Arthur, and for a brief moment we meet eyes, and I don't recognize the man standing before me.

With pale green irises, shaggy brown hair and a full beard that puts mine to shame, Arthur looks much older and more hardened than the eighteen-year-old man I've spent most of my summer with. He's wearing leather armor and wielding both Excalibur and Galantine, a sword in each hand. They look so natural in his grip, metallic extensions of his limbs.

No wonder my boyfriend became a top-ranking fencer in less than a year.

Lancelot wants to go to him — I can feel the tension between the two of them when Arthur pauses to regard us — but betrayal pollutes the air and hatred fills the room like smog. Whatever happened between them several hundred years ago is still a fresh wound in Arthur's mind.

"Your highness," I hear Lancelot say, as we take to one knee. "You have not changed at all."

Arthur's mouth moves in response, anger painting his face a rosy color. I still can't hear anything, but I get the vibe that he's not pleased at seeing an old pal who skipped town with his girlfriend.

Mordy and Morgana are still duking it out with the Merlin, who is clearly agitated by whatever it is they're doing.

"Wait," I plead. *"We still need to free Tammy, and help Viviane."*

"That witch? Absolutely not. If anyone should perish tonight, it should be the sea crone and her husband. As for your friend, I'm sorry, but that's not why I've come."

"You can't be serious! She's helpless. I don't know what the fuck he's doing to her, but she'll die if she's left like that."

"A wicker man. Besides, I thought you hated that woman."

"A what? What's a wicker man? And I don't hate anyone, except for maybe that asshole."

"What I mean is that I assume she's a sacrifice, and I assume he's going to sacrifice her, then burn down the house. Do you really know so little about our history?"

"*I'm Mexican American, remember? You and I don't share a history. You're a goddamn parasite that got inside my body somehow.*"

"*That's certainly an interesting take on the situation. How do you think you've lived for so long? How do you think you made it through those nights when your parents were too intoxicated to take care of you? How do you think it is that we made it back to Avalon in one piece? Surely you don't believe that all of this was left up to fate, now do you?*"

I remain silent, choosing to ignore whatever bullshit he's trying to manipulate me into believing.

"*Oh, you do. That's precious. Unfortunately, that's not the way the Wheel spins, Lance. You and I share a body, because for whatever reason, a botched reincarnation allowed two souls to inhabit one vessel. This vessel.*"

"*I am not a vessel, and I am through talking to you. If you don't want to help Tammy, then I'll fucking do it myself.*"

"*I hate to break it to you, but I am in control of this body, not you. You will do nothing but sit and watch as I ensure the safety of Arthur Pendragon, Holy King of the Britons. I will not allow anything or anyone to get in my way.*"

When Lancelot wheels himself around again — to face Arthur — the tall, bearded man takes two long strides toward us and peers down into our face.

"Lance," he mouths. "I know you're in there."

A feeling eerily similar to the one I got when my shirt was yanked in Arthur's trailer attacks my senses, and I can feel Lancelot struggling inside this body, swimming against the tide of rage now coursing through every vein.

"*I don't understand you. If I saw my boyfriend after a thousand years, I would rush into his arms without even thinking about it.*"

"*You are mistaken. Arthur was not my lover.*"

"What? You're a liar. I can tell by the way he looked at you, by the way you've restrained yourself this whole time, that you two love each other."

"No, he was in love with me, but I did not acknowledge it at the time. I never gave him any more than a handshake. Marrying Gwenhyvfar meant leaving behind a life of suffering and poverty that was forced on me at birth. Besides, we were men, and if I couldn't have him, no one could."

"What? You took Gwen so that Arthur couldn't marry her? Not because you loved her, but because you were jealous. If you couldn't have him, no one else could. You're so selfish. Do we really share the same soul?"

"No, we don't. Thankfully."

Arthur puts his hand on our shoulder, abruptly ending the shared telepathic squabble.

"Give me Galantine," Lancelot demands. "Now, Arthur."

I still can't hear anything, but I can hear when he speaks, I guess because we share a body.

"Arthur, the sword, please," Lancelot says, again. "Don't make me take it from you."

A few feet away, I see Mordy trying to break into the wooden cage, hacking at it with a small knife, carefully avoiding Tammy's arms.

Morgana is still trying to weaken the Merlin with magick, her arms in the shape of a vee, pointing up toward the heavens. If anyone can do it through witchcraft, it's Morgana.

Arthur and Lancelot continue to argue over the sword.

Their dynamic is weird.

Lancelot is nothing like I thought he would be. None of the legends align with anything I've read or heard. Or maybe my expectations of people are set too high. He's a goddamn paladin, for Christ's sake, a holy knight, someone who is sworn to protect their king in the darkest of hours. Not a petulant teenager who throws in the towel before the round even begins.

Morgana had said something about the three of us loving one another — Arthur, Gwen and me. That our love is pure and free from malice. Watching the two of them bicker like this over a sword — when they haven't seen each other in hundreds of years — grinds my wheat like nothing else. Arthur's eyes still maintain their light down here in the darkness, and every so often I catch him staring straight at me. Not Lancelot, but Lance. This isn't going to work for me. Waiting for Arthur to kiss me was torture, but four years doesn't seem all that bad when I compare it to how long Arthur's been waiting to reunite with his love, a love that is conditional and toxic.

The strange clamor inside my head is much louder than the commotion surrounding Arthur and me — a terrible combination of the Merlin's threats, the argument that Arthur and Lancelot are having, and Morgana's counter spells — and I know that Lancelot will not give me control over my body without a fight.

Meditation isn't really my bag, it's more of a Gwen thing, but I have a bad feeling that without deep contemplation of who I am and how I came to be standing in this very spot, Lance Lotte might be lost forever.

I close my eyes and reflect on my first interactions with Gwen, Arthur and the twins. The love I feel toward them swells in my chest, and I notice the first crack. At first, I assume it's going to be a war of wills, mine against Lancelot's, hundreds of years of angst against my twenty years of anxiety, but he gives in fairly easily.

"Oh, go ahead. He prefers you anyway."

"I do not have time to deal with you, Eeyore, and you don't deserve Arthur if you're not going to fight for him. You're supposed to be a Knight of the Round Table, the greatest warrior of all time, the greatest swordsman of all time, but I see now that most of that was fabricated."

"You have no idea what I've been through! How long I've waited for this moment, how long I've waited to apologize to him — for everything. But all he can see is you."

"Are you joking right now? Are you actually jealous of a soul? My soul? I'm sorry that in the end you got what you deserved for betraying everyone that I love, that you fucked things up the last time, that you weren't able to set the record straight, but we don't have time for a pity party. We don't have time for this. Whatever this is."

After I regain control of my senses and limbs, I assess the mayhem one last time before making the decision that what I must do can't involve Arthur or the holy swords, because when combined they make a fatal amalgamation, and I want everyone in this room to live.

Once I get acclimated to operating this enormous body, I reach into my side bag and withdraw the dagger that's been pulsating the whole time.

The Merlin is ensnared in some kind of psychic hold, and Mordy has managed to penetrate through Tammy's wicker fortress, her limp body now sagging lifelessly in his arms. The blood pooling around the two of them briefly punctures my confidence, and I consider the gravity of our situation, the unlikelihood that we'll all walk away from this venture unscathed.

"No," Lancelot shouts. *"We're going to save Arthur. Whatever you do after you've secured his safety is up to you, but right now I will not allow you to mess things up. Not when we've come this far. Take that dagger and stake him*

through the heart. Morgana has weakened most of his defenses, but she grows tired, and will not be able to do this much longer. You have to act now. Now!"

"You're the most selfish person I've ever met. Why are you so hell-bent on saving Arthur, and only Arthur?"

"What are you saying? Don't you care about him at all? I've watched you pine over him for years, while he made the most obvious, disgusting puppy dog eyes at you. But you were always making excuses, never accepting the truth. Now he's yours, and you want to save that woman, that woman who can't even get your name right?"

"Are you really lecturing me on this issue right now? You chose a life of luxury over the man of your dreams, and you have the audacity to tell me how to live my life? You're right. I was a coward, a wimp for many years, never believing that I was worthy or deserving of anyone's love, not just Arthur's. Everyone's. But my friends mean the world to me."

"She's not even your friend!"

"No, but she could be. And if I don't save her, we'll never know, because we won't get the chance to start over. I get it – you've had hundreds of years to stew and brood and blame the universe for your sorrow and misfortune – but I'm only twenty-one, and I don't intend on being angry for the rest of my life. These folks are what make life worth living."

"But – "

"Don't interrupt me, I'm not finished. I'm sorry – truly sorry – that your life was less than satisfactory, that you had to suffer because of an unjust society and unfair standards, but this is my life, and I won't let you, or some cycle, dictate how things are going to end."

"You are going to die, thinking like that."

"Don't you worry about me." I close my eyes and place my palms over my heart, still clutching the dagger in one hand. *"I'm no stranger to adversity. You know that better than anyone ever could."*

And just like that, Lancelot disappears. His voice shushes and I feel him return to the depths of my subconscious.

I glance down at my hands, flipping them over, admiring the signs of the zodiac on my fingers.

My fingers. My body. My choice.

"I'm sorry, Lancelot. Your pain made you bitter, but I won't let mine swallow me like a river."

Both Morgana and Emrys drop to their knees at the same time, the muffled sound a signal, promptly calling my attention toward them.

Morgana folds in two, her body no longer the great magickal bastion it once was. Her fading golden aura reinforces the severity of the circumstance—just how much she's sacrificed to be here, to do this—and I make the split-second decision to dive at the Merlin with my dagger in my mouth, cat-like reflexes manifesting all of a sudden.

But I miscalculate the distance between us, overshooting things by several inches, and soon find myself deeply woven into a nest of smelly velour and skin that feels like tissue paper.

The old man is a lot stronger than I'd anticipated.

When he raises his staff and whacks me on the crown of my head, a thunderous yowl rumbles inside my rib cage and rips through my throat, because it feels like my skull has just been fractured into a hundred tiny pieces.

Both Arthur and Mordy start screaming at the Merlin, hurling demands at the walking corpse, threatening to tear him from limb to limb, but their words fall on deaf ears and he grabs me by the throat. His movements are surprisingly fast, and knobbly thumbs jam into my windpipe, the asphyxiation restricting my airflow.

"A life for a life," I hear his raspy voice say. "You want the girl? Fine. He'll work."

The Merlin must do this sort of thing all the time, because I see a full galaxy's worth of stars in a matter of seconds. My legs go slack and everything clouds over, the strangulation cutting off my oxygen.

Holy fuck. Am I dying? Being choked out by a crusty old white dude is not how I imagined going out. Talk about lackluster.

"What are you doing?" a soothing voice asks. *"Wake up, Ocelot. No, no — it is not time for you to join me just yet."*

"Join you?" Mictēcacihuātl. *"Well, I had no intention of calling on you until this goddamn thing with Emrys was over, but I guess my plan wasn't foolproof, and here we are. What else could I do?"*

"What else? You have so much potential inside of that little body, so much to offer everyone, to offer the world. For the longest time you fought the darkness, the gloom, your other half. Now's the time to accept who you are, what you're going to become, and remember that when you do this, you're doing it for all of humanity, not just for yourself."

"Jesus, lady, way to push all of this shit on me. Why not Mordy? Or Morgana? Why me? Those two are far more competent, and established in who they are as people, and as witches. You've seriously got the wrong guy. I just got taken out by a geriatric wizard because I have shitty spatial awareness, and you expect me to somehow stop Armageddon."

"Who created the First Sun? Why is cacao so delicious? How was man able to steal fire from the heavens? Does it really matter why you were chosen? Sometimes things happen, and there's no real rhyme or reason behind them. All I know is that you are the only one who can stop this

madman. You don't have to be big, or famous, or strong, or even the most intelligent person in order to right a wrong. The mightiest of warriors are brave, courageous and willing to sacrifice everything for the people they love. But I'm not telling you anything you don't already know. Your power has just begun to develop, and if you look deep within yourself, you'll see exactly what I'm talking about."

"What do you expect me to do? Transform myself into something I'm not?"

"Yes, actually."

"What? I'm not a superhero, for Christ's sake."

"Our people believe that when a woman gives birth, they give birth to two spirits — man and animal. The nagual. The day you were born, your body became host to three souls, not two. Why the Divine Mother chose to do this, I'm not sure, and it is not for me to question. It is unusual, certainly, but nothing harmful. You've already met one of the two, and I can't think of a better time than now…to meet the other."

"You mean to tell me there's something else lurking in the depths of my psyche? Something not human, like a beast? No wonder I've been fucked-up all these years. My brain is a congested roadway. Well, how the hell am I supposed to rouse whatever else is in here? To turn into a werewolf or whatever? Mictēcacihuātl?"

When she doesn't answer, I know this is a task that I must complete on my own, so I concentrate on my goals — stopping the Merlin, saving my friends, waking my new roommate — and dam the flood of thoughts currently cascading around me. Treading through a sea of doubt, I delve into each memory, every corner of my mind, trying to unearth hidden meanings and anything that might be helpful to me at this time.

I have no way of knowing just how long I've been in here, no way of keeping track of time, and just when I'm about to give up — to turn around and say fuck it —

I hear a deep guttural meow. A cat. Not a wolf, or a falcon, but a cat. It makes sense—in some weird, practical way—that my nagual would be a cat.

A pair of white-ringed blue eyes appear before me, and the sensation is oddly similar to looking into a mirror.

Not just a cat, but an ocelot. Why didn't Mictēcacihuātl just say so, instead of holding some psychic pep rally?

I don't have to communicate with the animal because we share the same thoughts, which is actually a very good thing, because how the fuck do you verbally or mentally communicate with a wild cat?

Once we've established what we're going to do to the Merlin, I give myself over to the nagual and we leave the spiritual realm, or my subconsciousness, or wherever the hell it was we were.

The transformation is largely spiritual. My body doesn't undergo any special changes or mutations, no new hair growth or claws, no overbite accompanied by long fangs—nothing cool like that—just an awakening of instincts I'd never known I had.

Still squirming in the Merlin's grasp, the ocelot within tears at the old man's face, my fingernails digging into centuries-old skin. Enormous amounts of coalesced pus and blood run down my arms in a matter of seconds. The smell would normally sicken me, but something about it excites the nagual, and he overpowers the Merlin, knocking us both over.

His screams don't bother me nearly as much as they should, perhaps because he is literally trying to kill me, or perhaps because they fulfill some dark need of mine, a need I've suppressed all my life—but whatever the reason, I'm thankful that it's him, not me.

An ensemble of voices—from Arthur, Mordy, Morgana and Gwen, who must've appeared while I was speaking with Mictēcacihuātl—assails me, teeming with a mixture of relief and terror, adding to the intense anxiety I now feel.

The nagual sinks my teeth into the Merlin's neck. Salt and iron pour into my cheeks, and I gag on the taste, swallowing the thick, bitter fluid in one big gulp. After a few minutes of wriggling in my arms, the Merlin's body wilts, a tree whose roots have gone far too long without any rain. His body is heavy against mine and I roll him over, trying to catch my breath and to not vomit all over myself.

Arthur rushes to my side.

"G-God. Lance! W-what? Oh my God. Are you okay? I—I thought you were dead." His words come out in a jumble, half-sobbing, half-laughing. "What the fuck? It is over? Is he dead?"

"I think so." I'm covered in Merlin's fluids, and all I want to do is lie down somewhere. "Is Tammy okay?"

"Yeah, Gwen and Olivia got to her before it was too late. I tell ya, Gwen is somethin' else."

I lean my head into Arthur's shoulder, exhausted and broken. "Can we go home now? I hurt all over. I just want to sleep."

"And sleep you shall," a voice croaks beside me.

Before either of us have time to react to his voice, the Merlin bounds forward like a pop-up book, jabbing me in the side with Xiuhcoatl.

The pain is so severe that I can't do anything but weep, my words dissolving in my mouth before they have time to escape. I keel over and curl into a ball. Death has come to greet me, and I can feel this body dying, am aware that no prestigious knight is coming to save me—that no wild beast can shift me out of this reality.

The last thing I see before closing my eyes is Arthur ramming Excalibur into the Merlin's exposed rib cage.

* * * *

Now, I've read about out-of-body experiences before, listened to people's testimonies, researched the statistics and even watched YouTube exposés on the matter. They're a certain type of phenomenon where a person's essence leaves their body and essentially travels without it. Many have claimed to have done this, but left behind no paper trail or anything that could validate their claims.

I am not a skeptic, but at no point in my life did I ever expect to witness such an event. Clairvoyance and soothsaying—anything dealing with the third eye or psychic abilities, really—have never been a strong point of mine. Always something better left to Gwen. Or so I'd thought anyway.

Because here I am, floating above my body, which I assume is dying, given the fact that my loved ones are scrambling around me, trying to save me from succumbing to my injury. Their auras are so strong, so bright that it looks like a zigzag rainbow is occupying most of the room.

Down below, Arthur has my head cradled in his arms and is petting my face, while tears run down his. Mordy and Morgana are dragging the Merlin away from where Arthur and I are. Olivia and Gwen are standing behind us, in front of a wall that someone has smeared blood all over, in the shape of a pentacle.

A few moments later I see Gwen take Arthur into her arms, while Mordy and Morgana lift me by my arms and legs and place me in the middle of the room. Olivia bends down in front of Arthur and takes his hand as well as Gwen's into her own, then gently guides them up from their seats.

After I'm secured in the middle of the concrete floor, covered in a huge pool of my blood, Olivia holds out her hand, and within seconds her palm catches fire like a sparkler. An object materializes in her hand once the fire turns into smoke, and I'm soon able to identify it as a small chalice of some sort.

Their voices are barely audible, but I'm able to make out something about blood and a Grail.

Then Olivia instructs everyone to slice into their hands and dribble blood into the cup. Not a lot is needed, she explains, just a few drops.

A bloodletting ceremony.

The five of them form a pentagram — Olivia by my head, Mordy by my left hand, Morgana by my right hand, Gwen by my left foot and Arthur by my right foot.

Olivia kneels down beside my body, and parts my lips with the metal cup while everyone looks on with concerned faces.

"Lance," she says. "Oh, Lance, it wasn't supposed to end like this. Not again." I see Olivia's body transform into that of an elderly woman with a fragile, delicate frame, one that better fits her age. One that is as old as, if not older than, the Merlin's.

Viviane. The sea crone. The Lady of the Lake.

"With this blood I give thee life, a blessing from the horned god and his wife. Oh, please renew the balance now, restoring his life if ye shall." Then, turning to face my friends, Olivia says, "In order for this blood spell to work, you must each trade something precious. For me, the only thing left to give is my ability to return once this frail body fails me. Do you understand what I'm saying?"

"Viviane," Morgana speaks. "Are you asking us to give up our ability to be reborn? To end the cycle here, with Lance?"

Viviane nods. "That is precisely what I am asking."

Morgana laughs hysterically, and starts crying. "Of course we'll do it, you old hag. Do you not see how tired we all are? How worn thin we've become? We just want to sleep. For our spirits to finally rest. None of us expected my curse to have this effect, that it would last this long."

After that, the pentacle on the wall ignites and begins to spin in a counterclockwise motion, because even though Morgana was the only one to speak, I can only assume Arthur, Mordy and Gwen have offered their answers to the five-pointed star in silence.

"Farewell, you fools," Morgana barks. "I never wish to see you ever again!"

Before the ritual is complete, a loud rumbling calls our attention to the area where Emrys had been laid earlier by the twins. The floor beneath his body cracks, and quickly opens like a hungry mouth, trying to guzzle down whatever's in its path. Several seconds later a green shoot sprouts from the ravine, followed by spindly branches, and a tree that looks more like a hand with fingers than a burgeoning plant.

"The earth has come to claim him," Gwen says. "Blessed be!"

I'm so glad to hear her voice, to know she's made it.

"We'd better get the hell out of here before it claims us, too. Arthur, you grab Tammy. Mordy, do you think you can handle Lance?"

"But the ceremony," Olivia protests. "What about your brother?"

Looking straight at me, Gwen replies, "As far as I'm concerned, we've done all we can. The rest is up to him."

* * * *

Alternating red and blue lights rouse me and I bolt upright, awakened by the low murmur of voices in the distance. Stuffy and pulsing, my head feels like I've got the worst hangover of my life, and every muscle aches as though I've just ran a marathon, or what I assume it feels like after you've run one anyway.

Is this what happens to your joints when you die, or just when you've been brought back to life? Because fuck...

When I rotate my side, the skin across my rib cage burns, like a shave that's too close, a feeling that spreads across my lower back. I lift my shirt to inspect the area where Emrys stabbed me with Xiuhcoatl, which is extra-sensitive to the touch. But much to my surprise, the should-have-been-fatal laceration has already fully healed, and a white scar has taken the place of where the wound should be.

The rapid sound of boots clashing with gravel calls my attention to Arthur, who is now sprinting toward me.

"You're awake." His voice is unusual, an uncanny mixture of desperation and jolly. His arms slide around my shoulders and I rest my head against his. "Oh God, Lance. Thank you, Jesus."

"Hey," I say, weakly. "Where is everyone?"

Arthur shakes his head and puts up a finger.

"How's Tammy?" I ask. "Is everyone okay? Did anyone else get hurt?"

Arthur wags his head and I give him a moment. I suppose I would react in a similar manner if something like this had happened to him. To any of my loved ones. I can't begin to imagine what or how he currently feels.

When I finally pull away from his taut embrace, I see that his eyes are red and puffy, sagging and enclosed by dark circles. His pants are torn and he is missing his overcoat. There's no telling how long I've been asleep, but I can see that he's been crying the whole time.

I've never been so happy to see another human being in all my life.

He swallows and says, his voice breaking every now and then, "The cops are on the other side, looking for the Merlin. Olivia's been arrested, and Tammy was already taken to the hospital. They tried to take you, too, but Morgan wouldn't let them. She said you passed out from drinking too much. How do you feel?"

"Truly happy to be alive for the first time in my life, I think. Where are the swords? How are we going to explain everything?"

"There's nothing to explain. Olivia took the blame for everything. She told the cops we had come up here with beer and were drinking out back when one of us heard Tammy screaming. We found her tied up and called the cops."

"But what about Emrys?" I ask, the sight of a blue jay suddenly catching my eye. "What happened to his body?"

The bird lands on a branch in one of the oak trees that we tried to rescue, and turns its head toward me, as if it's interested in hearing what Arthur has to say. Mordy never fully explained who or what the bird was, other than calling it a spy, so I can't be certain of its true intentions, but I don't appreciate the way it's gawking at my boyfriend.

"Who knows? When we went back down into the basement, there was nothing there. No blood, no tree, no floor even, just a bunch of busted-up shit."

"Galantine? Excalibur? Xiuhcoatl?" I lower my voice and lean in toward Arthur, but keep the winged informant in my line of vision. "Are Morgan and Mordy both safe?"

"Gone. I'm tellin' you, it's looks like an unfinished construction site down there. I don't know what the fuck happened after we left, but it looks like everything went straight to hell. As for Mordy and Morgan, they're just fine. Exhausted, I think, but not seriously injured or nothin'."

"God, that's a relief." I briefly look away from the bird and survey the yard, noticing that half of the trees are still adorned with hand-painted paper charms. I don't ask Arthur if the police officers had anything to say about them, because of the likelihood that they wouldn't believe us anyway.

We managed to save our friends and Avalon from more death and destruction. The earth had probably swallowed the blades as well, when the tree came to take the druid to pay for his crimes. I don't share my thoughts aloud with Arthur, partly because the Merlin's name is one I'd like to forget, and because I can't shake the feeling that we might have some unfinished business.

"Damn. Did you just see that? That had to be the biggest blue jay I've ever seen."

Arthur's voice draws my attention away from the trees. "Huh?"

"That bird. It's gone now, but that wingspan. I've never seen anything like it in my life. Are you okay?"

I don't respond to his question, and instead close my eyes, letting my mind drift for a minute, absorbing the knowledge of Emrys' defeat and reflecting upon everything we had to endure in order to secure it.

Mictēcacihuātl, how can I ever repay you for what you've done? For how much you've helped? Thank you, Holy Mother, Queen of the Underworld. I will never forget this as long as I live.

"Oh my God, Arthur." I open my eyes when I feel his hand on my back. "It's done. It's over. We really did it."

He helps me up from the ground, placing my arm around his neck, and we make our way toward the front of the house, where Gwen, Mordy and Morgan are.

"We really did," he says, and kisses the side of my head with so much force that we both nearly fall over. "Let's go home."

Epilogue

A New Beginning

Lexington, KY

Have I ever mentioned that I'm terrible at goodbyes? Because I am. I suck at them. Big surprise, right? Maybe it's because I cry every time, or maybe it's because I can't deal with the idea of being separated from the people I love and cherish the most. Whatever the reason, they're always the hardest for me. Each desertion fills my heart with holes, and they're left empty until we meet again.

This morning I received a text from Mordy telling me that he'll be back for Christmas, and that he fully expects me to be here as well, that he'll drive to Lexington to kidnap me if I don't keep my promise to come back.

Mordy. Saying goodbye to Mordy had been harder than I'd anticipated. Nothing could have prepared me for the pain that would come after our last meeting.

He and Morgan had begun their drive back to California yesterday morning. All five of us had planned to have breakfast before they left, but Mordy had canceled an hour before we were supposed to meet, saying that if they attended they wouldn't have enough time in the morning to prepare for their departure, and that any delays might negatively impact the strict schedule he'd devised.

But I know the real reason for his desertion, because I'd nearly backed out three times last night.

It had been a lie, of course — he just hadn't wanted to say goodbye in person.

I hope he knows just how much I love him, how much I need him in my life.

After an early lunch with my parents and Gwen, Arthur and I head back to Lexington in his truck. Gwen had kept making jokes about his truck breaking down all during the meal, and I could tell that we'd needed to get out of there before he lost his mind on her. Ever since my near-death experience, Arthur has been somewhat touchy.

I get it, though — his boyfriend almost died, and what little time he had left with him was divided among his other loved ones. I'd be pissed, too, if I were in his shoes. None of this has been fair — to any of us.

Once we're well on our way, Arthur relaxes a little and turns on the radio, singing along to the terrible nineties country blaring from the station, and I roll down the window.

The sky is blue and expansive, and it's like I'm seeing it for the first time ever. Something about dying and being brought back to life has made certain aspects of living rawer, more vibrant. I try to soak in the sunshine and dry air.

For the first twenty or so miles we don't talk, instead absorbing the finality of everything, the possibility of things to come, the future that we'd fought so hard to secure.

"Gwen told me Morgan asked her to come visit," I say. "Said she could stay with her and Mordy's mom. Can you even imagine Gwen in a big city like that?"

Arthur chuckles. "Are you kidding me? Of course she did. I've never seen two people so attracted to one another and fight it like they do. Or at least how intensely Gwen resists it."

"God, she does, doesn't she?" I shake my head and start to peel the orange resting in my lap. "Morgan doesn't know what she's getting herself into."

"Hey. Can you do me a favor?" Arthur asks. He removes a hand from the steering wheel and gestures toward the glove box. "There are some letters in there. Can you get them for me?"

I lick juice from my fingers and arch my eyebrow at him. "You just had to wait until my hands were covered in juice, didn't you? Hang on a sec."

I wipe my fingers on my shirt, the citrus smell attacking my senses immediately, and reach for the plastic latch. When I open it, paper rains from the rectangular space onto the floor and I grab handfuls of letters, placing them on the seat beside me. The last letter on the floor, I see now, is from the University of Kentucky, and I take it in my hand, turn it over.

"What is this?"

Arthur doesn't look at me, and licks his lips nervously. "Go on, you can open each one if you want."

Centre. Transylvania. Eastern. Northern. Western. Georgetown.

There must be fifteen unopened letters here.

Since I go to UK, I decide to open that letter first.

"Dude," I say. "You applied to UK?"

"Yes, what does it say?"

"That you got the scholarship you applied for," I reply. "And that you should send a thank you letter to the donor because blah blah blah. Wait, why didn't you tell me you were applying to schools? Did you apply to all of these schools?"

"Yeah, and I got into each of them. Those are all letters for various scholarships that I applied for."

"UK is practically offering you a full ride, man. But how?"

"What do you mean how? I graduated with a 4.0 and have six years of mission work under my belt. Admissions officers live for that shit, especially when you're from a rural part of the state."

I sink back into my seat.

Arthur reaches for the radio and turns it off completely. "Are you mad at me for not telling you?"

"What are you even going to study?"

I am upset—not with him, but with myself, for not asking him about this stuff earlier. How could I have been so thoughtless? So oblivious? The topic had rarely ever come up, because I hadn't wanted him to think I was judging him for not going to school this semester. I'm such a doofus sometimes.

"Well," he says, "I like working on houses, and I think it's something I could do for the rest of my life. So I was thinking maybe architecture?"

I reread the letter ten times before responding. "Well, UK has a great architecture program, or so I've heard."

The mere thought of Arthur being so close nearly drives me to tears.

"Would it bother you if we both went to the same school? Because there's like ten schools to choose from."

I close my eyes. Gwen would be lonely if Arthur moved to Lexington and left her behind. His grandmother is also sick, and I'm not sure it would be right to take him away from her. Arthur means the world to me and so does my sister, but to separate them so that I don't have to be alone seems wrong, selfish. I don't know how I should answer his question.

"Oh, don't even start with that stuff. Wasn't it you who said that I let life pass me by?"

"Lancelot? I thought you were gone."

"No – unfortunately I'm still here, and now I have this cat meowing all the time, like it needs to go outside. I hope you're happy with what you've done to me. Now listen here, because I really don't like talking to you unless I absolutely have to. Your sister will be fine. You heard Arthur himself. Morgan has a vicious thirst for your sister. And his grandmother wants him to be happy. Don't forget that she's the one who encouraged him to move out of his parents' house. Be selfish for once in your life, and take what you want. You've earned this."

"You'd better not interfere in my life, or else I will have you exorcised the fuck out of existence. I know a couple of Santería priests, you know."

"Honestly, if it meant that I didn't have to listen to this cat anymore, I might take you up on your offer. But seriously, I have to wait until this body gives out to finally join my love, so there's no sense in repeating my past mistakes. Take him. He's yours."

"Lance?" Arthur's voice reins me back into reality. "Are you okay? Do you need me to stop at the next truck stop?"

I turn my head from side to side. "What are you going to do with Yin and Yang? Are you gonna give them up?"

Arthur's forehead scrunches, and he replies, "Absolutely not. They will come with me, of course, because they are my babies. Um—I am going to keep on workin' and savin' until I have enough to move into an apartment off campus. Everything on Craigslist sounds like a fuckin' scam, but I'm sure I'll find something. If I don't, I'll just ask Gwen to watch 'em until I do. She loves those cats as much as I do, and besides, she might appreciate the company."

Tears begin streaming down my cheeks and I look out of the window—because I'm not brave enough to say it to his face, not yet—and tell Arthur that I want him to move to Lexington, to choose UK, to choose me, so that we can be closer to each other, and that nothing in the world would make me happier.

A few seconds later the wheels of his truck hit a patch of uneven rumble strips and he pulls onto the shoulder, flipping on the emergency lights in a hurry. Then he unbuckles his seat belt and slides over to me, knocking my bits of orange peel and the pile of letters onto the floorboard in the process.

Arthur caresses my neck, then drags his index finger along my jawline and eventually tips my chin to greet his.

Eyes that are full of love and understanding peer into mine, and the burning intensity of them is almost too much for me to bear, so I close my eyes and fight back heavy sobs. Then, without warning, hot, wet lips smash into mine, and I grab the collar of Arthur's shirt.

"I love you," he says, after he finally pulls away. "And when you died, it was like the world lost its color.

I know it was only for like three minutes or something, but I want to spend as much time with you as I can. You heard Olivia. This is it. We don't get a do-over."

"I know," I say. "This is it."

After nearly a decade of misunderstandings and denying ourselves the happiness we had been seeking for hundreds of years, Arthur and I will finally be together, not as king or knight, but as college students. At this point, we've faced damn near every challenge known to man, and it's obvious to me that I still have some things I need to work on, but with Arthur's love and support, I'm sure I'll get there, that we'll get there, regardless of what gets thrown our way.

Want to see more like this?
Here's a taster for you to enjoy!

A Dragon's Treasure:
Cody's Dragon
K.M. Mahoney

Excerpt

Kirit's boots hit the pavement with a dull thud. He paused a moment and surveyed his surroundings with narrowed eyes.

Nothing unusual caught his attention from where he stood, hidden between two buildings. He didn't really expect it to. Old habits were hard to break, though.

He shifted his pack into a more secure position before diving into the crowded walkway. He would have to pick one of the busiest times of day to arrive — bad timing all around. At least the weather was still warm, and he wasn't forced to wade through knee-high snow. Denver was a bitch in the winter.

Kirit ate up the distance with long-legged strides, people unconsciously clearing a path for him. He knew his sheer size, along with his harshly carved features, didn't invite any pleasantries.

It took Kirit less than ten minutes to cover the blocks to his destination. He ascended a rickety staircase, which clung to the outside of the brick building with precarious tenacity. The metal door squealed loudly when he opened it, revealing a dim and narrow hall. Halfway along, he rapped firmly on the door marked 1207.

"Who's there?" A voice called from the other side.

"Kirit. Open up."

Locks clicked. Kirit counted six. That was, in his opinion, a bit unnecessary. Harper wasn't exactly helpless on his own.

The door swung open to show a short, stocky man standing there. He had well-tanned skin and a spiked mess of blue-tipped brown hair. "What're you doing here?"

"That's a marvelous way to greet someone. Are you going to let me in?"

"Will you go away if I don't?" Harper stepped aside to let Kirit enter his tiny apartment.

Once inside, Kirit dropped his pack to the floor next to his feet, not bothering to look around. He'd been here often enough and there wasn't much to see.

"Want a beer?" Harper disappeared into the tiny closet he called a kitchen.

"Hardly."

"Snob."

"Absolutely."

Harper reappeared seconds later, popping the lid off a bottle. He let it fall to the floor, obviously unconcerned when it bounced off the cracked ceramic tile and rolled under the olive-green couch. "So, what brings a high and mighty Draak to the human realm?"

"I'm on a hunt."

Harper's expression sharpened with interest. He let the bottle in his hand dangle at his side for a moment. "Dragon, Fae, or — "

"Not that kind of hunt."

"Oh." Harper returned his attention to his drink.

"I'm on a mate hunt."

"Good for you."

"In this realm."

Harper choked, spraying his last mouthful of beer across the room. The distance was impressive—Kirit had to sidestep to avoid being hit.

"Sorry," Harper said. "I think my hearing's going."

"Your hearing is fine. It's the rest of you that's…going."

"Yeah, yeah. Tell me something I don't know. But you're going right alongside me. A mate? On this side? Are you nuts?"

"It worked for Merrick."

"Merrick isn't Draak."

"Everyone keeps saying that. I'm sick of being alone. My mate is clearly not behind the Veil, and I'm not interested in waiting for the next generation to grow up. I didn't come here for a lecture. I've heard it all. Dozens of times."

Harper looked resigned. "Fine. Why did you come, then? Where do I fit into this grand scheme of yours?"

"I need connections. Information. What is the best way to meet the most number of people in the least amount of time?"

"Sheesh, you don't ask for much, do you?"

Kirit crossed his arms and raised one dark eyebrow.

"Do you realise how many people live in this frickin' city?" Harper pointed out.

"Shall I give you a precise number or an estimate?"

"Shut up." Harper groaned. He grabbed another beer before plopping onto the couch. The ragged piece of furniture echoed Harper's groan, creaking ominously under his weight. "Make yourself comfortable," he said, waving with his bottle. "This will take a while. Oh, and grab something to write with. You can make a list."

Kirit did as directed, settling himself gingerly on a chair which was slightly newer than the couch, but even uglier. "You may begin," he directed.

Harper growled. "Fucking dragon."

Kirit gave the witch an extremely toothy smile. "That's the ultimate goal."

"Next time, I'm not opening the door," Harper declared.

PUBLISHING

Sign up for our newsletter and find out about all our
romance book releases, eBook sales and promotions,
sneak peeks and FREE romance books!

About the Author

Jackson Garton spent his formative years in the Appalachian region of the United States, and has chosen to call Kentucky 'home' for the past twenty years. As a queer trans person living in this part of the country, he possesses a rather unique perspective, and this can be observed throughout the fantastical stories he tells. He also has a strong penchant for cats, tea, and the arcane.

Jackson loves to hear from readers. You can find his contact information, website details and author profile page at https://www.pride-publishing.com